He grunted, the sound drawing her gaze up. He still knew too much about shadows. They were in the dark, completely hidden from the rest of the world. She would never have realized there was such a place to escape to among the high security zone of the White House and yet, he'd found it. Now, he was a dark visage, tempting her to melt against him and share the moment.

Live in the moment. . . . reach for what you crave . . . take it now, before it slips away.

She shivered, the longing to do exactly that nearly consuming her. The delicate surface of her lips felt dry and she rolled them in, drawing his attention.

"Princess. . . ." his tone was harsh, edged with self-loathing and a lack of discipline she understood because she was experiencing the same thing. She felt his breath against her wet lips a moment before she felt his kiss.

Also by Dawn Ryder

Dangerous to Know

DARE YOU
TO RUN

DAWN RYDER

St. Martin's Paperbacks

This is a work of fiction. All of the characters, organizations, and events portrayed in this novel are either products of the author's imagination or are used fictitiously.

DARE YOU TO RUN

Copyright © 2016 by Dawn Ryder.
Excerpt from *Deep Into Trouble* Copyright © 2017 by Dawn Ryder.

For information address St. Martin's Press, 175 Fifth Avenue, New York, NY 10010.

ISBN: 978-1-250-07522-2

Our books may be purchased in bulk for promotional, educational, or business use. Please contact your local bookseller or the Macmillan Corporate and Premium Sales Department at 1-800-221-7945, ext. 5442, or by e-mail at MacmillanSpecialMarkets@macmillan.com.

Printed in the United States of America

St. Martin's Paperbacks edition / September 2016

St. Martin's Paperbacks are published by St. Martin's Press, 175 Fifth Avenue, New York, NY 10010.

10 9 8 7 6 5 4 3 2

To Angela Knight.
The gift of time is more valuable than
anything else. Thank you for a slice of yours

CHAPTER ONE

She didn't want to die.

Damascus Ryland shivered, the cold so bad it felt bone deep. In a strange way she was focused on it now because the misery confirmed that she was still alive. You couldn't hurt if you were dead.

Alive . . .

She drew in another breath and resisted the urge to claw at the sides of the concrete hold she was stuffed into. Above her head was a manhole cover, but all that was beneath it was a six-foot length of concrete water pipe that her kidnappers had dug out a hole for and used it to brace up the sides so she wasn't smothered. She looked up, waiting for the two quarter-sized holes in the cover to twinkle with daylight.

Not yet. It was still night. Blackness pressed in on her, threatening to smother her with how thick and impregnable it was, but she knew it could be worse. Her captors had made sure she knew it when they'd stuffed corks into the holes, because she'd screamed. She'd discovered what blackness was, spent what had felt like an eternity waiting for her night vision to kick in so she could see her own hands. It hadn't, she'd just had to endure the minutes that felt like hours while the idea of helplessness became more real than she had ever imagined possible.

Damascus stiffened and drew in a deep breath—she had to be stronger than her circumstances if she wanted to survive. So she put her hands on her face, jumping at the icy touch of her fingertips.

One . . . two. . . . three. . . .

She counted each one, allowing the cold to seep into her skin, and let the burning chill remind her that she was . . . *alive*.

There was a scraping noise, one she recognized well. The manhole cover was being twisted, so it might be lifted. The only difference was there was no light, just a strange red glow. She watched it anyway, desperate for a reprieve from the blackness. That red light came through it like the blade of a dagger, slicing it apart and giving her enough space to breathe.

It wouldn't last. She steeled herself for that harsh fact. No, the tube was hell and so were the faces that would look down on her when the manhole cover was lifted. They wore masks all the time. The old type of Halloween masks that were plastic with nickel-sized holes in the eyes. Gaily painted cartoon characters that took on a grotesque quality when coupled with the voices of her captors.

She continued to watch as the cover was lifted. It was done more gently this time, as if someone was trying to keep the noise to a minimum.

It was happening. Her mind was breaking.

It had to be, because the man who looked in on her wasn't wearing a mask. His face was darkened with some sort of black makeup. The red light came from somewhere over his ear. As she blinked, she realized he had on goggles of some sort, and a small light was attached to the side. He held a finger up to his darkened lips, a silent command, but there was a sharpness to it from the way he moved, hell from the very way he just, well, was.

She nodded, responding instinctually. There was a presence to him, one she'd never really felt before.

Yes, her mind was going. Not that she particularly cared. Not so long as her insanity came in the form of a man who cut the darkness away. He looked over his shoulder and then back down at her. A moment later, he'd reached right down into the hole and grasped the thick coil of rope that was tied around her body. It bound her arms to her chest all the way to her elbows and was tied in back, leaving her unable to climb the slick sides of the tube. It hadn't stopped her from trying though; her fingers bled from her efforts, her nails were shredded.

What had seemed impossible was suddenly happening. He sat her on the side of the hole as she blinked at him. He touched a finger to his lips again before he flipped open a knife and slipped it under the coil of rope.

A little sigh escaped her lips as he freed her. Just the softest sound, but he clamped his hand over her mouth in response. She smelled his skin, the scent making him more real. Her eyes stung but she was so dehydrated, there were no tears. He looked around and slipped his hand down to her wrist.

Her muscles were so cold, it felt like her tendons were going to snap, but Damascus ground her teeth together and stumbled behind him when he started to take her across the warehouse. He looked back at her, but she pushed her foot against the floor, ignoring the way something cut into the bottom of her bare skin.

Freedom was worth any amount of pain.

She couldn't hurt if she were dead.

She was a pitiful mess.

Not that Vitus Hale expected much else. A

Washington debutante, one who had managed to slip away from her escort and get herself abducted. A pampered princess like that didn't have a clue what the real world held.

Vitus knew. In fact, he was on very familiar terms with the seedy part of life. It was among the shadows that he spent most of his time, and there was something about it that gave him a kick in the pants. He liked the game, enjoyed the struggle and the sweet surge of victory that came when he was more patient than those he was hunting.

Like tonight. Damascus Ryland's kidnappers had finally given into boredom and popped their heads up out of their hiding place to indulge in a little online chitchat. Vitus couldn't help but grin. He really did love it when he caught bad guys with their asses flapping in the breeze.

The grin faded as he returned to the moment and ordered himself to focus. The operation wasn't complete, he needed to keep his perspective.

Vitus pulled her behind him, watching for the man set out on guard duty. He was leaning against a shipping container, the glow from his cigarette making him easy to spot. Vitus hunkered down, feeling the girl follow his example. It was a waiting game now, Vitus held her wrist in a solid grip as he watched the sentry. The lookout finished his smoke, then dropped it before pushing away from the container and wandering down the length of the dock in the other direction.

Now.

Vitus tugged on her wrist and led them across the open space to the edge of the dock. The waves were lapping at the side of it, making enough noise to cover their steps. He glanced back just once at Damascus and pointed down at the water's surface. Her eyes widened, until she saw the surfboard he'd used to come up along the side of the docks. No motor, no light, and no one with enough brains to look over the side of the docks, which was why he'd done it.

Vitus went down first. Once he was on the board he beckoned to Ms. Damascus Ryland, daughter of Congressman Jeb Ryland. He wasn't sure what he was going to do if she blew their position, but surprisingly enough she didn't hesitate to join him. It bumped up his opinion of her just a tad. At least she wasn't wailing all over him. He could smell the blood on her and the stench of being kept in that concrete tomb for the last week. When she joined him, he realized how cold she was, but she maintained her silence, even as she stiffened when her feet went into the salt water.

Vitus didn't have time to console her. He pressed her down onto her belly, lying on top of her so that he could paddle. She offered him another little unexpected jolt as she started to use her hands to help, digging at the water as much as she could beneath him.

So she had some guts.

And it was in a nice package . . .

Now that was crass of him but it was also the truth, and a SEAL needed to work with reality. Lying on top of her, there was no way not to notice just how good she smelled, even beneath the grime. She'd never find out, though. Hell, a daughter of a congressman was definitely not the sort he would ever take up with.

He needed some downtime, that was for damn sure.

"I owe you a beer."

Damascus blinked at the man who spoke. He considered her for a moment, in the same way her rescuer had before he reached down and hooked her wrist. They'd paddled up to another dock and this man was clinging to a ladder that went down the side of the dock and into the water.

What where they used for?

She had no idea, and what was worse, she realized just how much of the world she didn't understand the workings of. That ignorance was worse than all the aches and pains assaulting her because she could do something about it.

"Told you."

Her rescuer reached right up and flattened his hand against one side of her bottom to push her up the ladder. Her cheeks actually stung with a blush but not because of that contact.

Again, it was due to the fact that she knew she wasn't pulling her own weight. She reached up and grabbed the next rung and pulled hard to get herself moving. A face appeared above her, the man reaching down and grabbing a handful of her tattered evening dress to haul her up and onto the pier.

Jesus, they were strong . . .

And she just couldn't help but notice how built they were.

She ended up on her backside, blinking as the two men came up the ladder with an ease that was admirable. Her rescuer hunkered down beside her, looking perfectly at ease. "Commander Vitus Hale, United States Navy, ma'am. SEAL."

He had high cheek bones that were defined because of his low body fat. Most of his hair was trimmed away and his chin was clean shaven. Perfectly groomed and yet, there was a glitter in his eyes that proclaimed just how untamed he was. It made her shiver but in a very enjoyable way.

"Damascus Ryland." Manners had been drilled into

her young, and she stuck her hand out without thinking. Vitus's lips twitched as one eyebrow rose. He didn't take her hand but looked at it for a long moment.

"We'll get you cleaned up."

Vitus Hale was on his feet a moment later, turning to look back at the dock. The moon was behind them, casting a large shadow from the stack of shipping containers. Damascus pushed herself up, determined to do more than sit on the ground like a bedraggled kitten.

"How often did they check on you?"

Damascus blinked a couple of times before her brain engaged and she realized Vitus had spoken to her. More importantly, he hadn't offered her comfort. He was watching the sentry, one of the other men using a pair of goggles to do the same, while the third was facing the opposite direction to make sure no one snuck up on them.

Vitus let out a grunt. "Don't worry about it."

Damascus felt something inside her snap. Almost like a safety cap that had been on her for her entire life, keeping her oblivious and weak, unable to defend herself.

"Every night, just as the sun was setting." She answered up in a voice that didn't falter.

Vitus cut her a glance, obviously surprised. She straightened her back and resisted the urge to bite her lower lip.

"They wanted to force my father to vote in favor of the new port taxes."

Vitus nodded. "Yeah, I heard. It told me right where to look for you."

Understanding dawned on her and she smiled. "Right. Um, I mean thank you." She pulled her attention away from Vitus, which was much harder than it really should have been, and looked at his companion. "Thank you."

Vitus jerked his head, and the team started moving. "Well, we're not parting company just yet."

He'd hooked her upper arm and turned her around like she was a child before she realized what he was doing. Vitus Hale seemed to have no intention of explaining anything to her, just on moving her. He'd taken her across the docks, through stacks of cargo containers, and under huge cranes before they reached a car. One of the men opened the door, and Vitus put her into it.

Well, details didn't matter, at least not at the moment. It was a little more pertinent that they put some distance between them and the men who would gleefully stuff her back in the hole.

Only she was the one who was gleeful as they drove away.

"I can take you back to your father."

Damascus had been rubbing her head with a towel. She lowered it and looked at him while her hair sprang to life. She was a natural redhead, and a bright one too, who was naturally curly. Fresh from a shower, her head was covered in tiny corkscrews.

But that wasn't what attracted him to her, not the most anyway. Nope, what was drawing him to her was the way she blinked and lowered the towel without a hint of outrage over him showing up while she was wearing only a robe.

She could prioritize.

Which meant she wasn't as much of a spoilt brat as he'd assumed.

"Or . . . you could do what?" she asked him as she laid the towel down and reached for the medical kit he had forgotten was in his hand.

Fuck. He was spellbound.

Vitus pointed to the only thing in the room, which was a bed. Something flickered in her eyes now. She sat on it as he opened the kit and tore open a packet of antiseptic.

"We could keep you out of sight and try to trap your captors," Vitus said. "I take you back to your father, and they will scatter into the sewers."

"I like your plan." There was heat in her voice, and that stunned him because he honestly expected a wailing fit.

Damascus reached out and took some antiseptic from the packet while he was considering her, and began to smear it over one of her bloodied fingers. He should have looked away, to give her some space, but he was just too damn impressed—and that didn't happen very often. Damascus Ryland, debutante, looked at the mess that was her hands and smiled as he treated the oozing wounds. It had to sting like a bastard but she only smiled brighter until she caught him watching her. For a moment, their gazes fused. He saw the pain swimming in her blue eyes, proving she wasn't in shock.

"The pain . . . it means I'm alive," she offered in a soft voice.

"Yeah, it does."

Time shifted and he lost track of it for a moment while he looked into her eyes and fought the urge to touch her. The urge was powerful and seemed to have risen up past all of the mission protocol he'd had drummed into him.

She was a package, a mission goal.

But right then, she wasn't. Damascus looked like an angel who was welcoming him closer . . .

"Brought you some chow."

Saxon Hale was through the doorway as Vitus jerked. His brother came closer and went right between him and Damascus as he delivered a bowl of beans and rice that had steam gently rising from it.

"She's on board," Vitus offered as he turned and retreated.

Now that was a first for him, but honestly, Damascus rattled him.

"Send her home."

Vitus turned to find Saxon on his tail, looking at him with far too much knowledge in his eyes.

"And wait for these pricks to try again?" Vitus shook his head.

"I'm more concerned about you."

Vitus could have denied what his brother had walked in on, but dishonesty on a team leads to trouble. "She caught me off guard is all. I expected tears."

Saxon tilted his head to one side. "Yeah. Guess it's our lucky day. I do like the missions where the bad guys are our biggest headache."

Vitus was nodding, but Saxon wasn't nearly as gullible as he would have liked. His brother knew him too well.

"Just don't forget," Saxon warned. "She's Jeb Ryland's daughter. He's a conservative and won't take it kindly if you forget that he thinks his little girl is too good for you."

"Right."

It was the truth. One of those pesky little reality things. Sure, Vitus enjoyed pitting himself against the odds, but there were some things that a wise man just left alone. Like congressmen's daughters.

So why was he itching to find a reason to go back into that room?

Beans and rice had never tasted so good.

Damascus shoved two steaming spoonfuls into her mouth before she managed to quell the urge to swallow the entire bowl without taking a breath. Her mouth was so full, the broth was leaking from the corners of her lips as she chewed—and all she did was chuckle at herself without a care for how ill-mannered she appeared.

She felt so alive! Like energy was crackling along her circulatory system. It made her senses ultrakeen, and what she was noticing most with her hyperawareness was how amazing Navy SEAL Vitus Hale was. Her nipples were puckered tight, sensation prickling across her breasts, while she marveled at the level of intensity.

It was like she'd never felt before.

And there was one thing that burst inside her brain as she finished off that bowl. She was never, ever, going to be the stupid little chit she'd been before.

Life was to be lived and she couldn't wait to get down to it.

One week later . . .

God he smelled good.

Damascus just couldn't seem to get close enough to Vitus Hale. At least it didn't seem to be her problem alone. The SEAL watched her, not like Saxon or Dare Servant did—the way his eyes followed her was personal.

And she loved it.

"Shit," he said as he pulled his mouth away from hers.

She wanted to follow him and press her lips back against his to seal out any more words. She didn't want to talk, she just wanted to be immersed in his embrace.

"Damascus." Vitus caught her nape and held her back. "We've got to talk about this."

She let out a little sigh and heard him scoff at the way her lower lip protruded. "All right." She withdrew, her confidence restored by the look of raw rejection on his face as she did so.

"Your father is going to object to anything between us."

"I'm twenty-three," she answered. "Well past the age of consent."

He liked hearing that, but she watched as he held himself in check, sticking to his desire to have a conversation. It wasn't what she craved, epically since the first night that he'd kissed her like he just couldn't keep his hands off her. She sure as hell didn't want him to start now.

"You know what I mean. He's a congressman. I'm not the sort of man he has planned for you."

Damascus reached up and grabbed his shirt, twisting the fabric in her fist and pulling him down to her level so she could kiss him. Vitus didn't hold out very long against her onslaught, and he was kissing her back with all the hunger she'd come to expect from him. But she withdrew before it overwhelmed her.

"If you want a little girl who checks with her daddy, I'm not the woman for you."

It was hard to say and even harder for her to step away from him, more like ripping herself away from the thing that made her feel more alive than she ever had.

Vitus considered her for a long moment, drinking in the determination on her face. He saw her. Really saw who she was beneath all the layers of education and grooming her father had insisted she be encased in, right there, she was herself and she realized she wanted to get to know who she was and do so with the man who had made her realize she was moving through her life half asleep.

"I believe you." He reached down and caught the edge of his T-shirt and pulled it up and over his head, baring his magnificent torso for her. It was cut with ridges of hard muscle that she itched to stroke. "You are a woman."

She purred as he caught her back up against him. No, her father wouldn't approve, but she didn't care. The thought of returning to the life she'd had was intolerable, not when she'd discovered what living was truly about in Vitus's arms.

So she wiggled until she could get her hands between them and stroke him the way she'd wanted to. He made a soft, male sound of frustration against her lips and settled for releasing her so that she might have her way.

"Go on princess, stroke me,"

She did. Shivering as it felt like touching him was in some way completing a current. The moment she touched him, energy went pulsing through her, awakening a zillion points of awareness inside her that she'd been unaware of before.

Yet it wasn't enough. She broke away from him, fighting to free herself from her clothing.

"Oh no," he muttered in a husky tone. "Baring you is going to be my pleasure."

He caught her shirt near the hem and tugged it up and over her head. It went fluttering down onto the floor as he let out a little hum of appreciation. His attention was on her breasts, making her suddenly shy.

"They aren't . . . very big,"

She could have bitten her tongue in half. Vitus raised his gaze to her hers, granting her a flash of just how much passion was flickering in his eyes. Her confidence regained its wind in response.

"Do I look like I'm disappointed, princess?"

He'd closed the gap between them and laid his fingers on the swells of her breasts, where the edge of her bra ended.

Damascus shook her head.

He slid his hands around her and found the hooks that held the undergarment closed. She let out a little gasp as he freed them and brought his hands back around her body before pulling the bra down her arms.

"You're perfect," He muttered as he cupped her bare breasts, gently cradling them as he sent a jolt of pleasure

down her body. "So damned perfect. Why do you think
I call you princess?"

He didn't allow her the chance to answer but sealed
her mouth beneath his. The kiss was firm and she rose
onto her toes to answer him with a demand of her own.
She wanted him and needed to make sure that she did
her share of taking, craving that feeling of knowing she
was his partner, not just his responsibility.

They weren't close enough. Damascus needed more
of him. It was pounding through her and he seemed to
feel it too. He was stroking her. Using his hands to wor-
ship every inch of her body. She arched back, her eyes
closing as pleasure flooded her. He was moving slowly,
so very slowly that it was driving her insane and yet, she
enjoyed the torment because she was his sole focus point.
The intensity of it was off the scale, at least as far as any
scale she'd ever known was concerned.

He scooped her up, cradling her as though she
weighed nothing. Moving her toward the bed and settling her on its surface. He left her for a moment, rising
up like the hard warrior who had rescued her to tug her
pants loose and strip them from her.

She shivered, conscious of how easily he might bend
her to his will with his strength and yet knowing that she
was drawn to those same qualities because of what it unleashed inside her. She rose up, folding her knees beneath her so that she could reach for his fly.

"Damascus."

She liked the strained sound of his voice, enjoyed the
way it made her feel more in control than she ever had in
her life. She popped open the buttons and heard him draw
in a raspy breath.

His cock was swollen and hard. It sprung out as she
freed those buttons because he didn't have anything on

under his jeans. She ended up purring, reaching for it, marveling at the silky smooth texture of it.

But beneath that skin it was as hard as stone. She stoked it, enjoying the way he threaded his fingers through her hair, tightening his grip just enough to send a tingle of pain across her scalp. She started to lean down, intent on licking the slit on its head but he held her back.

"No tonight, princess." There was a firm warning in his tone. "Tonight, I'm the one introducing you to passion."

"But. . ."

She might was well have saved her breath. When she caught sight of his face, she witnessed a blaze of determination that sent a twist of anticipation through her belly. Her clit was suddenly throbbing as he shucked his jeans and rolled her back onto the bed.

It was all done in a moment, the bed rocking beneath her back while she gasped and he settled himself half over her. She moaned softly, overwhelmed by the amount of contact between them and yet, still unsatisfied.

"More." She wasn't sure that she decided to speak. Her brain was shutting down, impulses ruling her completely. That was what he was to her, freedom, in its purest form.

"Yes, ma'am," he muttered as he nuzzled against her breasts. At the same time, he swept his hand across her belly until he found the curls crowning her cleft.

She shifted, too full of pulsing need to stay still. He moved with her, locking one of his knees over her leg as he lifted his head and watched her. He teased her curls before delving into her cleft. She let out a soft cry as he found her clit, stroking it with a delicate touch that made her feel like a bolt of fire had gone through her.

"I'm going to learn just how you like to be touched."

There was a promise in his tone that she might have shivered at, except he returned to toying with her clit, making thought impossible. There was only the intense pleasure coming from that single point of contact, so searing she withered but it built something inside her. A need that was rooted deep inside her belly, where instinct rose up, taking control of her. She strained toward him, arching her back as she felt the pleasure building, twisting, intensifying, until it all burst like a huge firework that rained down fiery sparks.

"You never touched yourself princess?" Now there was a note of wonder in his voice. It drew her away from the stupor the explosion had left her wallowing in and she opened her eyes.

"No."

She felt stripped in that moment. For the first time in her life, completely honest about who she was. Vitus considered her for a long moment before he slowly smiled. There was a look of achievement on his face that struck her as some sort of gift that she'd expectantly given him.

"Touch me some more, Vitus."

His eyes narrowed, passion drawing his features tight. "Yes . . . , *ma'am.*"

He shifted, leaning down to kiss her. She reached for him, feeling like it was the most natural thing in life to do. They fit together in a way she'd never imagined two humans might. Both of them created to merge together in a moment of utter bliss. It far over shadowed the moment of pain when he pushed into her body for the first time. The ache lingered but she was too busy enjoying the building intensity that promised her another explosion of pleasure. She craved it with the need of an addict, craved him, and Vitus didn't disappoint her.

Not in the slightest.

***

Vitus didn't sleep.

Not yet anyway. His mind was turning a puzzle over

and that meant there was going to be no rest for him until he came to a conclusion.

He'd had sex before.

Tonight had been something different. Vastly different. He lay there stunned by his need to listen to Damascus breathing. He needed the scent of her body in some strange way that he'd never encountered before either. Yet it was there now, making the idea of slipping out of her bed repugnant.

A memory shifted and rose up from his brain. It was the look on his father's face when he watched Vitus's mother. Something Vitus had seen often but never understood completely.

Until now.

He got it now.

Because he was likely looking at Damascus the same way. It was devotion mixed with an emotion Vitus had avoided ever using in relationship to himself. That single thing that made more SEAL's hang up their boots and settle down.

Love.

'You've gone and done it now, sailor.'

He really didn't regret it, nope, he was too full of wonder and excitement. Of course, his brother was going to give him holy hell over it but that just seemed like a dash of spice on the whole thing too.

"Vitus." Saxon was growing frustrated.

Vitus heard it in his brother's voice and looked up at his sibling.

"You've got to stay away from her."

"I'm not putting pressure on her."

Saxon grunted at him. "I sure as shit didn't think so. You can bet I would have gone through that door the first time I heard you kiss her if I thought you were a bastard."

Vitus lifted his hands in surrender as far as the point went. "Okay, fine. I know how it goes."

"So what are you doing bedding her?" Saxon demanded. "Jeb Ryland can make a whole world of trouble for you."

"I love her."

Saxon's eyebrows shot up. "What the fuck?" his brother demanded. "You've known her an entire two weeks."

"I know," Vitus cut back. "Don't ride my ass. It's just as hard for me to swallow as you, but it's real bro. I don't know how to prove it to you, but it's eating a hole in me and it's not the first time you've ever heard of it happening."

Saxon muttered a word under his breath that made Vitus grin in victory, but his sibling pointed at him. "I'm not doubting you Vitus, but I am warning you, that little thing in there is a princess, and you know the ground rules are different for those. Brother to brother, I've got to tell you to walk away."

"I know," Vitus answered. "I can't."

"You mean you won't," Saxon argued.

Vitus shook his head. "No. I can't, Saxon. It doesn't make any sense, but I could cut my arm off easier."

Damascus was wringing her hands.

She paced back and forth across the tiny bedroom as time crawled by. She felt like her insides were knotted, but she turned and walked back toward the bed, determined to get all the nervous energy out of her system before Vitus returned.

He would return.

She concentrated on that idea, refusing to allow any doubt to wiggle around it.

"Miss me?"

She jumped, earning a chuckle from Vitus.

"How do you sneak up on people like that?" she asked, too relieved to see him to be anything but joyous.

He offered her a lazy shrug of his huge shoulders, but there was a cocky grin on his lips that made her smile brighter. "It's a gift."

He was pleased with himself. Damascus felt the tension dissipating. "And? What happened?"

He winked at her. "We got them."

Damascus was moving toward him, but he held up a finger. She froze, losing the battle to keep doubt from filling her mind. Was he going to tell her he was moving on? Give her the "dear Jane" conversation? She watched his expression, seeking any clue to his intentions, but all she saw was a flicker of determination in his eyes.

"You can go home now," Vitus began. "Or—"

"Yes?" she interrupted, unable to stop herself from leaping for the bit of hope he'd tossed out.

"Will you marry me?"

Vitus would have looked ridiculous on his knee. Instead, the SEAL was hesitating in the doorway with the first uncertain expression she'd ever seen on his face. He'd pulled something from his pocket, a small circle of gold that had a diamond winking at her.

"Yes . . . yes . . . yes!" Damascus flew across the room and launched herself into his arms. He caught her easily, holding her against him while her feet dangled somewhere around his ankles. She realized she'd never been truly happy before, because the way she felt right then was tons more intense, like the sun was suddenly shinning right in the center of her chest.

Vitus let her down and captured her hand. He slid the ring onto her finger. "It's not much—"

"It's everything," she insisted. Everything that she needed. "So, you going to take me to your place?"

He chuckled at her. "And chain you to my bed."

Damascus winked at him. "I should be so lucky."

Vitus's house was more homey than she'd expected. By the light of day, Damascus explored her new surroundings only to find her new fiancé watching her from the kitchen.

"I'm not disappointed," she told him.

He didn't really believe her. Damascus watched his face and read his uncertainty. She moved closer, catching the scent of fresh coffee.

"I'm not," she confirmed when she was close enough to lay her hands on his chest.

His expression remained set. "Enough to tell your father whose ring you're wearing?"

"Yes." She took a moment to straighten her ring.

Now he smiled, his eyes filling with a warmth that stole her breath. He reached onto the counter behind him and picked up a coffee mug. Vitus drew off a long sip before speaking again.

"In that case, let's roll."

"And if I'd said no?"

His expression turned wicked. "I would have taken you back to bed and given you more evidence to weigh"— Vitus cupped her bottom—"in my favor."

"Well, in that case, I'm not . . ."

A little *woof* was all that got past her lips when he tossed her right over his shoulder. She giggled as he carried her back toward his bedroom.

Her father would just have to wait.

Damascus stared at her father. They had never been close, but today she realized just how snowed she had been. Jeb Ryland was furious. The outrage flickering in his eyes didn't frighten her. No, all it did was make her feel incredibly grateful for the eye-opening experience life had handed her.

"I'm sorry you're not happy for me."

Jeb had settled behind his desk—a huge mahogany one—and she realized her father was trying to intimidate her.

Damascus straightened up. "But my mind is set."

"Unset it," Jeb snapped.

"I am not a teenager." Damascus kept her voice steady, deciding to prove the point by not turning the conversation into an emotional tirade.

Her father's lips twisted in a judgmental frown. "Apparently not, since you have decided to start bedding the help."

"Vitus rescued me."

Jeb offered her a shrug. "He's a dog of war, that's his job." He leaned forward. "Keeping his hands off you was also his job."

"I wanted him to touch me."

Her father slapped the desktop. "Slut," he accused softly. "No daughter of mine is going to be bedding a dog."

Outrage was moving through her, but Damascus maintained her composure. "I am sorry you feel this way. She gently fingered her engagement ring, the small token bringing her all the confidence she needed. "However, I am going to marry Vitus Hale."

"Do it and you'll be a widow within a month."

Her father's voice was cutting, but so certain that Damascus sank back down into the chair she'd started to get out of.

Jeb gave her a smug look. "That's right. He's active duty. I know plenty of admirals who will make sure he goes out in a flame of glory."

"You"—her throat was tight—"monster."

Her father slowly shook his head. "What I *am* is successful, Damascus. An idea you will learn to devote yourself to."

"You can't—"

"I can," Jeb informed her. "And I will."

"I love him." She'd lost the battle to keep emotions out of it. Her voice betrayed her, and her father's complexion darkened with outrage.

"If you do, you will make him think you want him gone, because if I ever see him again, I will pick up this phone"—he pointed to the one on his desk—"and send him permanently beyond your reach. Is that clear?"

It was. Like the pounding of a gavel in a courtroom. She was held in the grip of shock, but her eyes were wide, letting her see the determination in her father's eyes.

He meant it.

Nausea twisted her insides as she felt tears filling her eyes.

Damascus blinked them away. She wasn't a child anymore and it appeared that her new view of life included seeing her father for what he was.

Monster.

It was suddenly clear why she'd never been close to Jeb Ryland—he didn't have a heart.

"Your lover is waiting," Jeb informed her coldly. "I will be watching."

She was on her feet, without really thinking about what she was going to do.

There was only one thing she could do.

She felt that realization sink in and tear the bubble of joy around her heart to shreds. Vitus wasn't inside the house. No, her father had left him waiting in the driveway. She spied him through a window, leaning against his car with a hard expression.

He knew.

Knew the way the world worked. She'd been the one who'd made the mistake of thinking she had the freedom to choose her own life.

Well, you do.

She stiffened, realizing she had to be everything Vitus Hale was worthy of. Loving someone meant putting them above yourself, and she opened the door with that intention firmly in mind.

He read her body language before she'd made it down the front steps. She watched him stiffen before he moved toward her and took up a position in front of her that was military perfect.

"I will always be grateful for your service." The last word got stuck in her throat and felt like it left a raw spot when she forced it out.

His eyes narrowed. "It was my duty."

Clipped. Short. Cold words that cut her bone deep because he was going to just accept what she was dishing out to him. For a moment, she stared at him, trying to find her lover, but his expression was closed tight against her efforts.

She twisted the ring off her finger and offered it to him.

They stared at each other for a long moment. One of the worst in her life, because everything inside her wanted to leap toward him.

"Just like that?" Vitus asked her, his control slipping and giving her a hint as to how furious he really was beneath his stoic demeanor.

"Yes." She answered in a whisper because she knew if she spoke any louder, he'd hear how devastated she was. How it was killing her to send him away and Vitus Hale wasn't the sort of man to let her shield him. But she loved him, so she would. Even if he hated her for it.

Vitus Hale contemplated her for a long moment,

studying her with his keen eyes before taking the ring. Damascus watched the flames of rage flicker in his eyes, the ones fueled by the way she'd slashed at his heart. A man like him would never forgive her for such a wound.

"Guess you are a little girl after all." His expression had turned to granite, sealing her out. "Better run back to Daddy."

Damascus watched him leave, soaking up the details of his stiff posture. Saxon watched her from where he was leaning against a car, shooting her a look designed to gut her. It didn't though, because she was already mortally wounded.

But Vitus was alive.

Three years later . . .

"You're going to get out of this van." Special Agent Kagan had a frame that a professional football player would be envious of—or scared of, depending on what side of the field he was on.

Vitus only gave his section leader a mildly amused look, facing off with a frame that was just as wide and a confidence that was well earned. "It's been three years, a little late to be tossing me to the press at this point. Go find some kid fresh from Afghanistan to be your pretty boy. I don't need a medal. I sure as hell don't need a medal from Damascus Ryland. Can't believe you think her daddy is going to be too happy about having me anywhere near his precious little princess."

Kagan grunted and leaned against the side of the van. "I thought you were smarter than that."

From some men, those words would have been a dig, nothing more than a halfhearted attempt at getting him moving. But from Kagan, they were more. Any man with half a brain would be wise to remember that Kagan was a section leader for a reason. The man knew his shit, and some of the crap he had rattling around in his head, a wise man didn't want to know but was still curious about.

Vitus contemplated his superior for a long moment before he levered himself out of the van and yanked his dress uniform jacket from where it was resting over the back of one of the seats. "Explain."

Kagan snorted. "That time off softened your brain."

Vitus finished buttoning the tunic-length jacket and flashed Kagan a single finger salute. "Proven fact: Being pissed off lowers intelligence. Since Tyler Martin took my badge, I was at liberty to be pissed at him. There was little to occupy my brain."

Kagan offered him his hat before they both started walking toward the back entrance of the White House.

"It's simple really," Kagan offered softly. "Tyler Martin is still out there. You and your brother think it's Jeb Ryland who pulled the strings to get him freed after that business with the Magnus family."

"So do you," Vitus responded. "The good congressman is gunning for me, and in his entitled way of thinking the bastard believes he has the right to go after my family. Tyler seems to have signed on for the duty. Tyler was in control of assigning that Magnus case to my brother—he had a nice little vengeance death planned out. Tyler rolled over for someone who demanded it. Only person I can pinpoint on that list is Ryland."

"So what are you going to do?" Kagan asked seriously. "Sit back and wait for the man to make his next attempt?"

Understanding dawned on Vitus. They were getting close enough to see the glow from the lights. They passed Secret Service personnel with high-powered rifles, Vitus cutting a few officers salutes. It had been a long time since he'd been in uniform, even longer since he'd been

respectable. Congressman Jeb Ryland had made sure he
lost his shield when he returned his daughter to him, and
there wasn't a decent outfit willing to test the congressman's good will and hire him on. Which was going to
make tonight's award ceremony interesting to say the
least.

"Fill me in." Vitus said to avoid thinking about Damascus Ryland. He was on the congressman's turf now
and needed to stay focused. Thinking about Damascus
was a one-way track to disaster. Three years hadn't been
long enough to loosen her hold on him and apparently,
neither had losing his shield. Her face was floating
through his mind even as he tried to focus on Kagan,
on the very real fact that his brother Saxon had nearly
been taken out in some crazy quest for vengeance by the
congressman.

Nope. None of it mattered. He clearly saw her. Ginger curls that fluffed up when she didn't have a team of
servants to keep her looking perfect. Blue eyes that reminded him of the way the water looked on the beaches
of Hawaii. Lips the color of dawn in those moments when
you first woke up and believed that anything was possible if you just got moving.

"Simple," Kagan said. "I want you to push against the
bastard's comfort zone. See if it gains a response. If it
doesn't, he's clean."

"Or smart enough to know when he's pushed too
hard," Vitus countered, forcing his attention back to the
matter at hand.

His section leader cut him a sidelong glance. "Wouldn't
put money on that horse if I were you."

Vitus offered him a grin, but there was nothing nice
about the expression. It was pure intent, and Vitus
planned to enjoy it. "I'm still holding out on the bet I

made three years ago when Tyler Martin pulled my shield. I'm going to make sure Jeb Ryland has enough rope to hang himself. And I plan to be there when he does it."

"Vengeance is a double-sided blade." Kagan offered him a warning.

"So is hamstringing a man who was sent in to recover a kidnapping victim," Vitus replied. "I pulled his daughter out of a fucking concrete-lined hole. One her kidnappers never planned on her leaving."

"That wasn't the part the good congressman had difficulty with."

"Yeah, well, he can get the fuck over it," Vitus shot back.

"Sounds like you haven't."

Vitus didn't answer. He wasn't going to rise to Kagan's bait. His section leader was a master at shadow operations and as such, the man liked to know everyone's soft spots. Damascus was his.

What was Kagan up to? There was only one way to find out. Play the game. It looked like he was about to get a medal added to his record. It was overdue and that was a fact.

It was also a fact that he was perfectly willing to tuck tail and run in the opposite direction. That was a first for him. But then again, Damascus tended to be a whole bundle of firsts for him. The first time he'd fallen for one of his mission targets; the first time he'd been willing to overlook his field operating procedure; the first time he'd been unable to forget a woman who had so clearly written him off. He kept walking, his fingers curling into a fist as his jaw tightened.

A medal? It was going to feel like a goddamn brand being pressed into his chest.

* * *

Her escort was out of the front seat of the limousine before the car completely stopped. Damascus Ryland took
a deep breath to steady herself before her door was pulled
open, exposing her to the telephoto lens of the press. She
slipped one foot out of the car, making sure her evening
dress stayed over her thighs before scooting across the
edge of the seat and placing her other foot on the ground.
To some people it might have been overkill, the amount
of attention she gave to exiting the car, but those people
had never experienced the love the press had for tearing
apart any gaffe she might make.

And then there would be her father's reaction.

She stood with the help of one of the security men assigned to her. Her expression remained serene and poised.
Her dress settled into place, exactly one inch above the
polished top of her shoes, a testament to the skill of her
private tailor. Or perhaps it would be more correct to say
it was a blunt reminder of how much everyone lived in
fear of her father's wrath. Congressman Jeb Ryland didn't
suffer excuses, or even reasonable facts, well. If something was out of place, the reason was irrelevant.

Oh yes, everything had to be perfect.

So Damascus glided up the red carpet entry path to
the White House like a swan. The press remained behind
their barriers, snapping pictures as she softly greeted a
few with grace and poise.

Public Image.

Critical to her ambitious father.

Her smile faltered a little. She didn't like referring to
him as her father. "Sire" suited her feelings better. You
see, fathers loved their children. Jeb Ryland only viewed
her as a commodity, one to be used and exploited for his
benefit.

She refused to let that fact hurt her.

Her sire didn't deserve the benefit of her tender feelings. She'd learned that was the best way to face her life. Of course it had come at a high cost, but most life lessons did. Part of her enjoyed the way her heart ached from time to time, because it reminded her how very intent she needed to be if she wanted to avoid having life slap her again.

A ripple of pain, a familiar one, went through her. The reporter in front of her had asked something and she'd completely missed it as the shaft of anguish pierced her heart. She wasn't dwelling on it. No, it was worse than that.

She was savoring it.

She held the memory of Vitus Hale tight, even as the reality of her world tried to rip it away. Damascus made a polite reply and moved on. She refused to forget Vitus. Jeb might force her to do a great many things, but he would never be able to control her feelings. Just her life details, but that appeared to be enough for him.

Unfortunately, her memories would have to be enough, because there was no way to escape his reach. Not at the moment. She was working on that though. Her smile was sincere as she contemplated just how intent she was on making sure her future would be what she desired it to be.

"Soon."

She savored the word and everything it meant. Hope was something she lived on, cultivating it like the last shred of life left inside her. Honestly, she was pretty sure it was the only thing keeping her going, the knowledge that she was going to have a life beyond her sire's ambitions.

Well, she would if she managed to succeed.

The Secret Service milled around her, maintaining a security net that they believed protected her. In reality, it kept her exactly where Jeb Ryland wanted her. A woman in a smartly tailored navy blue suit was waiting just inside the open doorway for her. There was a smile on her lips and excitement in her eyes. The poor woman believed in what she was doing, that sparkle a testimony to how devoted she was to the position she had. There had been a time when Damascus believed too.

It was long gone.

"Welcome Ms. Ryland. I will be your liaison for tonight's ceremony." The woman extended her hand, engaging in a firm handshake.

Another thing her father insisted on was feminine attire. It was something she'd taken delight in for years, never questioning the wisdom behind wispy fabrics and stylish heels. Fate had taken a hand in helping rip away the rose-colored glasses her sire had secured so tightly to her head. Now, she knew that there were times she might have to rely on herself. A secret little smile lifted her lips as she followed the liaison into the White House. She could run now. That was something the next bunch of kidnappers wouldn't be expecting from her.

Ability.

Maybe resourcefulness was a better way to put it. All that Damascus cared about was never, ever, feeling as helpless as she had when Special Agent, former Navy SEAL Vitus Hale had rescued her. No, she was never going to be that frightened little girl again.

You will never see Vitus again either.

Well, that was wrong too. She saw him every night in her dreams. Her sire couldn't take that away, even if the ambitious congressman had managed to ensure she wasn't willing to cross him and return to the man she loved. It was a small thing, one little bit of defiance she held close to her heart because it was the only thing in her life that was truly hers.

She loved him and always would. Damn her sire to hell for making it impossible for her to go back to the man she craved.

Damascus held her secret close to her heart as she entered the world of politicians. She would swear she could smell the ambition in the air, feel it on her skin like a film of oil she wanted to wash away. The crowd inside the White House was an odd mixture of predators seeking a way to climb higher on the power ladder and people there to serve what they believed was a noble cause.

She was no different, just a resource for her sire to trade for his own success. It wasn't even a secret. There were people watching her now. Critiquing her with gauging looks as they contemplated how much trouble she might be to their own agendas. She didn't care. At least not about the ones who viewed her as a potential problem. What left her mouth dry were the men who swept her from head to toe like a prize racing horse. They were contemplating making a try for getting a saddle on her, which of course was what her sire wanted. All of her grooming and poise was designed to bring in a match that would add weight to her sire's bid for the vice presidency. That was why she couldn't marry the man she loved.

Her sire would kill Vitus before he'd ever see his chances for the vice presidency threatened. She didn't doubt his sincerity, which was why she'd left Vitus. It had been the only way to truly protect him. At least Vitus hated her now. She took that bit of knowledge and hugged it close to her heart. It was very dear, because Vitus Hale wasn't a man to bend in the face of a threat. Her lips curved into a genuine smile as she thought about him. No, he had a warrior spirit, one that would face off with anyone who threatened him.

Her smile faded as her belly knotted with the harsh knowledge of just how different her sire was from Vitus.

Jeb Ryland's concept of honor was twisted. Her sire wouldn't fight fairly. Oh no, he'd move to strike Vitus from any angle that would ensure his victory, dirty ploys perfectly acceptable.

So she'd left Vitus and let him think it was her choice. Being a liar was a small cost to pay in return for knowing the man she loved would live.

"Tonight's ceremony will be a little more personal than the last one you assisted with," the liaison explained to her.

Damascus felt a tingle touch her nape. She wasn't sure just why, only that it felt like the world was tilting off-center.

"I'm sure you're excited to finally get the chance to personally thank your rescuer . . ." The liaison continued without noticing what effect her words were having. She kept right on walking through the back corridor toward the reception room, which was already crowded with press. They were stacked deep, their security badges hanging around their necks in plain view of the Secret Service as they waited to capture a shot worthy of the front page.

"I don't understand," Damascus said, but she was getting a sinking feeling in the pit of her stomach, that gripping sort of sensation that only one man on the face of the planet had ever given her.

The liaison looked over her shoulder and flashed her a smile. "It does take time to get a SEAL to attend one of these medal functions."

Damascus froze. It felt like her lungs had just seized up, suspending her between breaths. Something deep inside her was stirring, straining against the bonds she'd imprisoned her emotions for Vitus with.

"Are you all right?" The liaison's voice rose in pitch,

drawing the attention of two of the Secret Service. They jerked their attention toward her, sweeping her from head to toe.

"Yes." Damascus pushed her response through frozen lips. The last thing she needed was attention drawn to the moment. Her sire would jump on that as proof she wasn't as docile as he believed.

There was no way she was going to see her carefully plotted plan turned into Swiss cheese.

And then what are you going to do?

She had no idea, only that she had to hold onto her composure or place the man she loved at risk. She would simply have to find a way to maintain her poise.

Which of course was something she had never been able to do when it came to Vitus Hale.

The press loved medal-pinning ceremonies. Well, at least they enjoyed them when there wasn't something juicier to sink their cameras into.

"Are you ready Ms. Ryland?" the liaison asked nervously.

"Of course," Damascus replied. But she knew what the woman was seeing. There was sweat on her forehead. Her professional makeup held up, but the little dots of perspiration were still there to betray her agitation.

Hell, it was full-on terror.

Damascus ended up running her hand across her forehead again and chided herself the moment she realized she'd done it. The press loved to get bad pictures of everyone. She knew better than to give them an opportunity, but her focus was slipping. The stage was set, the presidential podium in place along with the medals being awarded. Everyone was waiting for the president to begin the proceedings.

Vitus was there, so close and yet so far away.

Her heart was pounding, anticipation so gripping that she struggled to pull in each breath. The liaison was casting nervous looks at her, no doubt trying to decide if she was another fragile politician's daughter who would need delicate handling to make it through what should have been a breeze. Damascus cringed and focused on just how much she detested that type of woman. The ones she brushed elbows with on the White House lawn and in the ballroom. The ones who were too far detached from reality, rarely venturing to the bathroom without one of their personal assistants trailing them.

She refused to be that fragile. She had strength, had scraped it up from the darkest moment of her life when death shimmered like a reward. That moment when Vitus had rescued her from men who viewed her as a means to success in their venture.

So, she'd make it through today, through seeing him once more, through making it appear as if he wasn't the man she loved.

The press surged to life as a man entered the stage, moving across it with solid purpose. Camera lenses were lifted into position as he welcomed them all and introduced the president.

She knew the speech by heart, the accolades for service rendered above and beyond the scope of duty. The words outlining how grateful the nation was and how privileged the president felt at being able to award the medals waiting for their recipients.

She lost track of what the president was saying as four men came onto the stage. The Secret Service guided each one into position, stopping them precisely where small pieces of tape were secured to the carpet. They were all in dress uniform, but her attention settled on Vitus Hale. He stood at ease, even though she knew without a doubt he was anything but. His body was perfectly in position as the president turned to look at her.

"I think this medal is one I need to share the awarding with." The president smiled at her. "She's a lot prettier too. Don't you all agree?"

There was a rumble of amusement as the cameras continued to click away. Only the practice her sire had insisted she do ensured that she glided toward the president with poise and confidence.

All she noticed were the details she was starving for, the tiny little things about Vitus that she had missed for three long years. The way his chin seemed chiseled out of solid stone or the flecks of copper in his dark hair. His shave was perfect, his hair cut to a mere half inch all over his head. The president was waiting for her to take the Medal of Honor from his hands. The ribbon felt crisp and heavy as she stepped onto a step stool that had been provided for her so that she could secure the ribbon around Vitus's neck.

He smelled as good as she recalled.

Her fingers brushed his neck as she fumbled with the closure. It felt like it took too long, another round of amusement rippling through the press as she struggled to complete her task. She finally finished, and the president offered Vitus his hand. The president held the handshake for a long moment, ensuring that the press got enough shots before he stepped past Vitus to the next man. Damascus stepped down and held her position, one full step behind Vitus, while the rest of the medals were awarded.

It was only when the president was striding toward the edge of the stage that Vitus turned to look at her. His gaze cut into her, pinning her to the spot as surely as if he'd thrust a sword straight through her, eyes as blue as a

Caribbean lagoon but as cold as a glacier. Betrayal was there, hot, searing, and condemning enough to make her feel like she might just burst into flames and be reduced to a pile of cinders at his polished boots.

His anger was so scorching, it left her staggering back to the waiting liaison, who was unsure what to do with her. Damascus straightened her spine and walked toward the ballroom. At least there was something to be said for the number of times her sire had insisted she attend these functions. She knew what to do without having to think about it.

Which was good, because being around Vitus Hale made thinking impossible.

"I'm fine," Damascus repeated, but the liaison was still looking at her doubtfully. She'd already pressed a glass of perfectly chilled champagne into Damascus's hand and was contemplating what else might be needed.

Damascus took a sip of the champagne and then another. By the time she realized what she was doing, she'd finished the glass. The liaison looked at her doubtfully.

"So, the dance is next?" Damascus asked to try and cover her lack of composure.

The liaison nodded. "Yes. Commander Hale and the other recipients will begin the opening waltz."

Damascus tipped the glass up to get the last drops of champagne. The liaison's eyes widened as she bit back the question she was dying to ask.

It wasn't hard for Damascus to deduce what was on the woman's mind. Vitus had rescued her, and he was absolutely scrumptious. What was there to be skittish about?

Oh my, now *there* was a question.

For a moment, her memory offered up fragments of the stolen moments she indulged in with Vitus. Hot, passionate moments, when the only thing that mattered was chasing satisfaction, consequence nowhere in sight or thought. Just the freedom to be exactly who she was instead of what her sire wanted her to be.

But the cost had certainly shown up later when he'd brought her home, delivering her to what everyone believed was the arms of her loving family. She'd been struggling to finish paying off the debt ever since, but couldn't quite force herself to banish the memory.

Ha! As if you could . . .

That was a solid truth. Vitus was not a man easily forgotten. Of course, that was why he'd found her. His skills were almost unmatched. Little wonder he was a SEAL.

Or had been one. She let that thought settle into her brain because it proved just how much power her sire truly had. Vitus had mysteriously ended his career among the SEALs and ended up unemployed.

But not dead. She had to hold onto that bit of knowledge. The medal would help him reestablish himself. Maybe he could write a book.

She felt herself losing the battle to wring drops of hope out of the situation she was trapped in and it pissed her off to know that she'd infected Vitus just by reaching for him.

The ballroom was full of wives and daughters of politicians. Congressmen, senators, cabinet members all took advantage of the evening to rub elbows. The musicians were waiting for the signal to play a fanfare for the entrance of the president and first lady. A member of the Secret Service had been delegated the task of standing near the conductor. A message finally came through his earpiece, and he nodded at the conductor. The musicians lifted their instruments as a pair of wide double doors were pulled open to reveal the president and first lady. Their entrance was smooth and quick because the press was kept outside.

The conductor tapped his music stand, and the musicians all froze as they waited for the signal to begin. A hushed moment of anticipation held her in its grip as she waited for Vitus to surface.

He would. She had no doubt. He wasn't a man who knew how to shrink from duty. She didn't care for how bitter it felt to know she was nothing more than a duty to him tonight. Her heart was accelerating, her skin hypersensitive as she waited for him.

His hatred of her was the way it had to be, but that didn't keep her from lamenting it.

And she didn't have time to dwell upon her feelings. She felt him come close, the damn hair on the back of her neck standing up. There was always a jolt of awareness that hit her when he touched her, and tonight was no different. She gasped as he claimed her hand and turned her neatly into position right as the music began.

So very perfect.

Yet it felt so very forbidden.

"Try to play the part, Princess."

Vitus was just as she remembered him. He had her locked in his embrace, even though everyone around them wouldn't have found a single thing to fault him over. His hands were properly placed, looking quite gentlemanly, but she could feel the strength in his grip. So controlled and yet so very inescapable. He was worried she'd bolt and making sure she knew he wasn't going to allow it.

"Don't call me that." She needed to keep her wits. "I'm not a little girl."

He turned her in time with the waltz. For a moment, she felt like she was moving without any effort on her part, being swept along by the sheer power of the man holding her. His eyes narrowed, his lips thinning as his gaze dropped to her lips.

"You weren't a kid the last time we met either."

She'd been twenty-three and well past the age of not noticing how enticing Vitus was. Enticing was too tame a word. The moment he'd pulled the cover off the hole she'd been imprisoned in she'd felt like she'd been sucker punched. The memory was still vivid and haunted her dreams.

"So don't call me by a child's nickname."

He turned her again, controlling her body as the dance floor became crowded. Her heart was racing, the feeling of his arms around her making her breathless. The way he held her defied explanation. It touched off something deep inside her that bubbled up through the floorboards of what she thought was her composure. When it came to Vitus, there was no maintaining a grip on her reactions. She was the powder keg and he was the open flame. When they touched, the only outcome was an explosion. One that left her seeing stars.

Something flickered in his eyes. "If you didn't want me to think of you as a kid, you shouldn't have run home crying to Daddy."

His voice was edged with anger. She shifted, but he held her against him. "I didn't," she hissed through her teeth.

Surprise flickered in his eyes along with disbelief. That hurt her more than anything. He believed she was guilty of betraying him. For a man like him, that was unforgivable.

"Your father sure knows more than he should." The music climbed to its crescendo, the musicians finishing out the melody with a polished flourish.

He turned her under his arm, making her gown swirl away from her ankles. Just a touch of cool air hit her calves, setting off another ripple of sensation. Damned if he wasn't a master of keeping her on the edge.

"Thank you for the dance, Ms. Ryland."

She heard his boot heels snap together a moment before she was treated to the sight of his broad shoulders while he walked away from her. She was torn between the need to charge after him to make her case and behaving in a manner that wouldn't betray just how much his opinion mattered to her.

Her own private hell; it was a place she knew well.

Congressman McKinnon's son saved her by gliding up and offering her his hand. He was all of twenty-one years old but eager to please his family by making sure he performed well under the scrutiny of the Washington crowd.

He was perfect really, too young to truly be in the same league with Vitus. So why did she notice so keenly the lack of confidence in his grip on her hand? Or the very disappointing way he let her control their process around the floor?

Because you know what you want.

She did. And there was no way she was going to get it, at least, not without putting him at risk.

Vitus Hale wasn't the only one who knew how to protect others. She really would have enjoyed getting the chance to tell him so.

"Turn around," Kagan whispered. "You're about to miss what you came here to see."

Vitus stiffened. He didn't need to see her. Couldn't really. Every muscle he had was tight and his cock was hard. It shouldn't be so easy for her to get to him. He was an ex-SEAL for Christ's sake. Controlling his responses was what he excelled at.

Apparently not, at least when it came to Damascus Ryland.

He forced himself to do an about-face. And it pissed him off to realize how hard it was to do it. But his temper fizzled out as he took in Jeb Ryland standing next to his daughter. Controlling his personal reactions wasn't the only thing he'd learned to do while being a Seal. He'd also spent a lot of time reading peoples' body language. Damascus's said she was fighting the urge to shove her father away from her. The good congressman was gripping her elbow, trying to look like he was simply standing by her side, but a closer examination showed his fingertips digging into her arm.

"Whoa." Kagan shot an arm out, stopping him.

Vitus cussed under his breath as he realized that he'd been moving toward her.

"Daddy is a little unhappy." Kagan stated the obvious. "Want to take a stab at the cause?"

Vitus tightened his control. "We know he disapproves of contact between us." What stuck in his throat was the fact that Damascus was standing there taking it. She could have stayed with him. That was the thought that kept him standing across the room as Jeb Ryland finished up and handed his daughter over to another man. Vitus was grinding his teeth as Damascus went into the man's embrace and off across the dance floor.

"She's a little old to be jumping to do Daddy's bidding," Kagan said.

Vitus sent his superior a hard look. "You know the type. They might like to play dangerously when the press isn't watching, but the moment their lifestyle is threatened, they fall into line. Damascus is a politician's daughter through and through."

"Possibly." Kagan's tone left Vitus wondering if his section leader agreed with him or not. With Kagan, it was wise to question everything and double-check what you thought you were sure of.

Damascus came twirling by, claiming his attention. Maybe he should question what he thought he knew about her.

Then again, maybe he'd be the biggest dumb-ass on the face of the planet to venture anywhere near her. The woman was his own personal kryptonite.

"What do you think you're doing, Damascus?" Her father kept a smile on his lips, but his tone was biting.

"Being a good hostess," she answered back.

Her father's fingers bit into her arm.

"Need I remind you of the promise I made you?"

"No," she said. "It's hardly necessary to let one dance bother you so much. It was expected, and now it's over."

"It had better be," he warned her. "I can make sure that man's mother has a flag to hang over her mantle. You know I have connections with the right people."

"So you've told me."

Her sire wasn't pleased with her continuing to speak. His eyes were full of determination, a crazy sort that sent a tingle down her spine. He might just be a touch insane. In the capitol, only the truly dedicated survived. This was something different though. If he wasn't her biological father, she'd swear he was jealous.

Even knowing that, she still battled to swallow her distaste. She was pulling on her arm, the pain increasing to the point of agony.

"Ah, Carl." Her sire suddenly switched tracks, becoming the good-natured man he presented to the public.

It made her skin crawl.

"Evening Jeb." Carl Davis reached out and shook her father's hand.

If possible, her misgivings doubled, because the two men struck her as reflections of each other. Both of them as fake as hundred-dollar diamonds.

"I want you to know Jeb, I am just bold enough to challenge you for this lovely creature you are keeping to yourself," Carl declared as he held out a hand to Damascus. "Just because you're her father, don't go thinking you can monopolize her. I intend to get a slice of her time."

"You do tend to get what you go after," her sire joked good-naturedly.

Although it wasn't really a joke. There was true admiration in her sire's tone, something that could so easily translate into disaster for her.

Carl was grinning as he captured her hand and pulled her toward him. The musicians had struck up again, and he turned her into a waltz. But his hand slipped too low on her back, his little finger teasing the swell of her bottom.

"You are stunning tonight, Damascus."

The compliment unnerved her, sending a warning through her brain. There was a flicker in Carl's eyes that hinted at possessiveness. Something she wasn't at all interested in.

"I had a wonderful lunch with your father last week." Carl's hand ventured lower. She stiffened and watched his lips curve with satisfaction. "I think you and I should retire to some place more private to discuss the outcome of that meeting."

"Excuse me." She raised her voice enough so Carl was forced to release her or risk judgment from those close enough to hear. His grin faded but only for a moment. He flashed her a look that made it clear he was enjoying the chase.

"I need to go to the ladies room." She ducked through an arch and down a hallway, feeling like someone had just tried to stick her head through a noose.

Well, in a way that was exactly what had happened. Carl Davis was slated for the next presidential nomination in three years. His wife had passed away from cancer very suddenly the year before, and bachelors didn't make for solid campaigns. Her sire had been shoving her toward the man ever since the diagnosis went public. What chilled her blood was the interest flickering in Carl's eyes. All she saw was the difference between the way Carl looked at her and the way Vitus had.

It was a stark comparison, one that left her slightly nauseated because there was no way she was going to settle for what she saw in Carl's eyes.

But that left her dodging him, and the only place to go was the garden. At least the night was nice. She slipped through another hallway and out into the garden. There were whispers and a few breathless sounds from behind some of the immaculately kept plants. She steered clear of them and made her way along one of the paths.

"Exactly what I was going to suggest." Carl caught her hand and pulled her to a stop.

Damascus recoiled, her heels wobbling on the cobblestones. Carl used it as an excuse to reach out and cup her elbow.

"Really, Mr. Davis—"

"Carl," he insisted in a low tone. "Now that I have your father's blessing, let's dispense with formality."

She moved her hand in a wide circle and lowered it on the other side of his arm. Even though she'd only learned it from a book and practiced it alone in her room, the self-defense technique worked beautifully. Surprise flashed through Carl's eyes as she withdrew a few paces.

"I am focused on completing my doctorate," she said smoothly.

"Admirable," Carl answered. "And if I understand correctly, you should be receiving it within weeks. Which leaves you and I the summer to court before having an autumn wedding. I need to be a solid, settled man for the voters."

"No thank you, I intend to use my degree. Good luck in your search for a bride." Damascus turned to leave.

Carl's pulled her back, showing her an expression that was unyielding, betraying just how much he didn't like her hedging. "Let's cut the smoke screen, Damascus. I need a wife, the right wife. Your father wants to be my running mate. I want you, and I don't have time to play games." He held out his hand. "Let's go back inside and dance. The press will pick up on it. Just the sort of coverage we all need. The voters will eat up the image of a new family in the White House."

"That's the sort of thing you and my father"—the word stuck in her throat but she forced it past her lips—"need. Not me. Find someone else to be your first lady."

Carl chuckled ominously. "I'm going to be taking your father as my running mate. For that, he's going to pay up, and I want you." For a moment, his eyes narrowed, lust pulling his features tight. "I like knowing you've kept yourself clean. Can't have a first lady with too many lovers in her past. Your father and I already have an agreement, one he assured me you would honor."

Her temper was so hot, it was a wonder steam wasn't rising from her forehead.

"Think again." She was being daring, but she just didn't care. She was little more than an exotic pet to him.

"I always get what I want." He made a grab for her.

Damascus lunged to the side, taking refuge behind a large pot with flowers in it. She grasped the rim. "I'll send it to the ground. The service boys will be here in a flash and the gossip will flow."

He grunted but straightened up and fixed his suit jacket. "I like spunk," he offered slowly, his tone rich with promise. "It's going to make getting a saddle on you a whole lot of fun."

Damascus sent the pot toward the ground in response. It hit with a smashing sound that grated against the serenity of the garden.

"Bitch," Carl muttered before he cut off to the left and disappeared.

The scent of the soil was just tickling her nose when the first sounds of running feet touched her ears. Her sire wouldn't like her being the subject of the wrong sort of attention, but she didn't give a rat's ass at the moment.

Someone grasped her wrist and pulled her through the wall of shrubbery behind her. Only half a sound made it past her lips before it was smothered beneath a hard hand and she was folded into an unbreakable hold. For a moment terror surged through her, the memory of being tied up and helpless rising from her memory like a huge specter. Her blood chilled, her heart pounding so hard it felt like it might just break through her rib cage. She dug her fingernails into the hand over her mouth while she bit.

"It's me," Vitus hissed against her ear as she tasted blood.

She gasped, releasing his finger and sagging back against him. For a moment, the world spun and she dragged in a ragged breath to fend off the icy dread choking her. Vitus snorted before pulling her away from the men investigating the broken pot. Her feet didn't touch the ground until they were out of sight.

"You're jumpy," he said as he looked at the wound on his hand. Blood was spotting his white dress glove. He stripped it off and used it to apply pressure to the wound.

"The last time someone grabbed me like that, I ended up stuffed into a trunk." The memory was in control of her, spilling out of her mouth. She suddenly realized who she was facing and pressed her own hand against her lips to still them before she said anything else. He wasn't a man who would take her shielding him, no matter how wise it was.

"Fair enough," Vitus surprised her by saying. "At least your father seems to have gotten you some self-defense training. That was a nice little grip-breaking move."

His praise cut through the memory chilling her, satisfaction making her smile. "I learned it myself. Jeb would never have approved."

Once more, she was talking without thinking. She put her teeth into her lower lip as she realized the little bit of personal information she'd just let loose. She couldn't afford to make such mistakes. Especially not with Vitus—he was too astute, his senses too keen. She didn't doubt for a second that her sire would carry out his threat. And now, Vitus was studying her, trying to read her expression, breaking her façade down.

"I just . . . wanted to learn a few . . . moves," she added in the hope of closing the issue.

"You've got a few more to learn," he answered. "Like how to deal with an attacker who is behind you."

"Why did you do that?" she asked, unable to keep the question to herself. It felt like it was burning a hole in her.

He pulled his remaining glove off and stuffed both of them into his pocket. "Why did you push the pot over to begin with?"

"It was a mishap," she lied. It actually hurt because she wanted so badly to have someone to confide in.

Hah, you mean you want Vitus to be your hero.

She did, and she could never have that again, but the facts didn't seem to have much effect against her cravings.

Well, that summed up her dealing with Vitus all right. All impulse, no control. Straight forward with nothing but her cravings guiding the way.

"I would have thought you'd be happily on your way back to the dance floor with the good Carl Davis," he said. "You always are Daddy's good little girl."

"Don't embarrass yourself," she snapped. "You don't know anything about it."

One of his eyebrows lifted. "I know you told him all about what should have been private between us."

"I didn't tell him," she shot back before thinking. She realized her mistake when his eyes narrowed in contemplation. Vitus didn't know how to stay out of something, even when it was for his own good. That was why she had to get away from him before her muddled brain just delivered every last detail while she was intoxicated by him.

She turned to leave. "Flee" was a better word if she was being honest, but he caught her wrist and pulled her back. One second she was facing the path leading back to the lights of the ballroom, and the next she was colliding with Vitus. She put her hands up to break the collision, her wrist free just as suddenly as it had been captured so that both her hands flattened against his chest.

She shivered, the connection shaking her down to her heels as her toes felt like they were curling. He felt so good. So much better than the memory she'd been taking solace in at night when there was no one around to critique her.

So much better . . .

She was in bliss, there in his embrace. He'd closed his arms around her once more this time, molding her to him, stroking her from nape to the swell of her bottom with a touch that set fire to her blood. She wanted to purr. Wanted to arch back and close her eyes so there wouldn't be anything else in her world except the feeling of his touch.

He grunted, the sound drawing her gaze up. He still

knew too much about shadows. They were in the dark, completely hidden from the rest of the world. She would never have realized there was such a place to escape to among the high-security zone of the White House and yet, he'd found it. Now, he was a dark visage, tempting her to melt against him and share the moment.

Live in the moment . . . reach for what you crave . . . take it now, before it slips away.

She shivered, the longing to do exactly that nearly consuming her. The delicate surface of her lips felt dry and she rolled them in, drawing his attention.

"Princess." His tone was harsh, edged with self-loathing and a lack of discipline she understood because she was experiencing the same thing. She felt his breath against her wet lips a moment before she felt his kiss.

Her memories were bullshit, a sorry excuse for the real deal.

The real deal? She stretched up onto her toes to get more of it, slipping her hands up his chest, savoring the feel of him before finding his bare skin above the collar of his uniform jacket. That connection shook her to her core, breaking down the walls she'd built to keep her desires contained. Now they burst free as he kissed her, the way only Vitus had ever kissed her.

Boldly, passionately, and all the while touching her like she could take every bit of his strength. It was the thing that stroked her inner needs, that confidence in her ability to meet him and not need to be handled like a delicate vase. He held her like a woman and she kissed him back like one. Time froze, the seconds moving by like hours. There was only the taste of him and the way he angled his face so he could press his lips against her more completely. It was firm and spine-tingling. He moved his mouth across hers before boldly pressing her lips apart and tasting her deeper.

Just as quickly as it had begun, she was standing alone. There was a full foot between them though it felt like ten. She was breathing hard, and he was glaring at her. She would have sworn she could feel the heat of it.

"Good-bye Princess."

This time, the word was somehow different, his tone transforming it into an endearment, a very, very personal one. It stroked the memory of the hours she'd taken refuge in his embrace, those stolen moments when she had been a woman, his woman.

His . . .

He melted back into the darkness as she forced all her feelings back into the box she kept them in. When she emerged, she was everything she was expected to be.

But deep down inside, she was still his.

And always would be.

"The car is being brought around for you."

Her sire glided up to her side as the clock struck one. The good wives and younger children were making their way toward the exit while men like her father were getting ready to dig in for a long night of whiskey and information gathering. More business went down in the cigar rooms than anywhere else.

"Trenton will make sure you get home."

"Of course he will," Damascus purred. Her father's personal bodyguard was constantly dogging her heels. Her belly suddenly tightened as she realized what Carl had said about her not having too many lovers.

One look at her sire and she realized she wasn't wrong. There was a calculating look in his eyes, his mind working on a plan that included her playing her assigned role.

"You're having dinner with Carl Davis tomorrow."

Her eyes widened but her sire was striding across the polished ballroom floor without waiting for her reply. Oh no. She was expected to fall into line. Well, that wouldn't be happening.

"Ms. Ryland?" Trenton inquired softly from where the burly man had been shadowing her sire. He extended an arm toward the door.

Damascus took off, eager to be done with the appearance, and yet part of her longed for one last glimpse of Vitus.

What are you going to do if you see him? Run to him? You wouldn't dare.

No, and that was perhaps the saddest part of all. She was a coward. The car pulled up the moment she made it to the doors, the press snapping shots of her as she slipped inside and Trenton shut the door.

Damascus leaned her head back against the top of the seat in the limousine and allowed herself a moment of rest. She was wrung out, her cheeks aching from holding a smile so long. The delicate layers of her evening gown felt stuck to her skin with perspiration.

And her lips still tingled from his kiss.

Alone in the car, she could indulge herself and just let go of the façade that was her life in favor of recalling exactly how it had thrilled her to be back in Vitus's arms.

Maybe fate was finally being a bit kind. Granting her a last taste of what she wanted before she struck out on her own. She indulged herself in a smile, letting the knowledge of her coming liberation lift her spirits. Carl could suck her dick. Blunt, crass, and very definitely not the sort of thought her sire would approve of.

Which made it perfect.

She wasn't going to be Jeb Ryland's little princess bride, nor was Carl going to saddle her. Oh no, she had plans. Ones that were going to come into play very, very soon. Sure, there would be plenty of people who would condemn her for using her father's money to finish her education, but she'd paid him back in all the simpering he demanded of her.

That wasn't going to be part of her future.

No, she'd made her own plans and made her own arrangements. In some ways, she was her father's daughter all right. She'd learned to play shadow games and deal in secrets. There were advantages to knowing everyone in Washington, D.C. One of which was the fact that she had been able to arrange a posting to a very classified laboratory just as soon as her doctorate in contagious diseases was processed. She was about to become a doctor of contagious diseases when those little germs were rapidly becoming the weapons of the new era. Small pox, polio, Ebola, and even the Black Death. She'd studied them and was going to spend her life learning more about them and their containment.

She was going to serve her country and humankind, and there wouldn't be a damn thing her sire could do to stop her.

Her smile faded as she contemplated the other thing she'd get from going into a sealed faculty—protection. The one thing she needed if she was going to leave Jeb Ryland behind. He had enemies, ones who had proven they'd use her to get to him. That was why she couldn't go just anywhere. But a classified level-five laboratory? It was the perfect haven.

You mean prison . . .

No, she meant haven because her life with her father was a prison, and that was the only way she was going to allow herself to think about it.

She resented that fact, resented him for not being a decent person. Not that being angry helped her any. Thinking her circumstances through had. She'd devised a way to be free, and it was about to come to fruition.

Success, but it would not include the man she loved. Vitus Hale was not the sort of man that any woman should ever make a pet out of. So she wasn't going to even think about suggesting he join her. He'd likely face off with her father and be furious with her for trying to protect him.

She indulged in a smile. Yes, Vitus wouldn't accept her shielding him, at least he wouldn't if he ever discovered what she'd done. That didn't stop her from contemplating telling him. She always pulled away from reaching out to him though. The reason was simple. She'd told him she was a woman, so she'd shoulder her load, in the same way he'd come to her rescue and protect her.

After all, it wasn't his fault her family was whacked. Loving him meant letting him make a clean getaway.

So that was exactly what she planned to do.

"Something's got your attention," Kagan said.

Vitus considered ignoring his section leader as he opened the first few buttons on the top of his dress uniform. Back in the parking garage, he was finally free to dispense with the formalities. He dropped the Medal of Honor into his pocket, pissed off because he hadn't really enjoyed getting it. There had been a time when he dreamed of earning one. Being jaded sucked.

"The question is, what are you going to do about it?" Kagan continued.

"Keep watching Tyler and Ryland," Vitus answered. "They'll slip up one of these days."

"They already did, with that Magnus affair," Kagan reminded him. "We've got to get it to stick."

Vitus climbed into the driver's seat and started the engine. Kagan rode shotgun as they drove out of the parking area.

"Ryland showed his hand tonight," Kagan continued.

"That girl is his weak spot, because he needs to give Carl what he wants. Press on it."

"No." Vitus turned around a corner and onto the interstate. Kagan was cutting him a hard look.

"You can't afford to be picky."

"I'm not going to use her," Vitus said. "Shut the fuck up about it or you can walk."

He was being insubordinate, but Kagan liked his rough edges because when it came to dealing with bad guys, nice guys finished last. Sometimes, dead last.

Kagan let him drive in silence for a long time but Vitus didn't think he'd won the point. Kagan wasn't a pushover by any stretch of the imagination. No, his section leader was cultivating arguments.

"Damascus might have pissed me off, but it was personal. She's already been dragged through hell for the sake of who she's related to. I won't add to that," Vitus said as he started into the quiet neighborhood where his brother's team was operating from. The soccer moms never would have guessed that one of the sedate-looking mideighties homes actually housed an elite Special Operations team. Of course, that was the entire point.

Vitus pulled the van into the driveway and past the fence that kept the curious from seeing what was going on. A second car pulled in on his tail. His brother Saxon and Agent Thais Sinclair joined them in the driveway.

"Thanks for the backup," Vitus said. "Good night."

Saxon waited until his brother was out of earshot. "I'll do it."

Kagan offered him a small curve of his lips. It was high praise from a man who lived his life among shadow operatives. Anyone who wasn't sharp died pretty darn fast. That left only the best, and Kagan appreciated Saxon knowing something was up, even without solid intel.

"Be in touch," Kagan said. "Keep your suit pressed and your shoes shined."

"And make your peace with God," Thais added. The female member of their team was sleek and poised. The meager light made her evening gown shimmer, but neither man made the mistake of being duped by the picture she presented. Thais Sinclair was a deadly operative, a fact she'd proven more than once. She offered Saxon a long, hard look. "Ryland isn't going to like seeing you anywhere near him. Show your face and it will touch off an explosion."

"That's what I'm hoping for," Saxon answered.

Thais made a soft sound under her breath. "Be careful what you wish for, gentlemen. We almost got wiped out the last time Ryland came after us."

"Which is why I don't plan to wait for him to make another attempt," Saxon said. "There's also Tyler. He's somewhere close to Ryland. No one else could protect him or pull that many strings to get him released after that business with the Magnus case."

"In that case"—Thais offered a soft shrug—"count me in. Nothing I like better than facing an oncoming train."

She walked up the driveway, still looking perfectly poised in spite of being in heels for the better part of the day. There wasn't even a tiny falter in her steps, her body moving in a sultry motion that made both men fight to maintain their professional outlook on her.

"Be ready," Kagan said before he turned and walked down the driveway. A car was waiting, and he ducked inside it while it sat on the curb with its lights off.

Saxon nodded before moving on toward the house. He swept back his jacket to show his shield to the man standing in the entryway. There was a flash of red laser as the badge was scanned, and Saxon pressed his hand flat on a screen to confirm his identification. The screen chirped approval and the guard moved out of his way.

"You agreed?" Vitus was standing in the hallway. What would have been the dining room of the house was a communications center with computers and phones. Large flat-screen monitors were secured to the walls where family pictures would normally be. They lived the way they did so that the rest of the world could have normal dining rooms. Saxon didn't have any regrets.

"Leave her alone," Vitus said. "I mean that, brother."

"I'm not going to touch her." Saxon defended himself. "But you can bet I am not letting Tyler think we're just going to let him slide. Ryland is the key. I plan to make sure that bastard sees me watching him."

"That's dangerous," Vitus said.

"There was a time you would have called it ballsy," Saxon shot back.

"That too," Vitus agreed. "I just thought you were old enough to think with your brain these days."

"I'm not the one thinking with my cock," Saxon responded. "You're letting your association with that girl influence your decision. She's a good trigger point, and those are too hard to come by in men like Ryland. If we want Tyler, we're going to have to take risks."

Vitus knew it. He turned and went down the hall to the back door and went into the garage looking for his bike. He took a moment to pull on a leather jacket and helmet before taking off back down the driveway. The night air was crisp, chilling his neck. It was the time of night when construction crews were working on the roads to avoid tying up commuters. He checked the small screen that was in the side of his helmet for the road closures and avoided the traffic, slipping into the driveway of his house a few minutes later.

His teenage neighbor was still gaming, the window

flashing with the light from the kid's big-screen television. Vitus pulled his bike into the garage and walked up to the house. He disarmed the security system, then reentered it the moment he was sure he was alone in the house. He slipped the gun he'd pulled from behind the refrigerator back into its concealed hiding place before he stripped.

His jacket made a clunking sound when he laid it over a chair. The Medal of Honor was still in his pocket. He fished it out, taking a moment to consider it. When he'd first received his trident and became an active duty SEAL, he'd accepted the fact that he might earn such an award and that it very well might be awarded posthumously.

Part of him felt like that was the case tonight. There was something dead inside him, something he wanted to bury, but something that refused to go quietly to the grave.

And he'd been stupid enough to kiss her tonight, which meant there wasn't going to be any peace for him anytime soon.

Way to go Squid, thinking with your dick.

And his heart, but there was no reason to admit just how big of a fool he was. Damascus didn't need any help getting him to dance to her tune.

None at all.

"I have plans for my daughter," Congressman Jeb Ryland stated.

"So get busy telling her what they are," Tyler Martin answered him.

"I intend to," Jeb Ryland shot back. "You just make sure you keep those Hale brothers away from her. I saw both of them tonight."

The last of the guests were departing, allowing Jeb time to deal with details.

"I noticed," Tyler said. "Not that it was unexpected. The man was getting a Congressional Medal of Honor. His brother was sure to be on the guest list."

"I haven't changed my mind about what I want done." Jeb leaned closer to Tyler. "I want that family taken down. In name and blood."

"Sure you want to risk another attempt at that?" Tyler inquired softly. "It's a mighty risky thing, going after a decorated military hero. The voters won't take kindly to any hint of involvement."

"Which is your job to make sure it never happens," Jeb responded. "I told you the price for bringing you along and taking you under my wing. If it wasn't for me, you'd be rotting in a ditch somewhere with a bullet in your skull after that botched operation with the Magnus family."

"If it wasn't for you, I never would have been involved in that operation," Tyler answered. "I've got nothing against them."

The congressman's eyes narrowed. "I told you the price for becoming my head of security. Pay it or leave."

"I can't go back," Tyler answered. "You know that. Cut me and I'll draw blood on my way out."

Jeb smiled at him. "Wouldn't have you any other way. See? You understand this world. If I fail to deal with Vitus Hale, rumors will get around that I'm soft." He took a look around to ensure no one was close enough to hear. "I'd be a washed up shit-bag at that point, nothing to offer you except the chore of watching me fade away. That's not exactly what you signed on for, is it?"

"I'll work out some ideas," Tyler said. He didn't bother to make it clear that he'd also be considering some fallback plans. With a man like Jeb Ryland, it was a safe bet to assume he might need a safety net, but he didn't let that sour him to the relationship. The higher the risk, the greater the payoff. That was just the way life was, and he was looking forward to hitting the jackpot.

The congressman had nodded once before moving away from the White House to where his car was idling. Tyler pulled open the door for him before taking the passenger seat. He settled in, enjoying the prestige of being the congressman's number-one man. It was a position he'd worked hard for and one that he wasn't done paying for. Men like Ryland didn't play by normal rules. They expected a lot, but they offered more payback too.

Tyler Martin had no intention of risking his neck for thirty years as a special agent only to get rewarded with a meager pension and the joy of knowing he had to look over his shoulder for the rest of his life for anyone with a grudge against him. No. He was going to get more for the dirty work he'd done for men like Ryland and the president. When Ryland went to the White House, Tyler was going with him as his head of security.

It was going to cost him. That had never been in doubt, but the thing with Ryland's daughter was beginning to wear on his patience. So she'd fucked Vitus Hale. Big deal. She was back on the leash with enough promised repercussions to keep her there. From what he could see, Damascus didn't have enough spine to buck off the chains her daddy had on her. Maybe she was going to give Carl Davis a little run around the garden before getting caught, but that might just be her way of making sure she enjoyed getting put on her back.

Tyler didn't fucking care.

The only thing he had to care about was dealing with Ryland's insistence that he gain vengeance. That was a damn pain in his ass, but one he was going to have to deal with. He'd almost gotten it wrapped up when Kagan interfered.

He contemplated the Hale brothers. They were the best. It made it shitty that he was going to have to take them out, but a man had to do what he had to do to ensure his place. It was the new order, one where the superrich and powerful called the shots. Jeb Ryland was a prick with a serious control issue when it came to his daughter's snatch. Half the politicians' daughters in Washington fucked to their heart's contentment. No one gave a fig, so long as they kept it out of the tabloids and off YouTube.

But Carl Davis seemed to like the idea of having a pony no one else had ridden. Tyler shrugged, not really caring one way or the other. But recognizing that idea of exclusivity got him thinking about a way to deal with Vitus and Saxon Hale.

Jeb Ryland wasn't the only one who could see uses for his daughter.

CHAPTER TWO

A blender was running in the kitchen, and a moment later there was a squeak from her mother as the machine made a grinding noise and something hit the title floor. The shattering sound of glass was followed by a round of laughter. Damascus came around the corner but ended up being pushed back as one of the private security men went charging in to investigate what was happening.

"It's fine . . . fine . . ." Her mother was laughing so hard, she couldn't quite get her words out. "I'm just fumble-fingered."

Her mother laughed again as Damascus got through the doorway.

"Baby!" Her mother exclaimed, holding open her arms. Damascus ducked around the security man and into her mother's embrace.

"I wanted to make breakfast," her mother explained. A maid had emerged to clean up the remains of the blender and whatever concoction her mother had been trying to make. There was a splattered cookbook sitting on the counter along with about a dozen containers from the pantry.

"Yeah?" Damascus emerged from her mother's embrace and sent her a smile. There was a scent of something burning, and Damascus turned to see the security man yanking the oven door open. Smoke rolled out in a thick cloud as he reached in and pulled a baking dish out that had burnt butter bubbling ominously in it.

"That's great Mom." Damascus started steering her mother out of the kitchen as the staff dealt with the mess. The cook was rolling her eyes and biting her lip. "Let's get some coffee on the porch."

"Don't think I'm not onto you, Damascus," her mother muttered as Damascus ushered her out onto the back porch.

Damascus shrugged and sat down at a table already set with a coffee pot.

Her mother sat down with a little moue on her lips. "I am from the South. Cooking should be in my genes."

The maid had emerged from the house with a tray and a smothered snort. Her mother turned to look at her.

"Well, it *should* be," her mother exclaimed with just a hint of a whine.

"You just don't have the time to learn," Damascus said as she hid her smile behind a mug. Her mother was delicate and whimsical and completely perfect, so long as you didn't need anything cooked.

"That is for certain," her mother sighed "I can't believe how tight my schedule is. I am never home anymore."

"That's because you are in demand." Jeb Ryland joined them, playing the part of a loving family member. Damascus felt her skin prickle. Jeb was a different person when her mother was around. He smiled at his wife, dropping a kiss on her cheek. Damascus watched the way her mother smiled back at him; there was a sparkle in her eyes that needed no explanation.

She loved him, believed in him, and that kept

Damascus's lips firmly sealed. She knew what it was like to be denied the man she loved. There was no way she was going to shatter her mother's illusions.

"Well, I am happy to be doing my share for your career," Miranda Delacroix Ryland declared. Born and breed into a Southern political family, her mother had been groomed since birth to be the wife of a high elected official.

Damascus had never questioned that path until she'd met Vitus and been introduced to the other side of her father's nature. Jeb was shifting around on the porch, his hands in his pockets. The look he shot her over her mother's head was pure warning.

"Aren't you due in California tonight?"

Her mother sighed. "Yes. But honestly Jeb, I am never home anymore. I really need to ease up a bit."

"Can't do that." Her father deflected his wife's words easily. "Besides, Damascus is rarely home, her classes keep her at the university most of the time. That lab she studies in is a sealed one, the kind where the doctors have to wear those pressurized suits. Better for you to be out where you are doing good instead of waiting on her to finish."

Her father had stopped and placed a hand on her mother's shoulder. Miranda patted it. "You're right. Of course. Come hug your mother Damascus, I have to catch a plane."

She went back into her mother's embrace but caught her father shooting her a hard look. She was so tempted to let him see what she thought of him. The desire was chewing a hole inside her, but she clamped down on it, focusing instead on the moments she had with her mother.

There would be plenty of time to hate her sire later.

Of that she was certain.

* * *

"At last, we're alone," Carl Davis said.

Damascus lifted her glass and took a long sip, grateful for a distraction. But when she lowered it, she found herself looking across the restaurant at a man she recognized.

Saxon Hale.

She'd know him anywhere. He had Vitus's jaw, but his hair was dark as opposed to Vitus's. She looked into the same blue eyes, saw the same cutting condemnation she'd witnessed in Vitus before Saxon broke it off and returned to sweeping the area.

What the hell was he doing on security detail?

Her temper flared. The strain of maintaining her ruse with her sire was nearly more than she could shoulder, and now Saxon was there? She'd worked too hard to protect them both. Damn all men and their pride. And damn her for the way she squirmed in her seat. She didn't owe Saxon or his brother any apologies for going on a date, especially a date she didn't want to be on. But she still felt heat teasing her cheeks, like she was betraying Vitus somehow.

Shit, fate had a twisted sense of humor.

"I must say, I have been looking forward to this since last night," Carl continued.

Her temper was hot, which meant it was a bad time to open her mouth, but that didn't seem to register. Her patience was just worn too thin. "So have I."

Carl's eyebrows shot up in surprise.

"It's not often I get the privacy I need to tell someone like you exactly how much of a jerk I think you are."

There, it was said. The security men assigned to them likely heard her, but they were maintaining their stony, unreadable expressions as the waiting staff hung back and made sure they arrived only when Carl summoned them. The restaurant itself was a press-free establishment, members only.

"Your father has no idea what a little bundle of fire you are," Carl replied, his tone edged with anticipation.

It turned her stomach, destroying her appetite, which was a real shame because in his quest to use her as a pawn, her father kept her on a very strict diet. She was starving, and even sitting through dinner with Carl was worth it if she got to eat what she wanted. Instead of having the dietitian counting her calories.

"What's up Carl?" she asked as she laid her menu aside. "Can't you get enough women?"

He offered her a slant of his head. "Marriage and getting women are two separate things. For families like ours anyway," he sniffed. "You should know that—your mother is a Delacroix. No older family in Washington."

Of course, the Delacroix blood was what he was really courting. Her mother's family was so rooted in elected office, the only other name that even came close to matching them was the Kennedy's. She was business. It disgusted her and reaffirmed her confidence in her plans for her future.

A future that wasn't going to include Carl Davis. She pushed her chair back. "Excuse me."

Carl shot her an amused look. "Go hide in the ladies room for however long you like."

He sent her a wink. One that made her temper sizzle, but she turned her back on him, refusing to let him get a rise out of her. She passed the ladies room and walked to the door. She pushed right through it and ended up in the entryway of the club. The host looked at her with a frown on his face, then looked back down at his reservations list when someone moved up behind her.

She realized it was Saxon.

"What are you doing?" She shouldn't have asked. Should have kept the question to herself because she didn't need Vitus or Saxon knowing what sort of restrictions her sire had on her.

With her luck, they'd decide to do something about it.

Saxon didn't answer her. She made a low sound under her breath and took off toward the street. She heard him bite back a word of profanity before charging after her. He reached out and pulled her to a stop just a few steps from the sidewalk.

"Didn't you learn your lesson the last time you left your escort behind?" he demanded in a low tone as his fingers bit into her bicep.

"I learned a lot of things," she countered as she tried to yank free. "What I want to know is, didn't you and your brother learn anything? The only reason you'd be assigned to me is if you pulled strings to get the duty."

Saxon released her arm but positioned himself between her and the sidewalk. "Know so much about me, do you?"

"Babysitting dinner parties is beneath your skill level," she stated clearly.

There was a momentary flicker of appreciation in his eyes before he shifted his attention away from her gaze to the dragonfly in her hair. His eyes narrowed as he looked at it. The large gold insect had been her grandmother's, and she never went anywhere without it.

A private sedan had pulled up, thinking she wanted to leave. On impulse, she started toward it.

Saxon pulled her back. "Now you're just being stupid," he said.

"You're the last person I'd think would be telling me I should just fall into line with my sire's plans."

Saxon's eyes narrowed. "You don't know anything about me."

"Fine." She pulled on her arm, but he held it. "Maybe I just thought you were more like your brother."

"You don't know him either." Saxon released her, but still stood between her and the street.

"I know Vitus doesn't play political bullshit games." She shot him a glare. "And he's smart. Really smart."

She turned her back on him, returning to the restaurant. Carl Davis wanted to have dinner with her? Fine. She was going to make sure he learned the error of his ways.

"Your father would like to see you in his study."

Damascus wasn't surprised by the summons. For all of Carl's bragging about liking her spirit, she knew he'd go whining to her sire once their date was over. It was a small victory but one she savored because it helped bolster her confidence. Set to embark on her new life path, she was ready to leave everything behind. She'd gone through a lot of trouble to make sure she was ready, but there was still a tiny part of her that hesitated ripping away from everything she knew.

Well, it was time to grow past it.

She left her suite and went down the hallway toward the center of the house. It was a huge mansion, complete with indoor swimming pool. The carpet beneath her feet was plush and deep. There was no reason to knock on the study door. Her father's personal head of security, Tyler Martin, was standing there. He opened the door for her, his lips set in a smug grin.

The man made her skin crawl.

Tyler was a relatively new face, at least on a full-time basis. He had always come and gone, but now he was firmly attached to her father's hip. He didn't have the same detached manner about him that the other Secret Service members had. No, when Tyler was looking at her, he made sure she knew it.

And she felt like she needed a shower afterward.

"Shut that door," Jeb snapped the moment she crossed into the huge study.

Tyler shut the door but from the inside. The man actually pushed her forward so hard she stumbled.

"What the hell?" she demanded.

"That's what *I'd* like to know," Jeb snapped, drawing her attention off Tyler. "From both of you."

She looked behind her and caught Tyler wiping the smirk off his lips.

"What in the hell was Saxon Hale doing anywhere near my daughter?" Jeb tossed a picture down on the desk he was seated behind.

Tyler stepped close and picked it up. It was a full-color shot of Saxon holding onto her arm outside of the restaurant plastered across the front page of a tabloid.

CONGRESSMAN'S DAUGHTER DAMASCUS RYLAND CAUGHT IN LOVER'S QUARREL OUTSIDE EXCLUSIVE WASHINGTON D.C. CLUB

"And what were you doing leaving Carl siting at a table waiting for you?" her sire demanded.

Her temper was rising, burning away the layers of caution she'd wrapped herself up in over the last few years. "I was leaving."

It wasn't a wise thing to say, even less intelligent of her to voice it in front of a witness. Her sire didn't take lip from her, and he was the most dangerous when there was no witness around because he'd take his retribution where no one saw him do it. Jeb raised his hand and slapped her. She turned with the force of the blow but returned to glaring at him, the sting reaffirming her decision to never fall into line with what he wanted.

She would get out.

Her sire didn't care for her courage. He considered her for a long moment before he walked across the study and stood in front of the floor-to-ceiling windows that afforded him a view of his perfectly manicured grounds.

"You think you've got it all figured out, don't you, Damascus." It wasn't a question. She felt a chill touch her nape because she'd heard the tone before. Her sire was making ready to drop a bombshell on her.

Jeb Ryland turned around to face her. "Your mother hasn't been feeling well."

Her blood felt like it dropped ten degrees. Jeb didn't miss the reaction.

"That's right," he continued as he strolled slowly back toward her. "I'm becoming concerned. It's possible I might have to have her admitted to a very exclusive clinic where she will get very . . . personalized care. I plan to oversee it myself."

The way he said "personalized" horrified her. He knew it too, and gave her a long moment to allow his meaning to sink in.

"Defy me and the next time you see your mother, she'll be wearing a diaper and playing with finger paints. How hard do you think it will be to get a doctor to write up a diagnosis?"

"She's your wife," Damascus said in a hollow whisper, one that betrayed just how horrified she was.

"Yes, and she's been a good one. In fact"—Jeb lifted a finger and tapped her on the tip of her nose—"it would seem she hasn't yet outlived her usefulness. Yup, a good wife, that's what she's been."

He watched for a moment before looking past her to Tyler. "Take her back to her room and have Trenton make sure she stays there."

She wanted to snarl at him.

Wanted to unleash her anger on him.

But she turned and settled for shooting Tyler a furious look when he tried to grab her elbow. She walked out of the study even though it was one of the hardest things she'd ever done. She wanted to fight, needed to rage against the way her sire was trying to push her down and hold her there, beneath his heel.

She'd never thought he'd turn against her mother.

Well, you should have.

Back in her room, she paced around the cream and lilac–colored furniture. Her suite was over a thousand square feet of luxury that felt worse than the concrete cell Vitus had pulled her out of. It was a cage, just as surely as any cell was.

Just as a clinic retreat would be to her mother.

She sat down, feeling overwhelmed by circumstances. Her carefully plotted future was suddenly further from her reach than she'd ever thought it might be.

Maybe impossible . . .

No! She forced herself to stand. She refused to quit. She hadn't given up in the concrete cell and she wasn't going to throw in the towel now. There was a way around, something she hadn't thought of yet. Wasn't that what the field she was going into had taught her? Diseases had ravaged the globe for centuries, and yet people came along to defeat some of those germs. She wasn't going to give in, she was going to figure out a way to succeed. Just like those scientists had.

At least that was what she intended to tell herself until she believed it.

"I didn't expect to hear from you for another couple of weeks, Ms. Ryland."

Colonel Bryan Magnus pointed at the chair in front of his desk. Damascus fought the urge to look over her shoulder as she slid into the seat. She was taking a risk, but it was necessary. The colonel headed up the classified study program that she had secretly transferred into three years ago. The office was four stories beneath the surface of the university grounds, and very few people knew it was there. She certainly hadn't until the colonel had made contact with her. With her father insisting she cut her ties with Vitus, the offer had been the perfect retaliation, a golden ticket to a future of her design, instead of one her father laid out for her.

She'd made a grave miscalculation in overlooking the threat to her mother, and that just pissed her off because normal people didn't have to worry about their father using their mother against them.

But she did have to worry, so she looked the colonel in the eye. "I have a complication," she said evenly.

"At this stage of the game Ms. Ryland, you will be expected to fulfill your contract to us."

The colonel folded his hands and put them on the desktop. Bryan Magnus had always presented a controlled persona to her. Honestly, she couldn't recall ever seeing him smile, and now she caught a hint of disapproval in his eyes. One she didn't want to see grow.

"My father has threatened to have my mother admitted to a clinic if I don't proceed with an engagement he's given his blessing on."

There was a slight narrowing of the colonel's eyes. "You have been through classes that included classified materials and information. Were the terms of your commitment to us unclear?"

"No," Damascus answered firmly. "I am eager to fulfill them."

"Glad to hear it," Bryan Magnus said. "I'd hate to have to have you arrested on your graduation day."

His tone left it very clear that he wouldn't hesitate to do it. She shoved her misgivings aside. Nothing was free. Especially not the freedom and protection she needed. It had been made painfully clear to her that in exchange for her admittance into the classified program, she would be expected to take a position with them.

"Trying to slip out of my commitment to your team works a little better when I don't clue you in on my plans. I'm here because you said to come to you if I had a difficultly." She was grasping at straws, but at least the colonel represented a very sturdy, reliable straw.

"I did," the colonel confirmed. "I will look into the matter."

It wasn't a promise. Damascus tried not to dwell on the lack of satisfaction the meeting gave her. At least she had somewhere to go. Oh, it wasn't without its price. Wasn't that life? There was always something owed for something given. The calendar might say she was living in the modern age, but there were plenty of times when she felt like she had a lot in common with her ancestors from several centuries ago.

She made her way past doors that were locked and only had numbers on them. Learning to navigate the underground complex took concentration, because there were precious few details to distinguish one gray concrete-block hallway from another. Letting her mind wander was asking to end up having the military police rescue her.

She didn't like to admit how she knew that bit of information. It wasn't very flattering.

Navigating the complex had become easier with time and honestly, it was a labor of love because it was the one place her sire couldn't touch her. Part of her truly enjoyed knowing Trenton was waiting outside a door somewhere, fully confident that she was in the laboratory on the other side of it. The further she'd gotten in her studies, the more space Colonel Magnus and his staff had placed between her and her sire's security. At least while she was on campus. It was trained personal only inside the lab, and no exceptions. She'd never once thought the commitment she was making to the government was too high for what she'd get in return.

The knowledge had kept her sane, a tightly gripped secret weapon against her sire's strangling hold on her. The threat against her mother was just further proof that she had to escape or face a lifetime of abuse.

Her belly tightened as she thought of her mother. It was possible her sire was lying. She just couldn't afford to take the chance. Her mother was sweet and completely in love with being a congressman's wife. She did charity events, read stories to first-graders, served lunch in soup kitchens, and made sure the Ryland name was on the lips of the press for all the right reasons.

It was possible her mother was as fake as her sire, but Damascus had never seen it. So she held out hope that the only thing her mother was guilty of was loving and believing in the wrong man.

Damascus took another flight of stairs and went to exit the building through a different door than she'd entered it—one of Colonel Magnus's rules. Never be predictable, except for when it came to her home life. The colonel had given her plenty of suggestions for helping to lull her sire into thinking she was tamed.

The sunlight made her blink as her eyes adjusted. She'd closed the door before she could see completely. She'd started across the expanse of open lawn that the university boasted. Something caught her eye, and she turned to look toward one of the outdoor seating areas. Spring was just about to give way to early summer and the plants were taking advantage of the warm weather. The benches were partially hidden behind foliage gone mad, but she saw him. Saxon Hale was turning to take cover, but she knew without a doubt it was him.

How had he found her?

She stood still for a moment trying to figure the puzzle out, and when she did, her temper sizzled.

Her dragonfly.

The one thing she always had on her. It was around her wrist at the moment. She fingered its wings as she abruptly changed direction and went back through the door she'd just exited. She ran down a hallway and across another until she found a door that let her out near the library.

She made it into the building and up three flights of stairs, then pressed her nose to the window. Saxon came around the corner looking at his cell phone. Abruptly, he turned around and went behind another building.

She knew she was right—Saxon Hale was tracking her.

And right on the heels of that thought was a bolt of hard, cold fear. She felt like she couldn't breathe as it pierced her heart. She might have a plan for her future, but Vitus would be at her father's mercy if Jeb had any reason to suspect she might have gone off with him.

She couldn't leave him exposed. The damn fool would be a perfect target without realizing she was going to be setting in motion a plan that would enrage her sire. He would get caught in the cross fire.

What needled her was why he was back now. It would be so simple to think it was because he couldn't let her go any more than she could banish him from her heart.

But she wasn't that naive.

Vitus was a man, an experienced one. She didn't doubt that he'd been sincere in their interactions, but calling it a relationship was a true stretch. They'd had sex. Mind-blowing, spine-tingling sex that still made her blush three years later, but it had all been part of the mission for him. Unless she wanted to deal once more with the heartache that had nearly crippled her, she'd remember those harsh little facts.

Reality was a bitch, but she needed to keep a clear perspective. Her future depended on her using her wits. She was so close. Three years of planning and looking over her shoulder to make sure her sire's security personal didn't catch on to her training in microbiology instead of pediatrics. All she had to do was keep her mouth shut and her head down for two more weeks. Colonel Magnus had assured her that even the Secret Service couldn't interfere with his authority. Once she officially graduated, she'd be under the protection of the colonel's men.

Which only left Vitus and Saxon's very untimely arrival to deal with. Honestly, she didn't need the complication. She'd made sure she didn't have any close friends, no one for her sire to turn on once she revealed her plans.

It was so perfect and so close to being finished. But her sire knew she loved Vitus.

Damn it!

On impulse, she took the dragonfly off. It was from another era, the workmanship superior in every way. Made of silver, it had detailed wings and a solid weight not found in modern pieces. She walked around a huge shelving unit and scanned the journals. The security cameras would be simple for Trenton to hack into, so she milled around, selecting books and replacing them. Somewhere in the middle of her motions, she slipped the dragonfly into the spot behind the book she was pushing back onto the shelf.

She hated to leave it but it was only a thing. Vitus was flesh and blood and even if she couldn't have him, there was no way she was going to let him walk blindly into a shit-storm.

She owed him more than that, and there was no way

she could live with the guilt of knowing she hadn't tried to warn him, not when she was about to do something that would send her father into a rage and looking for a target.

She had to warn him.

But what bothered her the most was the way her heart accelerated and the anticipation that zipped through her.

You'd think she would have learned, but apparently, when it came to Vitus, she was still a complete fool.

Well, just wait until he looks at you with those cold eyes . . .

Now there was a solid bit of truth to sober her. Vitus wouldn't be happy to see her. She'd given back his ring, and a man like him wouldn't be rolling out the welcome mat.

Her heart didn't seem to care. Seeing him was seeing him.

You're an idiot.

Yeah, well, love did that to people.

Kagan rapped on the door, but didn't wait for Colonel Bryan Magnus to give him permission to enter. The colonel closed the file on his tablet before looking up.

"I have to admit," Kagan began as he slid into a chair in front of the colonel's desk, "I didn't see this one coming. You actually recruited that girl? Knowing who her father is? You're asking to get crisped in a backdraft, know that?"

"You must not have checked her IQ scores," Magnus replied as he tapped something into his tablet. He turned the device around so that Kagan could see the screen. A moment later, Kagan let out a low whistle.

"She's loaded in the brainpan," Kagan agreed.

"And she has a keen sense of being able to apply that knowledge to microbiology," Mangus added. "She's a perfect candidate, one I'm willing to take some heat to get. If she were at a private university, there would be a bidding war to get her. As it is, I've spent a great deal of effort blurring her scores to keep her undetected."

"Jeb Ryland won't let her go easily."

Magnus slowly smiled. "Can't really blame me for enjoying what fate has dropped in my lap. The good congressman has no idea his daughter is signed onto my program. I certainly found that an interesting twist of fate when my own daughter got caught up in that mess a few months ago. I will enjoy dealing with Jeb Ryland's displeasure, have no doubt about that. Truth is, I'm looking forward to it."

Kagan contemplated the colonel's response for a long moment before he pointed a finger at him. "You're offering her shelter from her father."

Bryan nodded once. "Not a bit ashamed of it. I need her on my team, especially with Ebola rearing its ugly head. She needs protection—something I can provide."

"That's not the only reason." Kagan dug into the colonel's reasoning.

Bryan Magnus offered him a tilt of his head, which was as close to a shrug as the world would ever see out of the seasoned officer. "Maybe the fact that I have a daughter means I have a soft spot for seeing Damascus offered a way out of the mess she's in."

"Maybe you just can't stand to see her potential wasted by that asshole of a father she's got," Kagan fired back.

"Are you telling me it doesn't make you itch?" Bryan asked. "Seeing that prick operate? Seeing Tyler Martin free as a bird when he tried to take down one of your teams and put two of your boys in the ground?"

Kagan took a long moment before he nodded. "So why have you brought me into the mix?"

The colonel held up two fingers. "Your man Saxon Hale is on her six. Why?"

Kagan offered the colonel a knowing smile.

Bryan choked on a chuckle. "Fine, I already reasoned it had something to do with Tyler Martin, but the girl is mine. I don't need her getting caught in a cross fire like my daughter did. Deal with Martin however you like, but make sure Damascus Ryland is clear of the action. Tyler has proven he isn't above using innocent blood to get what he wants. She's all set to make the run, I don't want anything scaring her out of doing it."

"Because even you will have trouble keeping her if her daddy cries to the right people. Something tells me you neglected to mention that to her."

Magnus didn't even blink. "Her father's been daring her to run for years. I just gave her a place to go to. She made the choice of her own free will."

"Well, I might argue that, considering what her alternatives are. Given true freedom, I bet she'd have married Vitus Hale," Kagan said. "But life is full of crappy poker hands. She won't be the first to have to decide how to play what she's got."

"Which is a genius-level IQ," Magnus said. "Sometimes, fate makes sure all the players have an ace in the hole."

There was a long silence as each man tried to impress the other. Neither was going to back off, each secure in the knowledge of his authority.

Kagan held up two fingers and pointed to the second one in question.

"The mother. Damascus was in here saying her father has threatened her mother with some bullshit about a private clinic," Bryan responded. "Something needs to be done. You have more resources than I do in the civilian sector."

"Why?" Kagan asked.

"Because you're right—if she buckles under her father's threat, he could make it hard for me to force her compliance, and I need her brains on my team," the colonel responded. "I plan to take Ms. Ryland under my wing in exactly two weeks."

"I'll let Hale know his timeline." Kagan stood up. "And I will deal with the other issue, if it becomes a reality."

The colonel slowly smiled, an expression that would have sent a chill down the spine of most men because it was pure intent.

"Tell Hale I can remove my asset any time he gives me the word, and I will be happy to watch his six when he takes Tyler down. I'd enjoy it after that mess he put my daughter through."

"He had your name targeted as well," Kagan reminded him.

"As I said, I'd enjoy it, and I'll bring a shovel."

It had been a long time since she'd been alone.

Damascus smiled as she looked around the crowded shopping mall. Most people wouldn't think she was alone, but to her she was practically marooned on a desert island. A fact she was going to make sure she used.

She walked into a clothing store and pulled a dress off the rack, making a wide circle around it and hitting all the departments. By the time she made it back to the register, she had everything from underwear to shoes. Her time with Vitus had been confined to a couple of weeks on the run, but she'd learned a lot from him in that time. She dug some of her emergency cash out of the side of her makeup case and paid for everything without there being a bank record. It was also a small, discount store and unlikely to have a security system, at least one linked to any major network. The Asian girl working the register was clearly the owners' daughter.

"No bag. I'm just going to wear it out."

The girl nodded and reached under the counter for a pair of scissors. She clipped off the tags and swept them into a trash can.

Damascus scooped up her purchases and headed into a dressing room. She changed out of everything and put on the new clothing, even sliding into new shoes. They were cheap ones and pinched her toes, but there was no way to know where her sire's security team had placed their bugs. She was going off-grid and she had to do it right, because if she got caught, there wasn't going to be a second chance.

She shoved all of her personal belongings into the bag and stuffed the cash into her bra. On the way out of the changing room, she dropped the bag in a box that was sitting by the door. Yeah, she'd learned a few things from Vitus, and she'd done a lot more research into avoiding detection in the years since.

The outdated strip mall was frequented mostly by university students. They were clustered around the food shops, sitting on the sidewalk with their tablets open to take advantage of the free wireless network offered by the local coffee shop.

"Hey, Damascus!" someone called. "Don't normally see you out this way."

She smiled at the boy who shared one of her advanced classes. He blinked at the welcome, his cheeks becoming flushed. He was fairly typical of most of her classmates—high intelligence scores and failing social interaction ones. The set of car keys dangling from his hand was exactly what she was looking for.

"Yeah, any chance I can hop a ride with you across town?" She moved closer to him. "I can toss in for gas."

"Um . . ." He looked like he was half frozen in shock. "Sure." He smacked his lips as he closed his sagging jaw. "I mean, don't worry about the gas. My parents support me. They claim it's so I make sure to put them in a nice convalescence home once they're old."

He pointed at a decade-old car. It had a Tardis decal on the rear window and a bobblehead Darth Vader on the dashboard.

He slid the key into the ignition and turned the motor over. "Where to?"

"Are you sure?"

Damascus nodded as she got out of the car. She leaned over and let her driver get a good look down her cleavage, small enough payment for using the guy.

"I'm good. Thanks a million." She straightened up.

"See you in class tonight?" he asked.

Damascus didn't answer. She crossed the street and started walking down an alleyway. No, she was going to miss class tonight, but it was the only way she was going to get the opportunity to sneak out. Advance bacteria classes were held in a secure laboratory, which meant her sire's security had to stay outside the building. They wouldn't know she was off-campus until at least midnight because the classes often went long and there was nothing to do but wait until she emerged.

It was the chance she needed and likely the only one she was going to get. She looked at the landmarks, her memory offering up the information she needed. Five more blocks and she turned east, making her way through a residential neighborhood as the sun set. Someone was walking his dog, and a pair of boys rode by on bikes. She ducked across streets and through alleyways, often looking behind her to make sure no one was following.

Her belly was in a knot when she first spied Vitus's

house. Tall shrubs obscured the windows. Not that she made the mistake of thinking Vitus couldn't see out. No, he was a master of disguise. The overgrown look of the place was just a clever duck blind.

Well, she wasn't going to be shy. She walked up to the door and rang the bell. Behind the door, she heard it echoing in the hallway. Seconds crawled by like hours as she waited. She felt exposed with the street behind her, as if at any moment Trenton or Tyler was going to skid to a halt in one of the unmarked, black, tinted-window sedans and haul her off the porch.

Well, she wasn't going to have it. She went around the side of the house. He used it more than the front door because the garage was set in the back. She didn't knock on the door but swept aside part of a shrub and pressed her hand against a section of the window.

She remembered like it was yesterday, the way Vitus had shown her how to unlock the door with her palm print. There was the small flash of infrared as her hand was scanned. Her breath was frozen in her chest as she waited to see if her print was still on file. There was a series of clicks as the door unlocked.

Her mouth was dry as she walked into the house, through the laundry room, and into the kitchen. The scent of coffee lingered, but there was only a single mug sitting upside down on a folded dishtowel. The rest of the counter was spotless—even the mug looked clean.

A ripple of relief went through her.

But that made her stiffen. She wasn't there to have Vitus rescue her. It was her turn to return the favor. She moved past the round wooden table that was in the dining room and came upon a huge, man-sized sofa that sat facing an equally man-sized plasma flat screen. There wasn't a coffee table. Instead, either side of the sofa had a footrest that came out to become a recliner.

She sat down, jealous of being able to have furniture designed for comfort instead of fashion. The leather of the sofa was scuffed and the floor had a few scrapes in it, but she found it more pleasing than the perfectly polished marble floor of her sire's entryway.

This was a home, and yet there were some things that were similar. The lack of personal items struck her as sad. There wasn't a single family picture on the walls, no knickknacks in sight, not a single dust collector on the mantle. Everything in the room had a function. There was nothing superfluous, nothing to give away the personal traits of the man who lived there.

Of course, that was the way he wanted it. The way he'd chosen to live. In some ways, that had fascinated her, making her think the small things he shared with her were more important than they really were. He liked Tabasco sauce on his eggs and she knew it, even if there wasn't a bottle of it on the table. No, Vitus would never leave his personal items out. He hid them, concealing who he was because that was the life he'd chosen to lead.

It would be hers too.

And she wasn't sorry.

Only sorry that this would be the last contact she would ever have with Vitus Hale.

His phone vibrated.

Vitus pulled it free and stared at the screen. His brain didn't freeze up very often, but obviously there was a first time for everything. He ended up cussing at the security flag from his home system. The thing didn't make mistakes, so if it said Damascus Ryland was in his house, she was there. He swiped his finger across the screen and selected one of the security cameras he had mounted around his property.

It was her.

And the *fucking* world tilted off-center.

He stared for another long moment at her face before he cussed and put the phone back into his side pocket.

He was home.

Damascus felt him. Call that what you may, but she was sure she felt his presence registering on her skin. The air in the house fairly crackled as she felt him drawing closer. She sat still, keeping her chin up and her hands on her knees. Her breath was stuck in her throat as she caught the first sight of him, just a quarter of his face as he looked around the doorframe. She was facing down the barrel of his handgun. He had his finger on the trigger, his left hand cupping the butt. His bare forearms allowed her to see the definition that proved he was just as hard and deadly as she recalled.

She bit her lower lip to keep from talking, her composure flying to pieces like it was being hit by a tornado. All the resolve and self-discipline she'd spent the last three years cultivating was being ripped away in chunks and strips by the sheer force of nature. He finished checking the house before coming back to stare at her. She felt his glare, like it was burning away the layers of the façade she'd built after realizing she had to leave him.

"You wanted my attention?" he asked at last, his voice a low rumble that suited the nearly dark room. The only light was coming from a red light. It had turned on the moment she entered the room, allowing her to see without killing off her night vision.

"Actually, that's my question for you," she said as she stood. He'd stopped across the room from her, the gun tucked against his center back behind his belt. She was quivering, being so close to him driving her nearly insane.

Get a grip . . . your father plays for keeps.

His brows lowered. "I don't follow."

"Your brother is trailing me," she informed him. "You bugged my dragonfly, didn't you?"

Surprise widened his eyes. It was a momentary loss of control, one he masked quickly but not before she saw it.

"I knew it," she said. "That was a low thing to do. The dragonfly belonged to my grandmother. It's important to me."

Which was why he'd used it, she realized as the words sailed out of her mouth. What the hell was wrong with her? Vitus sure wouldn't be sparing much empathy for her bruised feelings. She needed to get back on topic. Fast.

"I did place a bug in the dragonfly." He lifted a finger and pointed at her. "As a safeguard, when you were my responsibility. I haven't used it since."

"Well your brother is using it now. I caught him today, at the university." She shot his attempt to dodge the issue out of the air. "And Saxon wouldn't be watching me unless you were in on it."

"You're guessing, Princess."

There was arrogance in his tone. One that she wanted to hate, but she knew it was earned and that just pissed her off even more because of how it made her pulse jump. But it also wasn't a denial—he was dodging the question and trying to distract her.

"I saw him, and there was no way he would have known where I was unless he had a tracking beacon." She looked away from him, realizing she was saying too much. Her association with Colonel Magnus had to remain secret. She drew in a deep breath and turned to face him again. "Well, I'm here to tell you to stop."

"Saxon has a reason to keep an eye on your father. That doesn't mean he'd trail you."

"He was with me at the university," she said confidently. "And you have to stop before—"

She shut her mouth with a click of her teeth. A second later, Vitus had her by the forearms, his seemingly relaxed stance in the doorway nothing but a smoke screen to keep her at ease and spilling her guts.

"Before what?" he demanded.

"Before anyone else notices."

His eyes narrowed. It was a look she recognized, one that warned her he was filtering her words, peeling them away and getting ready to unmask her.

"Don't over think it." She flipped her hand in the air and took a moment to break eye contact so she could get a handle on her emotions. He released her, watching her as she moved away from him.

"Can't look me in the eye, Princess?"

Busted.

Damascus grasped at her resolve, drawing on the memory of just what her father had looked like when he'd pointed at his desk phone.

"There's no reason to. I've said what I came to."

There. It was done. She turned to leave. Vitus moved in a motion that was as fluid as it was sharp, intercepting her, stepping into her path so that she ended up recoiling into a corner between the doorjamb and the wall. He was suddenly too close for her failing composure. Her façade was coming apart at the seams.

"You took a damn stupid risk coming here by yourself. Thank God I had the system enabled to let you in or you'd have been stuck on the step like a sitting duck for who the hell knows how long. Don't be stupid like that, Princess. Your father has a lot of enemies."

He was hissing through clenched teeth. She tried to recoil from his temper, slapping at his chest when he held her without any real effort. Somehow, she'd forgotten just how bloody strong he was, but what she really needed to get away from was the way he was trying to protect her. She couldn't take shelter in his embrace. It would be the kiss of death for him.

"Well, I did do it," she shot back. "You and your brother aren't the only ones who know how to play shadow games. And no one taught me how to do it."

She was suddenly free and stumbled back a few paces, finally coming to rest against the wall.

"You shouldn't have to learn," Vitus said softly. So softly, she might have missed the sympathy in his tone.

But she didn't, and she lifted her chin, needing to be more than the helpless creature she was the last time she'd been inside his house. "You think I want to be the princess you always called me?" She shook her head. "I'm not a little girl."

His lips twitched, curving sensuously as his eyes narrowed in a purely male way. It had been three long years since she'd seen that look on his face, but she recognized it instantly, sensation rippling across the surface of her skin in response. There was no thinking, no deciding what she felt, there was only him and the way her body sprang to life when he was close enough to touch her.

"I have never "—he stepped closer, her senses so keen, she heard the soft sound of his boot connecting with the wooden floor—"never . . . thought of you as a little girl." All the tiny hairs on her skin were standing straight up as he closed the space so that he could flatten his hands against the wall on either side of her face.

His eyes were closed now as he leaned down and inhaled against her hair.

"I tried so damn hard to forget the way you smell . . ."

She heard the desire in his voice, felt it wash through her like a flash flood, sweeping everything else aside in a blink of an eye. There was only the moment and the

fact that she knew it would be her last with him. Wrong?
It seemed a far greater crime to turn her back on what
fate had delivered. All she wanted to do was cherish it,
until she was forced to resume being realistic.

"*Touch me.*" She couldn't have held the words back if
she'd tried.

"Don't say that," he warned, but it sounded like he intended it for himself. "I need to get you back . . . before
we both lose our heads."

"I can't think . . ." What she wanted was right there.
She could smell him, feel his body heat, and all she
wanted was a taste to go with it all, to send her into
sensory overload where reality could just fucking drown.
". . . when you're this close."

"I know." He answered in a tone coated with hunger.
It was like a living, breathing thing between them. He
closed the distance, surrounding her with his scent.

She lost the battle and reached out, finished with waiting and being cautious. He was too close, too real to be
ignored in favor of doing the wise thing. His chest felt as
good as she recalled, hard and sculpted. His T-shirt was
a thin barrier, but it frustrated her because it kept her
from what she craved.

So she dug her fingers into the soft jersey and yanked
it up. The tail came free from his belt, rising up to give
her exactly what she wanted.

"Fuck it and everything else we both should do," he said
and reached down to take control of his shirt. There was a
rustle of motion, a bunching of his abdominal muscles
as he pulled the shirt up and over his head, chucking it
across the room with a motion full of barely controlled
strength. He was breathing as hard as she was, both
of them a hairbreadth from some sort of explosion.

Damascus felt it building inside her as she licked her lips with anticipation.

His face tightened as his gaze settled on her tongue and made the journey across her lower lip. She was fingering the fabric of her dress, and suddenly couldn't bear the impediment of it between them. She tugged it up, pulling it above her head before she felt him grasp it and finish the job.

The cool air hit her overheated skin, but only for a moment before he caught her up against him. He captured her mouth in a searing kiss. She moaned softly, unable to contain all the sensation inside her any longer. He pressed her lips apart, licking across her lower lip before threading his hands into her hair, thrusting his tongue into her mouth to stroke hers.

She shuddered, the bluntness of it making her clit pulse. Her heart was hammering with a crazy rhythm, but she didn't care if it burst. The only thing on her mind was to get closer to him. She reached for his belt, fumbling with it as she struggled to free what she craved.

"Fuck . . . no," he growled as he put her at arm's length. "Too fast."

His voice was raspy and his face looked like it was etched in solid stone. There was a fury in his eyes that should have scared her, but the only thing she had room for in her brain was the need to touch him again.

But Vitus wasn't letting her decide anything. He scooped her off her feet like she weighted as much as a pillow, cradling her against his chest as he carried her through the dark house to his bed. Her belly tightened as she realized what he was doing, excitement curling her toes even as she fought off a twinge of frustration for the way he was taking command.

She couldn't expect anything less from him, but he

wasn't the only one with desires. She flipped over and rose to her knees the moment he tossed her onto the mattress. It bounced, the springs groaning as she reached behind her and unhooked the flimsy bra she'd bought. Her cash fluttered down as she enjoyed the way Vitus had frozen, his gaze riveted on her breasts, his mouth a thin line of hunger.

"Shit," he groaned, his voice thick with need. His fly was only half open but he leaned across the bed and fastened his lips around one nipple, drawing on the point like he was starving.

She gasped, sensation flowing from that connection down to her clit. He crawled right over her, slipping his knees on either side of her hips as he closed his arms around her and sucked on her tit. She arched back, offering it to him, offering every bit of herself to him.

His . . . she just wanted to be his.

And Vitus didn't disappoint her. He pulled her against him as he leaned over at what should have been an impossible angle to suck her nipple. His fingers were spread wide across her lower back as she heard her own breathless cry echo off the ceiling. And then she was falling backward onto the bed as he pulled his hands along the curve of her waist to catch the edges of her underwear. He was stripping it down her legs before she finished settling completely onto her back.

She shivered, feeling exposed. He sat there on his haunches, between her legs, stroking the insides of her thighs.

"I do like it," he said bluntly. "Seeing you like this . . . knowing you're mine."

Maybe she should have taken offense, but it would have been a lie. Her pride might have raised a protest if her belly wasn't knotted with anticipation.

He stroked her from knee to upper thigh and back

toward her knees. A slow, long stroke that made her clit twist. She was so desperate for contact with that little bundle of nerve endings, so needy for one firm touch to end the torment.

"I've thought about it . . ." He started moving his hands back toward her core, slowly, so slowly it made her lift off the bed.

He smiled, his lips parting to give her a glimpse of his teeth. "Thought about it enough to make me a prick." He'd made it to the very top of her inner thighs, where her skin was intensely sensitive, the folds of her sex tingling with the need to be next.

"I wanted to smell you." He leaned down and she shied away.

She heard him make a soft sound as he pushed her bottom back onto the surface of the bed with an open-handed grip on both of her thighs. He held her there, spread wide as he lowered his head until his face was a bare inch above her sex.

"Vitus." She had no idea exactly what she was pleading for. Release? Yes, but what form? It was all a twisted, bubbling mess inside her.

He looked up her body to lock gazes with her.

"I want to do so many things to you . . . *Princess*."

She jerked, the first contact nearly sending her into climax.

"And I want to watch you fight to control yourself." He found her slit, his fingers slipping easily into the folds because she was so wet. "You always fight to control yourself. . . . . Why?" he demanded.

She couldn't think. He was stroking her slit but never moving all the way to the top where her clit was throbbing intensely. He would get just a hairbreadth from it, the little bundle of nerves would tighten, taking her right to the edge of climax, before he trailed his fingers down to the opening of her body, rimming her in a delicate, slow motion that made her shake.

"Because . . . because . . . oh damn you, Vitus! Stop fucking with me!"

He chuckled, leaning down and pinning her against the bed with his body. She was snarling at him, bucking against the restraint, and the beast held her there as he thrust two thick fingers up into her.

"I'm not fucking you yet, Princess. You'll know when I get my cock into you."

"You know damn well what the hell I meant," she insisted with another attempt to buck him off her. For one second she was free of him, and it was a moment full of torment because that was the last thing she wanted, to be without him. It felt like he'd been ripped away, the sting of the parting making her whimper.

"I wanted to hear that sound out of you too, even if I'm a fucking Neanderthal to say so."

She felt the touch of his breath against her wet folds a second before he claimed her clit between his lips. She twisted, clawing at the bedding as he pressed her thighs apart and sucked her off with hard, slow motions of his lips. Nothing delicate, no. He ate her out. It took only a few moments before she was groaning, the pleasure so deep inside her, all she could do was utter a sound that came up from the most primitive part of her soul. She felt like she was dropped back onto the bed, a gasping heap of useless muscles as she basked in the glow of satisfaction. It was just so intense, her brain wasn't capable of thinking.

There was a soft sound of fabric as Vitus shucked his boots and pants, and then he was smoothing his hands along her quivering limbs again, rubbing her like a mare that had just finished running. Easing the ache from her muscles and replacing it with soft enjoyment. He was there surrounding her, controlling her, anticipating the way she'd twist when his touch became overwhelming. Allowing her to move just enough away from him to ease that tension before coming at her from a different angle. He knew her too well, or maybe she didn't understand herself. She didn't know, all that she did know was that she needed him inside her. She wasn't satisfied, not by a long shot. He'd only taken the edge off her desperation.

"Now." Her voice was a husky croak, her lips dry as she tried to pull him to her.

"Yeah . . . now," he agreed, rolling her onto her back and pinning her down with his weight.

She whimpered as his cock touched her. So hard, so much of everything she'd been hungry for since the last time she'd seen him. She was wet and eager, but he wanted her at his mercy. She sensed it, felt it in the way he spread her wide and took a long moment to consider her waiting for him before he pressed his length into her body.

She let out a sound that was guttural. She was tight, as tight as the first time, but that didn't stop her back arching as she tried to take more of him. His cock was splitting her, stretching her open again, pain zipping through her like the sting of hot spice. It stung but thrilled at the same time. Still, it wasn't enough.

"Stop treating me . . . like a . . . princess."

She got her wish when he came down on top of her, pinning her wrists to the sheets and pumping against her until she felt his balls smacking against her bottom.

"I want"—he grunted and drew in a breath that hissed out of him as he shook above her—"I want to take . . . my time."

But his body was shaking with the effort of holding back. She was lifting to meet him, caught completely in the need to finish what they were doing. She was rushing toward the zenith, no more will to do anything else. She was a bubbling cauldron of need, and he was what she needed.

"More," she insisted, her voice cracking like a whip. "More!"

He reached beneath her and gripped her bottom, lifting her up so that he could drive himself deeper, ride her harder.

"Yes!"

Damascus had no idea who actually said it, because the word felt like it was ripped from her soul. She was straining toward him, groaning as she took what he thrust into her. Caught up in the motion of their bodies slapping against each other. When her orgasm hit, she felt like a house that was having every one of its windows shattered in a single second. There was only the feeling of being ripped apart and flung in a thousand different directions all at once. Her core gripped around his cock, pulling from it what her flesh craved.

He snarled as his cock pumped a measure of hot seed that set off a deeper ripple of satisfaction inside her. There was no coming back from it and she didn't want to. She surrendered completely and let the wave tumble her into blackness.

She'd changed.

If Vitus hadn't already noticed the difference maturity had bred in her, getting a glimpse of her bare body without passion clouding his judgment certainly did.

The curtains were open a bare inch. Moonlight was shining onto the bed, bathing Damascus in a yellow glow. She was too thin. Her breastbone showed clearly and her breasts were no longer the plump handfuls he recalled.

His lips twitched up as he recalled just how sensitive those mounds still were. The sound she made when he cupped them replayed across his memory like a favorite song.

But it wasn't enough to distract him from noting all the details of her body. Her arms were defined now. It was the sort of thing a person only got one way, through resistance training. Diet alone wasn't enough, neither was cardio. She'd been doing push-ups and pull-ups at the very least and often. The definition went down to her wrists. He looked at her abs. They were flat and there was a faint outline of three ridges. His gaze swept lower to her legs where he found further evidence of an intense training program. One he knew her father wouldn't have approved of.

At least not the Jeb Ryland he knew. The man was a throwback conservative. One who didn't like to see females in pants much less exerting themselves through exercise.

What are you doing Damascus?

Hell, that was the question tonight and it applied to more than just the condition of her body. The entire situation needed an explanation. But he was loathe to get to the part where he forced himself to go after it. Her scent was still filling his senses, the moonlight washing over something he'd seen in his dreams a thousand times, only this time, it was real. She stirred, a little sound escaping her lips that hit him like a double shot of whisky, instantly dulling his wits, tempting him with the promise of ecstasy if he'd just surrender to the mindlessness of her effect.

Tempting.

Too much so, really.

The toll the last three years had taken on his emotions had left thick scars, ones that her presence soothed. It was a balm he hadn't realized he'd been yearning for, and he frankly didn't give a shit about anything else beyond indulging himself in the opportunity to be free from pain.

Except for the fact that she'd taken a huge risk in coming to him tonight.

Why?

As much as he wanted to sink back down onto the bed and enjoy holding her, he couldn't sleep while there was something going on, something dire enough to send her into the city on her own. That could have cost her dearly, and he knew she understood the risks.

Which led him back to asking why.

He picked up his cell and sent a text to Saxon.

"If you're tailing Damascus . . . you've lost her."

"Fuck."

Vitus stared at the screen, not wanting to believe the confirmation. But it was there, and he let out a soft exclamation of profanity.

"Told you."

Vitus jumped. Damascus indulged herself in a brief moment of victory, because Vitus wasn't a man you got the jump on very often. She did make sure she didn't move until he'd focused on her completely. Once he had, she drew herself up, cringing a bit as her abdomen muscles protested. It was just enough of blunt reality to recall her to the purpose of her visit. Her father's face flashed through her mind, chilling her blood.

"Your brother needs to back off," she said as she rolled off the bed and picked up her underwear, desperate to avoid eye contact.

"Why?" It was a short, clipped word, but she didn't trust for a second that Vitus was anywhere as calm as he sounded. She felt him watching her, trying to dissect her motions and get at her reasoning.

Which she couldn't allow to happen. So she pulled on

her panties and put on her bra, scooping up the bills she could see and stuffing them into one side of it.

"Just do it Vitus. There isn't any reason for you to be trailing me, and it was really hard to get over here to tell you that."

He'd pulled his jeans on and buttoned the fly. No zippers for him, the sound was something he wouldn't take a risk on. Even on civilian ground, just a tiny detail but one that made him the man he was.

The man she couldn't resist.

"Where is the dragonfly?" he asked.

"I left it in the library. That will be where your brother is sitting outside of right now. Don't bother to deny it. I'm on to him."

Vitus looked back at his phone. It took him half a minute to decode Saxon's location. He cussed again, and she started to smile in triumph.

"It was a damn stupid risk you took, Damascus." He cut into her moment of victory.

He was tying his boots but watching her as he did.

"I told you, I am not a child." She left the bedroom, going back into the front room to get her dress.

Vitus caught her the moment the garment fluttered into place. "Then don't act like a stupid kid by going solo. Your father has a lot of enemies, men who will happily cut pieces off of you to send to him."

A dark memory tried to crawl out of the pit she'd locked it in, like the claws of a dragon appearing on the rim of a wall. She shuddered, recalling the way light reflected off the polished blade of a knife when it was being brandished just inches from her face.

"I know." She pulled her arm free and forced her attention on to the matter at hand, slamming a lid down on her memories with the force of determination. "Get your brother off my tail so I can get on with—" She was saying too much. He always had that effect on her. Her thoughts just spilled out of her mouth because she trusted him. Well, for his own good, she had to stop.

"Get on with what?" Vitus demanded as he pulled his shirt on. "Dating Carl Davis?"

She fought to contain the cringe that tightened her muscles.

"I don't have to explain myself to you." Couldn't, actually.

His expression hardened. "So what was this exactly? A last celebration of your free will? A little rebellion screw before you get down to the business of making Daddy's dream match for you a reality?"

His words hurt. As in, the pain was nearly unbearable. She was hugging herself to keep her feelings inside, biting her lip to stop all the denial she wanted to spit in his face.

He snorted when she didn't answer. He grabbed a gun from a hiding place behind the sofa and shoved it into his belt at his back.

"Fine. Glad to be of service. Nice to know I rank higher than what you think you'll be getting from Davis." He ripped a jacket off a hook by the door and yanked it open. "Since you seem to be finished, let me get you home before I have to put my neck on the line again to rescue you."

Her classmates looked at her strangely as she joined them on the way out of the lab, but one thing a level-five classified lab training class was good for was teaching everyone to not question what was happening around them. That little word "classified" had a magical way of sealing lips, since all of her fellow soon-to-be doctors were heading for the same high-risk sort of research. She was bone weary and emotionally drained, but her father's security men didn't notice anything out of place.

Idiots.

Except that she felt like a bigger one. The man she loved hated her now. It was what had to happen and still, she couldn't embrace the wisdom of it. Her heart felt like it had a fresh, raw wound. She should have seen the bright side, should have focused on the fact that Vitus could move on now. Honestly, she didn't want to be the sort of woman who left a man longing for her.

But that left her wondering just what sort of woman she was. She'd gone to him with the best intention and even if she could be objective enough to realize he'd only been pissed when he'd insulted her, the fact was, she hadn't had the self-discipline to keep her clothes on.

So maybe he'd move on, but she had a very bad feeling that there was no way she ever would.

Love totally sucked.

Forget her.

His self-discipline was letting him down, which was a shocker all in itself because there had been times when the only thing that kept him alive was his will to persevere. Vitus growled and opened up the cabinet above his pantry. He stared at the liquor bottles stored there as his fingers tightened around the handle until the metal edges were biting into his skin.

Shit.

He slammed the door shut, cursing Damascus for stealing even his enjoyment of a good double pour of whiskey. That was just hitting below the belt.

His cock stirred, reminding him rather bluntly of just how she affected him below the belt.

Ten fucking minutes and he'd had his hands on her again.

He was a moron.

A glutton for self-punishment.

Even now, as he moved through his house, he detected the soft touch of her scent. He stood for a long moment, looking at his bed. He leaned down to pull the sheets off and toss them in the washing machine, but a discoloration caught his eye. Turning around, he flipped the light on.

She'd been tight, but he hadn't realized it was tight enough to bleed. He stared at the stain before pulling the sheet free and walking back toward the laundry room.

There hadn't been anyone since him.

You don't know that.

He did. He'd suspected it before seeing the stain, and now he knew. The knowledge didn't sit well on his shoulders. She'd walked away from him. The last thing he needed was to think about her in some light that cast her as the woman of his dreams. He needed to think about her screwing her way through half of Washington, or holding her little body up as bait for the highest bidder.

Instead, she'd come to warn him. That stuck to his mind, long into the night when he should have been sleeping. He was thinking about why, trying to sort it out and find the pieces of information he was missing.

He rolled over at daybreak and sent a text to his brother. *"Meet me."*

He was tired but there was no point in lying in bed. His mind wasn't going to let it go, so he was going to find out just why Saxon was trailing Damascus.

Maybe then he'd be able to close the chapter of his life that included her.

Somehow, he got the notion it was going to be a whole lot harder than he anticipated. Something was off, something he couldn't quite put his finger on. But whatever it was, it was twisting deeper into him as images of their encounter replayed across his mind. She was hiding something. It had been too dark to get a good look into her eyes, but she'd been hedging. He'd made the mistake of thinking it was guilt.

You're just seeing what you want to . . .

Possibly, and then again she'd risked her neck to come to his house, while no one knew.

Which meant he'd missed something. A mighty big something, because whatever it was, Damascus had slipped her escort and crossed town to find him. To warn him. She'd taken a risk for him and he'd lost his head.

And that sent him off to see Saxon, because there was no way in hell he was turning his back on her when she needed help, even if she'd walked away from him.

Moron.

Fine, but there was no way he was going to allow that feeling to become one of regret because he failed Damascus in her darkest hour.

CHAPTER THREE

Tyler Martin knew a lot of people. Good ones, bad ones, but what made Tyler more valuable than others was the fact that he knew how to overlook just how seedy a man was in favor of how useful he might be. Under the right circumstances, even the worst scum had merit.

New Orleans had a long-standing tradition of the right kind of scum. They were connected and just organized enough to make them effective when it came to operations that needed someone not affiliated with the law.

The streets of the French Quarter were narrow with houses that rose up on either side. Bar after bar had music spilling out of their open doors, no matter what time of day or night it was. There were strippers in some, musicians in others, and the scent of food mixed freely with the music as street venders offered local cuisine while restaurants tried to lure in customers.

Tyler stopped to consider a menu. A woman walked by him, her skirt flipping back and forth across her thighs. He grinned, enjoying the view as he followed her inside and through the wooden door that led to the kitchen. She kept on walking, taking him into the maze of back alleys. It was steamy hot with the scent of moldy concrete because of the lack of sunlight. The woman kept walking, her heels tapping as she moved. She finally came to rest against the side of a building, leaning back and raising one leg so that her knee was bent and the bottom of her shoe rested against the brick wall. She'd tipped her head back, letting the moonlight shimmer off her throat while she looked up at the sky and kept her eyes off his face.

"You pick your pieces of fluff well," Tyler said once he was inside.

There was a husky chuckle from the man sitting at a pub-style highboy table. He wasn't by far the biggest man, but the twin scars running through the stubble on his chin added strength to his persona.

"She knows to keep her eyes off business," he said, tapping the tabletop in invitation.

Tyler slid onto a stool and resisted the urge to investigate the shadows around the room. For sure there were men there, men who wouldn't hesitate to kill him on Pratt's orders. But he'd known what sort of scum he was meeting. He aimed a firm stare at the man known only as Pratt, who was the Raven's right-hand man. Arms dealing, guns for hire, high-profile hostage trade—that was his world. He was among the best in the business.

"So . . . this business. It will cost you," Pratt said.

"Didn't think you were into favors," Tyler responded.

Pratt grinned, reveling chipped teeth. He snapped his fingers and someone appeared with two shot glasses and a bottle of whiskey. "Every man owes his share of favors. I am no exception." He flipped open a knife and cut into the wax seal on the bottle. "But I do not owe you any that I know of."

There was a faint Russian accent to his tone. He peeled the wax seal off and poured two measures. Tyler reached for one glass without hesitation. There was a momentary flicker of surprise in Pratt's eyes before he scooped up his own.

"Little point in suspecting you of trying to poison me before payment is made," Tyler explained as he took a sip.

"Unless I have decided it is too risky to do business with the head of security for Congressman Jeb Ryland."

Tyler set his glass down. "If your balls aren't big enough, I'm wasting my time."

Pratt lowered his glass a little too fast, and it clunked against the tabletop. "I am man enough."

"Good." Tyler tossed back the remains of his drink and set the glass down with a solid thud. "I need the job done right. The girl is to be returned."

"Yes, yes . . . unharmed." Pratt waved his hand in the air between them.

"I don't give a shit what you do to her, so long as she's mostly in one piece and mentally together enough to be of use. Don't do anything permanent that is too extreme. Just make sure you leave her face alone."

Pratt chuckled, a dangerous little sound that was rather evil if Tyler cared, which he didn't. Damascus needed to get busy making her father happy. Life was going to be mighty hard for her until she learned that lesson. He already knew which way the wind was blowing and he was going to do what he had to in order to make sure he had a place on the ship.

"The Hale brothers—" Tyler began.

"Die," Pratt said flatly. "In front of her, preferably. So she learns her place."

Tyler nodded and tossed a thick envelope down on the table. "First installment. Cash, used bills. As requested."

Pratt had already pulled a bundle of money from the envelope and was flicking through it like a deck of playing cards. He flipped to the end and nodded.

"There are two security passes in there. The girl will be at a bridal shower this weekend. Those will get your men in as caterers. Van will be left at the agreed location."

Pratt poured himself another drink. Someone shifted behind him, opening a door. There was the glow of a red light just behind him. A woman sat there on the end of a bed, wearing a lacy bra and garter belt. She had her long, trim legs crossed and a black mask over her eyes. Tyler didn't move. Pratt raised an eyebrow before rapping on the tabletop with his knuckles. Another body shifted into view, this one was a male, wearing just as little and with his eyes covered also to protect Tyler's identity.

"Whatever you want . . . it can be had," Pratt explained.

"Just the deal," Tyler said as he turned and left.

Keeping perspective was key. His cock was hard but he walked away, taking cover in a crowd of people making their way down Bourbon Street. They wore tags from some convention around their necks—most had their ties stuffed into their pockets—and cheered when their guide pointed at a bar.

Perspective had kept him on the rise for years. He never mixed his fucking with work. There would be plenty of time for that later. Tyler was going to get what he wanted.

Tyler planned to enjoy the moment.

Vitus stopped short of going into the house Saxon was using as a command center because his phone was buzzing. He caught Kagan's identification code and felt a tingle go down his spine. It might just be another assignment, but his gut told him it wasn't.

"You want me to what?" Vitus demanded a half minute later. His cool was slipping. Okay, it was fried because his temper was in full flare-up mode. He'd missed something the night before, that was for damn certain now.

"What part of your assignment is unclear, Agent Hale?" Kagan asked calmly. "Damascus Ryland is a high-profile target. I want you to sit on her."

His misgivings doubled, but he decided to see what information Kagan might spill.

"Fuck the bitch," he bit out. "I'm not laying my ass on the line for her."

"I noticed that she prefers your company. Fine by me."

"Zip it!" Vitus growled back. "She's a lady."

"Not with you she isn't." Kagan spoke with just enough knowledge in his tone to make Vitus shut his jaw. Vitus knew his section leader. Kagan didn't bullshit around. He knew what he knew and had amazing timing on letting you know when he was wise to you. So far, Kagan hadn't really admitted anything but he was doing exactly what Vitus was doing himself—jabbing at his opponent in the hope of gaining a response. Kagan knew something that had to do with Damascus.

Which meant Vitus was taking the assignment. A pack of wolves couldn't have stopped him. "Details?"

"She's going to a private party. I want to make sure she's got eyes on her. Tyler has been making some interesting contacts. I think he's making ready to pull something. Sending you the facts."

His gut tightened in response to Kagan's tone. There was another thing he knew about his section leader— Kagan didn't waste his time. His reservations shriveled up in the face of that hard, certain trust he had for Kagan. Nothing was going to get between him and Damascus now.

* * *

"We've gotten off on the wrong foot," Carl Davis said as casually as he might have ordered salad dressing.

Damascus couldn't have agreed more, but she bit back the response she wanted to make. Carl was grinning at her, looking like he knew what she was thinking.

He was walking beside her, his shirt sleeves rolled up to bare his wrists since the weather had warmed up. They were in her father's gardens. A place she couldn't very well escape from. Of course, both he and her sire knew that.

Just two more weeks . . .

"I really don't want to be rude," she said. "But I didn't invite you to lunch."

"And I followed you out here?" Carl finished with a smile. "Damascus, be very sure that I know exactly what I am doing. I've been planning to make a run for the presidency since I was four."

She got a very unsettled feeling in her belly as she noticed the flicker of enjoyment in his eyes. "I don't get why you're amused, Carl."

It might have been wiser to keep her mouth shut. Okay, it definitely would have been a better choice, but part of her rebelled at playing games. She stopped and faced him, completely exhausted being someone she wasn't. "I told you the straight-up truth. Are you really into games?" she asked.

"The right games," he answered as he reached out to tap her on the end of her nose.

It wasn't what she'd expected. Some sort of attempt to kiss her maybe, but Carl took a few steps away and pushed his hands into his pockets. He made a slow survey of the area before bringing his attention back to her.

"Well, I'm not into toying with men," she told him firmly.

He flashed her a knowing smile. "Yes you are."

Her insides twisted with something that felt a lot like forewarning. There was a glitter in his eyes that hinted at him making ready to drop something on her.

"I want what I want, Damascus, but that doesn't mean you can't get something you enjoy out of the bargain."

He leaned back against a retaining wall that had ivy trailing over it.

"I intend to use my doctorate, and I know having a career won't mix with being your first lady," she said slowly.

"True," Carl agreed. "You'll just have to get over that part."

"We seem to have a difference of opinions on the definition of the word 'bargain.' In my book, it means I get some of what I want too." She was wasting her time but couldn't keep her mouth shut. Part of her really wanted to know what he was getting at. Curiosity was likely as good for her health as it had been for the cat.

"You want Vitus Hale for a lover. That's acceptable. Just keep it quiet."

Her jaw nearly dropped. Shock held her in its grasp for a long moment as Carl chuckled at her. He straightened up and managed to stroke her jawline while she was busy attempting to figure out just what the hell he was thinking.

"You're quite clever," he continued, his tone edged with admiration. "Managing to slip out and back right under the noses of your father's men. Genius. My man was quite impressed with your ability to cut and run so completely. He nearly lost you too."

Her stomach felt like it dropped to her knees, the impulse to sputter out an excuse strong. That would just be letting him see her bleed though, and Carl was a shark. A dangerous one.

"I see I have your full attention." Carl had turned deadly serious. All hints of playfulness were gone. She got her first full look at the man she'd suspected he had to be in order to be interested in working with her sire. Ruthlessness shone in his eyes just as brightly as she'd seen in her sire's.

"Now, Vitus Hale." Carl forged on. "You want him for a lover? Can't really blame you. He is a magnificent creature."

Her jaw dropped a second time as she caught the unmistakable glitter of lust in his eyes. Carl only grinned wider.

"You're gay?" She just had to know for sure.

Triumph flashed in his eyes. "You're cleaver Damascus, but I've been playing this game a little longer than you. Don't feel bad that you never guessed. I've spent a lot of effort making sure there isn't even a whisper out there about it."

"Okay, your point. Fair and square," she conceded, more than a little impressed. The Washington crowd was masterful at ferreting out juicy personal information. A chill touched her nape as she realized she now had another obstacle to deal with on her way to freedom, and Carl wasn't going to be simple to outwit.

Well, guess this is where you say how much you love a challenge . . .

Sarcasm wasn't helping very much. She was still standing there, facing Carl Davis and his plans for her.

He chuckled again. "I like your straight-to-the-point way of talking. No messy emotional tirades. See, that's what I need in a wife, the brains to know what to keep under the covers, both with the press and with me." He shook his head. "I don't want to babysit your feelings."

"You won't have to," she said. "Because we're not getting married."

"What? Because I want you for your brains and not your body?" he sneered. "Isn't that the cry of women everywhere? 'Love me for my mind and not my body'?" He snickered softly but not so softly that she couldn't hear the disgust in his tone.

"As I said"—she cut into his amusement—"I am set on having a career."

"One your father will never let you have." Carl cut through her argument. "Better negotiate with me, at least I'm willing to give you some of what you want. You can have your lovers, so long as the children are mine. I can manage *that* much of a relationship with you."

It was suddenly hard to breathe, like a rope was tightening around her throat. She put her hands behind her, as if that would somehow keep him from putting a ring on her finger. She needed to think, needed to keep focused. She had a plan, a solid one.

"Good." Carl stated. "We've got things straightened out between us. My assistant will work out a courting schedule with your father's people."

There was a clear warning in his tone. He stepped toward her then leaned over her.

"Don't make the mistake of thinking I will let you go now that you know my darkest secret, Damascus. Be your mother's daughter and we'll get along perfectly. You can have your lover and I will have your mother's Delacroix connections." He reached out and stroked her cheek. It took all her effort to hold back the nausea that gripped her. "Home, hearth, family. That will translate into votes."

And deceit, secrets, and games.

She drew in a deep breath and ordered herself to get over the feeling of impending doom. Colonel Magnus wouldn't let her go. She'd pledged herself to him, and he had warned her that he'd arrest her if necessary.

That idea gave her back her poise, which Carl took as

a sign of agreement, walking up the path toward the house with a happy whistle on his lips.

Well, at least he wasn't interested in her body.

What a fucking relief.

"My reason is simple." Saxon took another sip of coffee. There were dark rings under his eyes but he wasn't groggy, not in the least. "Tyler Martin is working for her daddy and I want his ass on a platter. I saw Ryland's reaction when you got near his little baby, so I'm sticking close. Maybe he'll lose it and try to take me out. Nothing I'd like better."

Vitus considered his brother for a long moment. Agent Greer McRae was listening in, twirling a pen between his fingers as he tried to arrive at a conclusion before Saxon divulged his motives. That was one of the reasons Greer was a top-notch agent; it was also a reason why Vitus was considering smashing him in the jaw. The latter action was likely only going to get him a good fight, since Greer thrived on flesh-on-flesh contact.

The problem was, Vitus was spoiling for some sort of outlet for the emotional storm brewing inside him. What he needed was to apply his brain to the situation. His gut was telling him that and he needed to listen to his gut. Things went really bad when he didn't.

"I'm not waiting for Tyler to get set up for another shot at us," Saxon explained.

Vitus nodded, understanding bursting inside his brain. "That little mess with Zoe Magnus was almost perfect."

Greer was nodding. "Give the fucker too much time, and we'll get those toe tags he has picked out for us."

Saxon pointed at Greer while hitting the coffee again. "So, I'm going to push on his sore spot. The Princess."

Vitus frowned. He had his arms folded across his chest, and ended up gripping his shirt sleeves. Saxon didn't miss it. "What did she want bad enough to seek you out?"

"To tell me to pull you off her tail."

"She's got four men dodging her footsteps," Saxon replied. "Understandable, considering how many enemies her daddy manages to make. Since she's had a taste of just how willing they are to use her to get to him, it was really stupid of her to go on a solo outing."

"She gave you the slip. No matter what else, that's worthy of notice."

Saxon's eyes narrowed as Greer snorted.

"Or courageous," Vitus said, getting back on topic. "But if that's the case . . . I have to start thinking about why she's worried about me."

Memories surfaced from the previous night. Could he have misjudged her responses? Mistaking temper for fear? He didn't like how much he was returning to that question. It was starting to raise the hairs on the back of his neck.

"Don't go there," Saxon warned him. "The bitch left you."

"Don't call her that." Vitus didn't wait to see if his brother was going to toe the line on that one or not. He sat down and logged into one of the computers sitting in the house they were using as a base of operations. It was pretty quiet at the moment because the mess from their last case was taking a long time to mop up. Tyler Martin had almost pinned stolen classified Intel on them and he wasn't above shooting an innocent girl in the process. He'd picked Zoe Magnus for the operation because the situation suited his needs, and those needs seemed to be exacting revenge on Saxon and himself.

But details were still murky. He and Saxon had plenty of suspicions but not a lot of hard data. Which left them with the fact that Tyler was working for Congressman Ryland when he should have been dead after a very hushed trial and an equally quiet execution. When you signed on with Shadow Operations, you accepted the fact that they meted out of their own justice. Someone had pulled some strings to save Tyler's neck and now the bastard was running Ryland's personal security. It wasn't hard to deduce who had pulled those strings.

"You've got no reason to get that look on your face." Saxon followed him.

Vitus looked up, locking gazes with his brother. "Except that Kagan told me to stick on her six. Officially."

Saxon's expression hardened, and the pen froze in Greer's finger. The tension in the room tightened, drawing curious looks from the newer members of the team who were working in what would have been a living room of the house if it were a home.

Saxon's jaw tightened and so did Greer's. The reason was simple.

Shit just got real.

Kagan toyed with a couple of shots of Tyler Martin in New Orleans.

"You do realize Martin is after your men?" Dare Servant asked from where he was sitting on the other side of room. "And you just assigned one of them to the very target who is going to lead him to the man gunning for him?"

"The girl has always been bait. Vitus Hale isn't stupid," Kagan said.

"Shouldn't you clue your men in?"

"I don't have any iron-clad evidence," Kagan explained. "Tyler wiggled out of the mess he made last time because of his contacts. The only way to get him is to follow the bait. The Hale brothers know not to turn their backs on Tyler. In fact, I'm pretty sure they understand exactly why I assigned them to the bait."

Dare let out a low whistle. "That's a dangerous game."

Kagan snorted. "This isn't the Boy Scouts."

"Not even close." Dare picked up a print showing Pratt. "This guy works for the Raven. I've been on the case for weeks now and no one alive has seen his face. His damn screw partners don't even know what his dick looks like. Makes them wear a mask."

"That means he's someone with a public image, the kind of face even a gutter rat would know and exploit," Kagan reasoned. "And someone who can pull strings."

"I've got a feeling I'm going to be digging in for a long haul on this one," Servant finished up. "But it was a spot of luck seeing Tyler down there. Since someone sponged his record clean, no one would have told you."

Luck. Yeah, Kagan remembered Lady Luck. She was fickle, but every now and then she blew him a kiss. He considered the photo of Tyler in the French Quarter of New Orleans.

"I'm coming for you," he said softly before he turned around and looked at a pair of pictures tacked to his office wall. There was nothing else on the wall, just the two service photos. Pictures of the men Tyler had gunned down while trying to set up Saxon and Vitus through the Magnus family.

Tyler might think he was safe. Maybe Lady Luck would desert Kagan and let Tyler slip away from the retribution he so richly deserved. Hell, it wouldn't be the first time the bad guy won.

Maybe. Then again, sometimes, the good guy won. And every now and again, the hero even got the girl.

They'd just have to see which way Lady Luck wanted

it all to go. Once the ball was in play, it would all be in her hands.

"You strike me as a man who gets things done."

Tyler turned and considered Carl Davis. The man had a practiced happy-go-lucky good-guy expression on his face, an expression he wore most of the time. He scanned the area before letting it slip into a more serious one.

"I could appreciate a man of your talents," Carl continued.

"Good to know," Tyler replied.

"I like knowing you were smart enough to track her over to her lover's house." Carl grinned when Tyler's eyes widened. "She's my future bride. Of course I had a man on her."

"Should have thought of that."

Carl nodded an agreement, then fished something out of his pocket. "This might make a nice little addition to the evidence you're planning to plant."

Tyler considered the oblong item before letting out a low whistle. "Only the SEALs have these. Must have been a bitch to get it off-base. Nice resources you have."

"Remember that," Carl said as he came in closer. "Remember that I'm the man going to the White House. Who I take with me as a running mate can change, but one thing that won't change is who I'm planning on being my first lady."

"That a fact?" Tyler asked to keep the man talking. It was always best to let others do the chattering. He learned so much more that way than when he was asking questions.

"It's the only fact that should really concern you in the coming days," Carl replied smoothly, but there was a hard promise in his eyes. "Mind you, she's my choice because of how the press loves her. Sweet little blue eyes and those ginger curls coupled with her desire to help sick children." He lifted his hand to his mouth and kissed his fingertips before opening his hand. "Press candy all the way. And her rescue from the clutches of evildoers will spike my support numbers."

He tapped Tyler on the shoulder with one fingertip. "Just make sure she comes home in mostly one piece and runs into my arms."

"Got it." Tyler turned and walked away before anyone noticed them talking.

He did enjoy it when life wasn't boring.

There was cake.

Damascus smelled it as she came around the corner and into the garden where the bridal shower was being held. Frosting was her fatal weakness, and the damn nutritionist her sire kept on staff never let her have any. She sniffed at the air, the scent of buttercream frosting tickling her nose.

She was so having two pieces.

There was a huge, gleaming white gazebo with lilac netting and ribbons adorning it. Music was coming from a string quartet sitting in the shade of a large tree while the bride-to-be welcomed her guests.

"I'm so glad you could make it!" Laura exclaimed as she leaned in to hug Damascus. "Rumor has it, you might be next. I am so jealous."

Laura gave her a knowing wink before moving on to the next VIP in line without a single care for the fact that she'd happily dump her current fiancé for a bigger fish. Laura was everything Jeb wished Damascus was. The perfect opportunity-seeking daughter.

Damascus happily handed off the large box that contained something from Laura's extravagant gift list.

There were two uniformed caterers assigned to the duty of cataloging the gifts and taking them away to a waiting van.

Damascus took a glass of champagne off a tray and felt the tension lifting from her shoulders. Just ten more days. It seemed impossible in a way and yet her careful planning was about to come to pass.

Would it bring her peace?

It certainly wasn't going to bring her the man she loved.

She frowned as she lifted her glass, but the scent of the champagne only made her belly roll. She didn't want to numb her wits. If that was all it took to placate her, she would have fallen in line with her sire's plans and happily accepted Carl's offer, because she could run to the liquor cabinet anytime she needed an escape.

No, she wanted more from life. Freedom. Choice. Her gaze moved to the cake.

Frosting.

And no one got everything. Vitus would move on. That thought would have to satisfy her. At least until they cut the cake.

It was a private house, but there was an army of suited men prowling the perimeter.

"Worse than mosquitoes in the south," Saxon groused.

Vitus considered the group of private security milling around the edges of the garden. The women attending the shower looked like a bunch of koi in a sunken pool at a sushi restaurant. Inside the pool, they thought they were the masters. But in truth, they were the ones being contained.

A touch of pity caught him unaware.

His temper had been hot enough to keep him from really dwelling on his feelings, but now he couldn't dismiss just how much empathy he felt for Damascus.

Okay, and the feeling that she still needed him to rescue her too.

Shit.

He didn't need to go down that thought path. It was only going to lead to trouble. Damascus didn't want his help. That was the reason she'd come to see him, to tell him to leave her alone.

Yeah, but what had her actions said?

That was what was chewing on his insides. People said a whole lot of stuff, but truth, well, that was found in their actions. He moved and caught Damascus in his sights. She'd broken away from the rest of the group and perched herself on the edge of a large garden bench. There was a blush on her cheeks and a small smile curving her lips as she eyed the slice of cake in her hands. He was fixated on her as she used a polished fork to slice off the pointed tip of the cake and scoop it up. Enjoyment sparkled in her eyes as she opened her lips and closed them around the cake. Her eyes had even shut, like she was enjoying some forbidden pleasure.

Which she was.

He recalled her bare body perfectly. The low body fat didn't take to cake very well. But realizing what her joy stemmed from only left him with more questions. Was it by her design? The intense training? That would hold a lot of water considering the mess he'd pulled her out of three years ago. A person only had two choices after something like that—build up your strength so you could cultivate enough confidence to feel safe or turn to medication to dull your wits so you could sleep at night.

"I learned it myself."

He recalled what she'd said at the White House and felt his misgivings double. He would put money on the fact that her father wasn't having her trained to be anything but the perfect politician's wife.

One of the catering staff appeared, diligent to the core. Damascus was startled, bringing a small grin to Vitus's lips. Sometimes, she was so damn innocent. Caught with her plate of cake she blinked at the waiter, taking a glass of champagne and mumbling out a hasty thank-you to send the guy on his way.

She actually looked both ways before going back to her treat, making him want to go get her the entire damn cake just to see her smile.

She was sneaking cake. It was pretty pathetic. Damascus lifted a forkful up and considered it. Everyone wanted something. Some women might envy her for her slender figure while she was stuck noticing how unfair it was that she had to slip away to eat a slice of cake.

She took a sip of the champagne and then another because the sugar had made her mouth dry. A contented smile curved her lips as she became fascinated by a butterfly. It was fluttering about, moving among the milkweed. She got up and started after it, enthralled by its colors and motions.

So free . . .

So . . . beautiful . . .

"Something's wrong," Saxon said.

"No shit." Vitus answered his brother but he was already in motion. Saxon hooked his arm and held him back. Vitus dislodged his grip with a hard and efficient motion.

"We need some backup," Saxon hissed into his cell phone.

Damascus was wobbling. The plate of cake was facedown in the grass where it had tumbled from her fingers. The glass of champagne was about to join it as she wandered after a butterfly, her normal poise gone as she staggered with half-closed eyes and a bemused smile on her lips.

It was the last thing he saw as the waiter passed them, and then it felt like lightning hit. The burst of light was so bright, it sent a shaft of pain through his skull that slammed him into unconsciousness like a baseball bat to the back of the skull.

"Shut up. I need to piss."

Damascus blinked, but it was still dark. It took a while for her to realize she had something tapped over her eyes. Then she twisted and felt the bite of cold metal on her wrists. A strange whine was coming closer. She bit into the gag that was between her teeth. Fear was bubbling up so thick, it threatened to choke her.

Get . . . a . . . grip!

She shouted at herself, frantically trying to maintain her composure. It was up to her. She knew it, had faced it before.

"Awake?"

Someone yanked her off of whatever she was lying on and sat her up. Her breath was coming in little rasps, giving her away.

"Good. You can use the can before takeoff."

A rough hand gripped her upper arms and pulled her to her feet. She got twisted up because she was so disoriented.

"Walk, bitch. Because I don't really care if you wet your pants and sit in it for the next day. Just don't really want to smell it all the way to the Quarter."

She believed him. His tone left no doubt that he considered her a thing. Something he was dealing with in order to get paid. The job. Men like him could do the most horrible things once they applied the mental label of "job" to some person. She had ceased to be a human being in his mind.

Damascus forced her feet to work and stumbled in the direction he shoved her. She hit her shin on something, and something else jabbed into her thigh.

"Gonna unlock you, but if you give me any grief, I'll let you sit in your shit after this."

There was a click as one of the handcuffs was unlocked and then she was shoved forward. A door closed behind her. She ripped at the blindfold and gulped in some deep breaths once she could see again.

She hated the dark.

It was the one thing she'd never quite banished from her first abduction.

Well, you can see now, so get it together.

She had to. The small bathroom was somewhat clean. She also realized what the whine was. It was the engines on the plane warming up, a small private jet of some sort.

She turned around and used the bathroom, because wetting herself wasn't something she needed to add to the moment. She looked at herself in the mirror and stared at the dragonfly. It had torn part of her dress but was still attached. She grabbed it and unpinned it, moving it to the inside of her bra. It made a slightly uncomfortable bulge against her breast but she decided it was the best feeling in the world.

Because it meant she wasn't alone.

"How can my daughter be missing?" Jeb Ryland demanded. "It's your fucking job to handle security."

"The culprits had forged IDs," Tyler Martin replied. "Allowing them right onto the grounds of Senator Forrest's home. Those radical extremists are resourceful."

The congressman was pacing around his office. Tyler

made sure the doors were locked before he continued. "I made sure they won't be traced back to me."

Jeb flipped around, his mouth hanging open.

Tyler offered him a half smile. "You can send the Hale brothers after her. It's a rather dangerous assignment, might even cost them their lives, but when all the evidence is sorted out, there are sure to be a lot of questions as to why both brothers were at the scene of the crime and knocked out. Seems rather clumsy of two former SEALs to get downed so easily. In fact, some might conclude that they were in on it."

Jeb shut his mouth, his eyes narrowing. He made a continue motion with his hand.

"Your daughter gets a couple of days in captivity to remind her how good she's got it and the Hale brothers die trying to rescue her. Once the official investigation kicks off, the fact that they both were at the scene of the kidnapping will lead the investigators down a carefully laid path of evidence to incriminate them."

Jeb was nodding.

"Which should make sure your daughter settles into her engagement without any more night excursions."

Jeb looked at him, clearly confused. Tyler tossed a couple of black-and-white photos of Damascus on his desk.

"Some families are still traditional," Tyler explained. "Your daughter made the mistake of doing her quick change in the store of one. The father found her clothing and took her picture off his security system. Brought it up here to the house because he felt a father should know what his daughter was up to. He did me a favor. It was a shame to have to cancel his family's visas but we can't have them around when the election heats up."

"Where was she going?" Jeb demanded.

"To see her lover," Tyler replied. "Vitus Hale." He

tossed another set of photos down. "Tracked the kid's car across town through traffic cameras. He dropped her off about five blocks from Hale's house. That's proof enough. Nowhere else she would have been going to."

Jeb had turned red. He was crumpling the edges of the photo as he nodded.

"As you can see, I have the situation in hand."

"You'd better!" Jeb snapped.

Tyler slowly grinned. "Let's get one thing clear between us." He leaned over the desk and grabbed the photo, ripping it out of Jeb's hand. "I am not your bitch."

"You are what I say you are," Jeb responded. But there was a tremor in his tone that betrayed his fear.

"I am the best," Tyler continued. "Start treating me like it or I will be out your door and through another one so fast, you won't have time to wipe your ass before I let out some evidence that will have the hounds nipping at your cheeks for a pound of flesh."

Jeb started to say something but thought better of it.

"Good." Tyler straightened up. "I'm going to get back to performing the task you set for me. You need to insist Special Agents Saxon and Vitus Hale be assigned to the case of retrieving your daughter. After all, there is no one else you trust with the assignment."

Jeb nodded and reached for his phone. Tyler whistled softly on his way out of the office. Things were running as smoothly as could be.

Time for phase two.

"There isn't a fucking mark on either of us," Vitus growled.

Greer was considering the area, down in a low crouch as he looked at the plants. He moved forward, using a pen to move a branch of rosemary aside. "Someone was here."

Saxon frowned, trying to recall the moments before he'd blacked out.

"And I saw a flash." Greer stood. "My guess is the waiter took you two out with a flash grenade. Or a hand-held version of it. The security footage is nothing but an overexposed frame."

Vitus exchanged a long look with Saxon. "She had the dragonfly on."

Saxon pulled out his phone and tapped in a password. Vitus moved next to him, but there was no signal to be found.

"She's in the air," Vitus said. "Above the cell towers."

Saxon nodded. Vitus was already moving when his phone vibrated. He pulled it out. Kagan's identification code was flashing on the screen.

"Seems you two have made the special-assignment list," Kagan said. "The good congressman has requested you both to be put on the team looking for his daughter."

"That stinks," Vitus replied.

"Agreed," Kagan responded.

"Especially when you factor in that Saxon and I were taken out by a flash grenade," Vitus continued.

"A nice little classified weapon that only a SEAL would have access to," Kagan finished.

"Exactly," Vitus said. "I don't need to look far for who is behind that."

"You have full resources. Go off-grid. Far far off," Kagan instructed.

The line went dead. Vitus felt like something inside him woke up. If Tyler wanted to dance, fine. But the man had made a huge mistake in using Damascus. Because now, killing him was just too good.

"Put that blindfold back on before I open this door."

Damascus jumped, but ordered herself to remain

calm. "Okay," she stammered out, wincing when she realized how scared she sounded.

Maybe that wasn't such a bad card to play.

"I'm . . . doing . . . it." She made sure her voice shook as she nodded with satisfaction. Let them think she was paralyzed by fear. That would be an advantage. She swallowed her distaste for the dark as she put the blindfold back in place.

"You done yet?" her host called from the other side of the door.

"Yes."

"I'm going to bust your jaw if you're lying to me."

She heard the door being opened. "Okay," he said in response to finding her as he'd instructed. He pulled her back down the aisle and pushed her into a seat. There was a moment of fussing around with the seat belt before she heard him drop into a seat nearby.

"Let's get this can off the ground!"

"Yeah. . . . Waiting on the boss man," the pilot responded.

There was a buzz from the guy next to her.

"Yeah, we got her. . . . Okay. I'll get it."

There was a sniff and a shift of fabric. "Open the door back up, boss is sending Reni back for a little evidence."

There was a click in front of her face that made her wince. "Now you listen to me bitch. You're going to sit there and take what I give you or the next time the boss wants a piece of you, I'll take something you'll miss more. Like one of them fingers. Doctors need fingers the last time I heard."

The word "piece" set off a panic inside her but her host had already jammed his arm under her chin and pinned her against the side of the plane. She felt the knife touch her upper ear a second before pain blinded her. It was white hot, her scream strangled on the gag as she bit down on it, actually grateful for it because it saved her tongue.

"So shut the fuck up."

She was free, and the scent of blood filled the air. She fought off a wave of nausea out of desperation because she didn't want to choke when the gag trapped the contents of her stomach inside her mouth. Her head spun in a dizzy circle, making her grateful for the seat belt. It gave her a fixed point. Something to help her feel grounded as the pain centered on the top of her ear in a throbbing mass. Tears had made wet spots in her blindfold as the plane rocked and someone came aboard.

"That's what the boss wants you to deliver."

She was still reeling as she heard the door close and lock. There was a sniff and another rustle of fabric as the guy sat back down. She felt him looking at her, and she turned toward the heat of the sunlight coming through the window. The pain was nearly overwhelming, but she drew in deep breaths and steadied herself. As her brain cleared, she decided to let out some whimpers.

"That's right, you remember what you get if you even think about giving me shit."

The plane jerked as it moved, the engines revving up.

"You didn't have to take that much."

Damascus stood still, which took a monumental amount of self-control as she was being inspected. Someone had a hand in her hair, pushing it back to look at the slice missing from her left ear.

"Just a bit off the top." Her airplane companion replied in a bored tone. "Never miss it with that mop on her head."

"Better hope the client agrees with you. He made a point of making sure we know her image is important."

"If you wanted me to take a toe, you should have said

so," he groused. "You were pushing for us to get off the ground, so I didn't take a lot of time thinking about it."

The quarter. It made sense now, the French Quarter in New Orleans. She connected the accents with the scent of boiled crawfish in the air.

"We won't have her for long," whoever was looking at her ear said as he released her. She made a point of shivering. "But we have to wait until the rest of the deal comes together."

He suddenly gripped her hair, pulling it with a savage grip while his breath hit her lips. She recoiled as nausea gripped her.

"Got a little warning for you," he said as he shook her head with his grip. "Learn to do what you're told. When you don't, the price will be higher than you like."

She tried to jerk free, but he held her by tightening his grip until she couldn't control the cry that escaped as a muffled sound through her gag.

"I'm going to wait for your lover to come looking for you and then I am going to let you watch me splatter his brains all over the place."

She cried out as her captor snickered.

"You heard that right." He cooed against her ear. "So you just spend a little time thinking about what happens when you step out of line. Give me any trouble and I'll cut you, until you stop."

He released her and gave her a hard shove. She stumbled, running into a wall before he pushed her again. This time she went a lot further, not stopping until she hit the edge of a bed and landed on it in a tangle of limbs.

"Stupid cunt. I feel sorry for the poor bastard that was dumb enough to not know you're out of his league." There was a grunt of disgust. "Maybe I'll cut you a few times anyway, for being a slut. You should know enough to be a smart whore and get the right price before giving out any samples."

There was a slam and the sliding of a bolt. She wanted to vomit. Horror was gripping her, twisting her into a quivering ball of reactions, reducing her to nothing but raw emotion.

She had to resist it.

Damascus forced herself to sit up and swallow. No one was dead yet, so she'd better concentrate on making sure that didn't happen. Vitus wasn't stupid.

Yeah, well neither were the men holding her.

But you aren't either . . .

That thought helped her get a grip. Right. She'd found a way out of her sire's plans for her and she wouldn't be rolling over. No today, not ever. Vitus sure as shit wouldn't, so neither would she. The cut on her ear throbbed and she focused on it, letting the pain cut through her fear and fuel her determination.

What she needed was a plan.

Damascus was suddenly grateful to her sire's nutritionist because her butt was small enough for her to slip her arms over it and up in front of her. She yanked off the blindfold and gag, quelling the urge to throw them across the room. She might need them later so she put them back over her head and let them hang around her neck. She shivered with revulsion, but ordered herself to keep a grip. The lump of the dragonfly gave her enough hope to maintain her poise as she investigated her surroundings.

It was a dingy room to be sure—if the paint was less than ten years old, she'd be surprised. It was peeling in spots and long, dusty cobwebs decorated the corners and pretty much the entire perimeter of where the ceiling met the walls. The only window was eight feet up and covered with an iron grate. It was ornate, with leaves and acorns, but it was also very solid-looking, like it had been cast in the early part of the century.

Well, she wasn't going to let its look intimidate her. There was a chest of drawers in the room. She eased one of the drawers out, happy to see that it was as solid-looking at the iron grate. She sat it on its side and climbed up onto it. She slid the window open, but the grate was attached to the outside of the building.

But she could feel the screws.

She climbed down, cursing the handcuffs, which made it a lot harder. She looked around the room but there wasn't anything else. Despair tried to choke her right about then, rising up and pushing at the barrier she'd placed between herself and it.

No. . . . Keep your head.

She could bet her entire ear that Vitus wouldn't sit down and cry. But she did sit down, the evening setting in and taking the last of the sunlight with it. The bed groaned as it took her weight, and she stood up as the sound registered.

The bed was just as old as everything else. She got down onto the floor and looked beneath the mattress. There was a dated spring system holding a grate that the mattress sat on instead of a modern box frame. She flipped onto her back and started pulling at the springs. She had numerous cuts by the time she freed one, but she held it up to the light spilling in through the window and smiled. The curved end of it was sharp and hard. She climbed back onto the drawer and pushed her hands through the window to where she could feel the screw-head holding the grate in place. The outside of the building was brick. The clay crumbled a little as she dug into it, but the bolt stuck in place.

Well, she wasn't giving up.

Not until she was dead.

*   *   *

Vitus touched down in New Orleans. Frustration was driving him mad as he went down the stairs of the private jet and onto the tarmac. Saxon was right behind him, cell phone in hand as he waited for it to grab a location from the local cell tower.

Seconds ticked by like hours, the little icon on the screen going around and around while Vitus ground his teeth.

"She's in the French Quarter."

Greer had already gone ahead and climbed behind the wheel of an unmarked car. He had the engine going before they made it into the vehicle and told him where to go. It was seamless teamwork, smooth, deliberate. The only thing missing was the detachment he'd always had when going out on an assignment.

That was a good way to get killed.

An even better way to tip off their perpetrators and arrive in time to find the body of their target still warm because the kill was that fresh.

He knew the facts, had trained until they were part of his thinking process, but tonight it didn't seem to mean a goddamn thing. His emotions were riding high, impossible to control.

His phone buzzed, and he opened the line on speaker.

"Proof of life was delivered while you were in the air," Kagan informed him. "A piece of her ear. Got it at the lab now for DNA, but blood type matches."

"Fuck," Vitus growled.

"Shit," Saxon added.

Greer grunted something in Gaelic that really needed no translation.

There was a pause on the other end of the line. "Why does it look like you have Intel on her location?"

"We'll be in touch." Vitus killed the call and shoved his phone into his shirt pocket. "If anyone wants out, now is the time."

There was a long moment of nothing but road noise. Vitus cut Greer a hard look. "This is personal for me."

"For us," Saxon corrected him from the backseat.

"*I* screwed up," Vitus insisted. "Not you."

"Tyler has already come after me once, no way I'm sitting this out." Saxon's tone made it clear he was digging in for the long haul. It was a stubbornness Vitus knew very well and very personally because he had his own share of it.

"Greer—"

"Shut your jaw." Greer turned a corner and tightened his hands on the wheel. "About damn time I got to have a bit of fun." He offered Vitus a grin. "You Americans spend too much time following the rules."

"Well, we're about to go off the reservation," Vitus declared. "So lock and load."

Someone was going to die. The fact that it might be himself didn't really concern Vitus. There was also a chance that he might come out on top, and that was worth the risk.

Hell, Damascus was worth his fucking life.

Sweat was making her fingers slick.

It might have been blood, but Damascus refused to think about it. She had to focus on something other than the way her fingers were trying to cramp up or the fact that her neck was killing her from the angle she was holding it or the half-dozen other things that were screaming all over her body. She took a deep breath and dug the end of the spring into another place. She heard the brick crunch, felt a sprinkle of dust stick to the wet surface of her fingers before there was a pop and the bolt finally went flying into the alleyway. It clattered onto the pavement, making her cringe because it sounded so loud.

She froze on her perch, listening for any approaching footsteps. Her heart was hammering as she put the spring between her teeth and tested the iron grate. It pushed out but not enough. She set her sights on another bolt and went to work. Digging in, listening for the crunch of the brick, feeling the crumbling dust and waiting for the first hint of give on the bolt. She felt it and moved the spring a tiny amount around the head of the bolt to begin again.

Dig in.

Her confidence was growing, the way the grate vibrated feeding her resolve. She could smell the metallic scent of her blood, which only fanned her determination. She would get out. She would join Colonel Magnus's team.

She would be more than a princess.

The second bolt went sailing into the alleyway as she leaned against the wall. Her fingers were in agony, but that didn't stop the wave of accomplishment that swept through her. It left her smiling as she sagged against the peeling paint. Pleased with herself in a way she'd never really realized she might be, in some dark part of her mind, where the remnants of her last kidnapping still lived. She'd known it was there, all the doubt and helplessness that she had never been able to banish.

Tonight, she had to stand up against it or she was going to lose more than another piece of her ear. She let the throbbing pain take precedence, focusing on it as she determined which bolt to attack next. When that one popped free, there was enough music outside to cover the sound. She pushed on the iron grate, biting back a cry of victory as it pushed out a full two feet. She pulled her hands back inside and tucked the spring into her bra before reaching back up and lifting her body up to the window. She didn't dare move the dresser. Someone might hear that, so she struggled to hold her body weight and shove through the window. It was awkward to say the least, but she held onto the side of the grate that was still bolted to the wall and pushed with her feet against the side that was free. The windowsill gave her a narrow perch as she used all of her strength to hold tight to the iron grate; it also gave her the leverage to push her feet against the open side.

Her legs slid out as the iron gave way. Her knees and then her hips went through as she twisted and pushed herself out to her waist with her hands. The iron tore at her dress, leaving gouges in her skin. She kept pushing, stuck at her shoulders as she lost the angle to use her hands while her feet dangled uselessly in the air. She pulled her knees up and pushed against the outside of the building. The iron grabbed at her hair as her shoulder moved, and then gravity did the rest.

She landed in a heap, pain jolting through her as she hit the ground and her heels crumbled under her weight. Her hair was a mop that covered her eyes as she went rolling through the gutter. There was a foul stench she decided she adored because it meant she was outside. When she came to a stop she scrambled to shove her hair back so she could see and get her feet under her. The alleyway was only a few feet wide. She drove toward where it opened into a wide street, the sound of people tantalizing.

But she ran into a body. A solid, hard male, who gripped her shoulders and set her back a pace into the alleyway.

She hissed at him, struggling, fighting for her life. He sucked in his breath and yanked her toward him, wrapping his arms around her.

"Princess."

She froze, blinking as she tried to decide if her brain was playing tricks on her. Was she cracking? Hearing what she wanted to because she just couldn't deal with defeat?

"Not too bad." Vitus eased his grip, letting her push back from him. She stared at him, still unwilling to believe her eyes, although maybe "unable" was the more appropriate word.

"No too bad at all." Saxon echoed his brother's words.

Vitus let her go slowly, making sure she could stand before he slid his hands along her sides and tugged her dress down. It popped the shock bubble she'd been caught in.

"How—" Her brain was firing off faster than her lips could form words. "Oh, the dragonfly." It was still tucked into her bra.

"Yeah."

"Here." Another man leaned past Vitus, reaching for her wrists. There was a click as he unlocked one side of the handcuffs. Damascus jerked back as Vitus lifted her hair away from her ear.

"You have to go . . . now," she insisted, a cold dread filling her. "They are going to kill you."

"Shut up, bitch," someone said behind her as a hard hand grabbed her hair. Vitus grasped her bicep at the same time he leveled his gun at the man behind her. She was stuck between them.

"Federal Agents," Vitus announced. "Put your hands up."

The man behind her only snickered. "I know who you are. Been waiting on you."

"That so?" Vitus was trying to distract the man, starting to move past her and put himself in the line of fire.

"Stay right the fuck there," the man behind her

warned, his fingers digging into her hair. Damascus bit her lip to contain the cry of pain trying to get free. "I'll put one through her head before you get a round off or take more than one step."

"You won't shoot your hostage," Saxon growled.

"Sure will," the man behind her confirmed. "No way around it. Three against one, which leaves me only one choice."

"You can surrender," Vitus said.

There was a soft chuckle from the man behind Damascus, sending an icy chill down her spine.

"I'd be a dead man," he rasped. "No one fails the Raven. You'll do me fast. You can be sure I won't get that sort of deal from the man. No, he likes to make examples of the men who fail him."

Damascus's heart had started racing. Vitus, Saxon, and the other agent were all focused on the man behind her. Sweat was trickling down her back as she tried to think of what to do. There was a shifting of the shadows behind Saxon. A man emerged, moonlight shimmering off the polished casing of a gun. Saxon's body tightened as he shifted, turning on him while the other agent ended up muzzle to muzzle with another gun. She was gripped by horror, feeling helpless against her sire's need to strike at Vitus. The trap was too tight.

"Just go." She wasn't sure when she decided to say it, only that the words were out of her mouth as she took a step backward.

There was a gasp and a round of giggles as a group of women rounded the corner and came barreling down the alleyway. They were chattering and obviously several drinks into the night.

"Oh yes!" one of them said.

"Eye candy!" another chimed in.

"Grade A viewing! Right this way."

The man holding her hair grunted, releasing her as he recoiled from the group. Vitus pulled her hard and she stumbled forward as another round of giggling bounced off the brick walls. There was suddenly a crush of bodies as the newcomers just plowed into them all.

"Ladies!" Someone called from where the alley opened into a street. "That's the wrong way!"

"Shit," one of the men said as he shoved his gun under his jacket. "Yeah, wrong way. . . . Get back to your tour."

The man at the opening to the street illuminated the scene with a high-powered flashlight. Guns went under jackets as Vitus shoved Damascus forward, into the light.

"Oh . . . sorry."

"Opp-sy!"

There was a shift next to her and then the hard sound of flesh hitting flesh. As the group of women turned, Saxon and Vitus struck, leaving the gunmen on the ground while they shoved her toward the front of the group.

"Move, Princess," Vitus said next to her ear. They all popped out onto the street as the group of women laughed and the tour guide tried to get them back under control. Vitus wasn't really waiting for her to follow his orders. He pulled her along as the night crowd swirled around them.

"You can bet they're setting up a way to drop us," Saxon muttered next to her.

"And there isn't much we can do about it," the third agent growled.

The three men had her caged among them, their gazes darting around as they tried to find an escape route.

"Get closer to me." She grabbed Vitus and Saxon by their forearms. "They want to shoot you, but not me."

"What?"

She wasn't sure who actually voiced the question. She was a little more focused on pulling them both closer. She was stepping on the sides of their shoes and had a death grip on both of their belts. Personal space be damned.

The street was full of people partying in New Orleans style, making it easy to crush together. The doors of the bars were open, the music spilling out and cars tried to thread their way down the crowded streets. She was stumbling, hearing every step she took because her senses were heightened while her heart continued to pound. She was panting and she was missing a shoe. She hopped and kicked the other one off because it made keeping up easier.

"There." Vitus gave a short jerk of his head toward a large hotel. "The roof. PD helicopter is setting down."

She started to look up, but Vitus tightened his grip on her nape to keep her head steady. "Don't give us away, Princess."

"Oh . . . um, right." She had to do better, had to be smarter.

"Can you fly that bird, Greer?" Saxon asked.

"Sure can."

With a destination in mind, the three men suddenly tightened their focus. She was herded along as they drove around groups of people, weaving in and out along the sidewalk and across traffic in sudden motions all designed to make it hard to follow them. The hotel was a Marriott. It was on the edge of the French Quarter, its tower rising above the historic area. Vitus pushed her through the large revolving door and into the lobby without blinking an eye. The bar was full, as some sort of convention was in progress. Greer dropped his suit jacket over her shoulders from behind to cover her torn dress as they swept her in a fluid motion toward the elevators. Saxon made a detour to the security desk. A guard there looked at him like he was crazy before Saxon flashed his badge, and the man handed over a card.

"Roof access," Saxon muttered as he slid into the elevator and warned a group of people back. Vitus took the card and pushed it into a slot on the control panel as the doors closed.

The soft music filtering into the elevator seemed like a cruel joke and the final straw. She was struggling to piece together everything that had happened in the last hour. Every inch of her body suddenly felt like it was on fire, the scrapes down the side of her body making it seem like her dress was stuck to her with blood. She made the mistake of looking down and felt like she wanted to vomit when she realized her dress *was* covered in blood.

"Easy Princess." Vitus hooked an arm around her, pulling her back against his body as he cupped her chin and raised her head.

"Don't call me that." Her voice was a strange little squeak, which irritated the hell out of her. "I was doing just fine. You have to get away from me."

But now that he was there, she was shaking, her body giving out as though she hadn't just gotten out of a locked room, in handcuffs no less. Vitus lifted her chin until their gazes met. At last she had something steady to rely on. It was there in his eyes, an unwavering strength that stabilized the trembling that felt core deep inside her.

"You were doing good Princess, but I'm getting you out of here now."

It was the promise she needed, even if her pride rebelled. The doors of the elevator opened, letting the night air brush the wet fabric of her dress. She looked out at the helicopter, watching the way Saxon and Greer steamrolled their way past the police officer standing near it. They flashed their badges and swept the guy's protests aside, even reached out and grabbed his shoulder radio when he tried to call in for a badge check.

"Classified," Saxon insisted as he opened the door.

"Blackout mission," Greer said as he climbed into the pilot's seat.

"Say one goddamn word before we make contact and I'll have your shield." Vitus was lifting her up into the seat of the aircraft while the officer was still sputtering. He turned back to him. "Total blackout, got it?"

Vitus had his badge out, holding it two inches from the officer's nose. The man finally broke, gripping his belt as he backed up out of the rotor's range. She tried to scoot across the seat, but her body had suddenly lost every ounce of strength. She'd made it only halfway when Vitus leveled himself into the helicopter beside her and moved her. The seat was padded, but it felt like she'd landed on solid stone, pain jolting through her abused flesh as the aircraft vibrated and began to lift off. Vitus pulled a harness around her shoulders, somehow getting it into position while she struggled to make her limbs respond to the simple order of putting on a seat belt.

There was a click as he secured her in place and a second one as he took care of himself. Greer took them over the edge of the roof and up into the night sky as Damascus lost her grip and tumbled into unconsciousness.

"Ready for my two cents' worth?" Greer cut a look at Saxon as he kept the controls of the helicopter steady. All three men were watching the sky, because they all understood just how precarious their position was.

"If it involves a plan, yes," Vitus responded.

"Dunn Bateson, heard of him?" Greer inquired.

Vitus bit back a word of profanity. "Yes."

"He's a friend of mine," Greer continued. "His jet's ready for a hop back to Vegas."

"That sounds too good to be true."

Greer made a sound in the back of his throat. "Yeah,

every now and then, fate likes to hand out a little luck. But mostly because the bitch is enjoying watching us try to stay alive."

"I'd have to agree with that," Vitus replied. It was what they needed. One hour and they'd have Damascus in international waters. That would change the game rules, dramatically.

"Call him." Vitus made the decision, catching a look from his brother as Greer fumbled with his cell phone.

"Wait." Greer was still finishing up the last few details of shutting the helicopter down. The rotor was winding to a stop, allowing them all to remove their headsets.

The section of the airport they'd landed at was used by police, federal agents, and fire services. Men in uniform milled about as they made their way to an unmarked aircraft.

"There are cameras everywhere," Saxon muttered, the sound of his voice making it clear he didn't like that fact.

"All we have to do is get across the airport to my buddy's plane," Greer said.

"That's a tall order," Saxon responded.

"Where's your sense of adventure?" Greer inquired.

Damascus looked out of the window, feeling like she was about to try to cross a war zone. It was a more modern form of battlefield, one that would have her trying to avoid smartphones and security cameras instead of bullets and land mines. "Where . . . are we going?"

At least her voice didn't sound as tattered as she felt.

"Off-grid," Vitus said. He reached over and unsnapped the harness holding her in the seat. "Get down, behind the seat. We don't need your red hair seen."

She slid off the seat, feeling every strained muscle and every scrape. Whatever she'd rolled through in the alley reeked, and the blood spotting her dress mixed with it made her want to gag. She hunched down in the footwell instead, finding herself grateful to the damn nutritionist again.

She was probably never eating cake again.

Vitus reached behind her and tugged the suit jacket Saxon had dropped over her shoulder up and over her head. She hated that the fabric blocked her view. Her heart accelerated as she battled the need to escape from the darkness. It was far worse now, panic clawing at her insides as she tried to force herself to remember that it was behind her now. She looked at Vitus, using the sight of him as an anchor.

"Think about Alaska in the summer."

She blinked and moved her face so she could see Vitus through the opening of the front of the jacket where she was holding it closed. His expression was set, but she found that comforting because he was in control, something she desperately wanted to be.

"Alaska?" she inquired.

He turned and looked at her through a pair of sunglasses. "Eighteen hours of sunlight a day."

"We'll get something to move her in," Saxon said.

The two front doors of the helicopter opened and the aircraft jiggled like a rowboat on a lake as Saxon and Greer climbed down. Vitus moved his attention to the window, keeping his gaze moving, watching her, protecting her.

But he was the one in danger. "You need to listen to me," she said.

"I will." He glanced down at her before he returned to watching the area. He had his hand under his jacket, on his gun. "Just as soon as I get you secured some place your father can't reach."

"He wants to kill you. . . . You have to get away from me." What she needed to do was leave on her own. The idea burst in her brain and she fumbled with the jacket, turning toward the door.

"Don't make me cuff you, Damascus."

"You wouldn't." She turned back toward him with a hiss.

"I would, but it isn't going to be necessary." He cut through her argument with a soft tone that was nonetheless granite hard. "You're in shock and about ten seconds from passing out."

"I am not." But her tongue felt like it was swollen and too big for her mouth. She opened and closed her jaw a few times to try and figure out why it felt so strange.

He glanced down at her, his expression softening just a tiny amount. Her pride smarted because the last thing she wanted was his pity. "Don't you dare feel sorry for me."

She couldn't take that. She just couldn't, not on top of everything else. Her head felt like it was bursting from all the events of the last few hours, it was all spinning around and around and around until she felt like she was falling off the edge of some merry-go-round. Just like a kid, she went happily falling away from it, enjoying the way her insides clenched and her toes tingled before she landed in a black void that wrapped around her like a blanket.

Saxon came back driving a small luggage truck. Vitus stepped out and pulled Damascus from the helicopter. She made a half sound of protest before she settled against his chest. He slid right into the front seat of the truck as his brother considered Damascus.

"I believe her," Saxon said as he put the truck in gear and started driving across the airport.

Vitus tugged a hat down onto his head as he let Damascus settle into his lap. "About what precisely?"

"About the fact that those guys intended to kill us," Saxon answered as he stopped to allow a passenger liner to cross in front of them.

"Ryland is showing his hand at last."

"The problem is, he's managed to cut us from the herd," Saxon said. "We go back to Washington with her, and Tyler will dig in."

"Taking her off-grid gives Tyler time to regroup," Vitus answered.

Saxon nodded. "And I don't care for it any more than you do, but the way I see it, we're stuck between using her to control the action of the game or handing over our one ace and sticking our necks out when we do it."

His brother took a look down at the crumbled form of Damascus. Her hair had flipped back, reveling the missing part of her ear. "Not that she's escaping her share of the risk."

"Tyler might leave her alone now. Find some other bait."

Saxon shook his head. "You know he won't. My guess is, Daddy wants his little girl to learn what happens when she steps over the lines he draws."

"Is there a team that can take her while we draw Tyler's attention?" Vitus asked. He was frustrated, his recent return to duty meant he was operating with old information. At the moment, that meant the difference between success and failure.

"I wouldn't trust them. There have been too many leaks when it comes to Tyler Martin. The guy is connected. Obviously he's been working on this move to Washington for a couple of decades. You know that means he's got dirt on people who wouldn't normally roll over. We leave her, we have to accept a margin of risk."

"I'm not willing to do that," Vitus answered, feeling his belly knotting. Tyler should be dead. The fact that he wasn't was almost admirable, because the situation was a fucking work of art as far as setups and double-crosses went.

He couldn't. Step back that was. His temper was raging and he needed to get a handle on that immediately so that he could think . . . clearly. The last thing he needed to do was hand Tyler a victory because he was too busy seeing red to outsmart the man.

"This idea of Greer's—"

"Is the best we have," Saxon answered back, his gaze on the airport traffic. They'd crossed over into the civilian area now. Large passenger jets were butted up against concourses as sky-dining trucks and luggage trains streamed around them.

"Ryland's reach might be weakened if we take Damascus to one of Dunn's properties. The guy is a recluse."

"But we bring an unknown into the operation," Vitus cautioned.

"Greer knows Dunn. In fact"—Saxon cut his brother a sidelong glance—"from what I saw, the relationship is tight."

"I hope so."

Because he was about to bet both his and his brother's life on it.

"She's a little rough around the edges."

Vitus looked up from Damascus. The man standing in the aisle of the private jet was considering him. Vitus stood up, judging the man for a long moment. Tension filled the air, but the man in front of him didn't flinch. He stood there, his lips twitching up just a tiny bit to prove that he was enjoying the way Vitus was trying to cut him down.

"Dunn Bateson, a friend." Greer stressed the word "friend." "Stop glowering."

"No offense taken." Dunn said as he offered Vitus his hand.

Vitus shook it. "We owe you."

Dunn grunted. "I owe Greer. He was right to hit me up." His gaze moved down to where Damascus was lying across the sofa that ran along one side of the jet. "Would have done it anyway, just because whoever did that to her needs his ass kicked. Happy to be invited to the party, I get sick of playing polite games."

He reached up to open the latch to an overhead compartment. "No staff on board, so, self-service." He pulled a blanket down.

Vitus took it and laid it out over Damascus.

"Good timing too," Dunn continued as he started toward the private office at the back of the plane. "I was going to cancel this flight."

"Glad you didn't," Vitus replied as he tucked the blanket around Damascus. She was shivering, but he had to focus on getting her into the air before dealing with comfort concerns. "Your flight plan is already approved."

"More than one actually," Dunn confirmed. "There are some aspects of my business that have to be handled in person, and sometimes I don't get a lot of advance notice. Once we land, there will be three other planes waiting to take off. No one will know just where she is."

"Something tells me you enjoy keeping people guessing on just where you'll show up," Vitus said.

Dunn flashed him a grin before he started heading back to the office. There was a chirp as he pressed his thumb against a print scanner and the door popped open. He disappeared behind the wall.

"Dunn likes his privacy," Greer said from the cockpit. He was going through preflight checks. "Trust me, he's one of the good guys."

It wasn't as if he had much of a choice. Vitus leaned

over and buckled a seat belt around Damascus's waist. He tucked the edges of the blanket around her, smoothing her hair back before moving into the cockpit. "I'll take the first shift as copilot."

Saxon considered him for a moment before he nodded and took his headset off.

At least the act of getting the plane into the air was something he had control over. Saxon settled into the back and leaned his seat back so that he could rest. Vitus listened in as the tower gave Greer clearance to take off. His lips curved up as they taxied toward a runway.

The only thing he regretted was the fact that he wouldn't get to see the look on Ryland's face when Tyler confessed that he'd lost Damascus.

"One bitch was too much for you to handle?"

Pratt didn't often get nervous, but he was smart enough to know when the moment had arrived. He was in one now, facing the wall as his boss let him know how displeased he was.

The Raven didn't show his face and a wise man never tried to sneak a peek. Pratt kept his attention on the wall. "Should have handled her myself."

Pratt's men made the mistake of bristling under his comment, one of them twisting around toward the Raven. There was a soft whistle as a bullet discharged through a silencer. His man got a good look at the Raven, his eyes widening with recognition before his knees gave out and his body slumped to the floor, a dark puddle of blood running across the tile.

The other two men watched it spread, their faces tightening as they waited to see if they were going to join their comrade.

"I'm disappointed," the Raven announced softly. "And now, I am in the position of dealing with this."

"I will clean it up," Pratt said.

"How?"

Two shots rang out. This time, Pratt had fired. His other men slid down to join the body on the floor. "I will find them and finish the job."

"You sound confident," the Raven said. "Why?"

"If anyone saw them, I will find them," Pratt answered. "No one knows the Quarter as I do."

"That is why you are still alive."

There was a soft crunch as the Raven left. Pratt stayed in his seat, making sure he gave the man plenty of time to clear out of the area. Pratt had never seen the Raven's face, but he suspected the Raven was someone with a public image. Like the girl. Someone he might recognize and in that moment he'd feel a bullet tear through his heart, giving him just enough time to know he was going to die, a slow minute of torment as he was trapped and helpless to avoid his fate while the knowledge of who he'd been working for filled his mind.

He would rather live in ignorance and thereby keep drawing breath. He considered the bodies for a long moment, making sure he soaked up just how important it was that he succeeded. Death was such a final thing, he sometimes wondered why he fought to avoid it. Life was a struggle, a continuous battle against the demons that walked as men. For sure there were good men as well, but he did not have the luxury of making his living beside them. He had killed a few of them because a man such as himself didn't always have the choice of who to spare. Today would be another one of those days. Vitus and Saxon Hale were good men, but it was his task to kill them.

So he would.

Life was not fair.

CHAPTER FOUR

Damascus woke with a start, feeling like she had been dropped several feet onto solid stone, the jolt shattering her slumber like glass hitting the pavement. There was a roar all around her, and something was binding her to whatever she was on. She struggled against it, trying to rip whatever it was off her waist.

"Easy Princess."

She looked up to find Vitus watching her. His eyes were clear and unwavering, so collected. Her cheeks flushed as she recognized how flustered she was by comparison.

"We're landing."

She looked around the interior of the jet in confusion. Blinking didn't change the view. She pushed herself up and froze as pain shot through her body. It was actually stunning just how acute it was.

"Bet you're feeling the effort you put into getting out of the building."

Vitus's tone was the only thing that made it possible to sit all the way up. There was a note of admiration in his voice and that wasn't something he handed out lightly.

She felt her pride glowing. Just a bit, as she managed to sit up on the sofa she'd been lying on. Reaching down, she hit the release on the seat belt buckled across her middle. The aircraft was slowing down, making a turn before it wobbled as it parked and the engines began to wind down completely.

"You're dehydrated."

A water bottle appeared in front of her face while she was attempting to take everything in. The cap was off and Vitus didn't wait for her to grab it. He reached down and grasped her wrist, lifting her hand up and putting the bottle against her palm. The moment its chilled surface connected with her skin, she realized her mouth felt like she'd been chewing on cotton balls. She lifted the bottle to her mouth, losing the battle to drink it in any sort of way that might be considered polite.

She guzzled it, gulping air only when Vitus pulled the bottle away from her lips.

"Slow down or it will just come back up." He was cooing now and she grunted at the placating sound of his voice.

"I was—"

"Doing just fine," he finished for her. "Yeah, we've established your take on the operation, Princess."

She opened her mouth to argue with his use of the endearment, but he pushed the bottle back toward her lips, and the need for water overpowered her pride.

The slim door between the cockpit and the cabin slid open. Saxon considered her as she looked at him over the rim of the water bottle. He had a lot in common with his brother. One of those things was the way he cocked his head to one side and lifted an eyebrow while he contemplated her.

Judged her.

"You look rough around the edges, Ms. Ryland," Saxon said in a tone that lacked a lot of the icy disdain she was used to hearing from him.

It was all she could do to keep from sticking her tongue out. She finished off the water as Greer appeared behind Saxon and sent her a wink.

Greer clicked his tongue. "Redheads go well with drama."

"Gee, thanks." She tried to stand only to discover her head was swimming. Vitus was there before she realized she was woozy, clasping her bicep and helping her toward the aircraft door. Saxon had lowered the steps and disappeared down them with Greer on his tail. She blinked at the sunlight and the nearly deserted airfield. There were several private planes but no larger aircraft in sight. A large van was pulling up, the driver popping his head out the moment he parked. Damascus felt every bit of grime more intensely as the driver swept her from head to toe, his face exposing his shock.

"Greer . . . I've got to say, by the looks of her, your rescuing technique needs a bit of refinement."

"Thanks for the warm welcome." Greer spread his hands out wide as Damascus made her way down the steps, hopping once she made it onto the pavement as rocks jabbed into her bare feet.

She turned to Vitus. "Where are we?"

He cut her a sidelong glance. "Getting you off-grid takes an extreme amount of effort considering how visible you are in the media. We're in the California mountains at a friend of Greer's property."

"Happy to be of service." Another man appeared at the top of the stairs. He had dark hair, a little longer than she was used to seeing on a clean-cut guy. But there was no way to dismiss him as shabby, even with his hair brushing his collar. There was still order to it, and yet there was something about the longer length that hinted at just how uncivilized he enjoyed being. The suit he wore was impeccably tailored to his frame, something she knew more than a little about, but it wasn't a high-profile label. No, unless she missed her guess, the suit was custom.

He made his way down the stairs as she took him in, his eyes a startling green. "Dunn Bateson," he introduced himself once he stood on the pavement, towering over her as Vitus helped steady her.

"But, you aren't here," Dunn said with a shrug. "Shame. You're not boring. I think I might have enjoyed your company."

It seemed to be his form of a compliment. He considered the mess of dried blood on her dress, and one side of his lips twitched up.

"I took out the cameras," the driver said as Saxon opened the side door of the van. "But there are still a few folks around here, so maybe you should get her into the van before someone notices all that blood?"

Vitus was moving her toward the open van, in his normal "no arguments" hold. She made her way inside as Saxon and Vitus followed.

"Do I owe him a thank-you?" she asked as the door slid shut.

"You thank Dunn by not being tedious. We got lucky. He was already scheduled to fly back when we hit the airport. No one will suspect the flight plan," Greer supplied from a seat in the back of the van. He'd stretched out his legs and leaned back against the seat, his eyes closed. "Long flight, I'm beat."

"Um . . . thanks," she muttered as the van peeled around in a circle that had it tipping to one side before leveling out. She ended up locking gazes with Vitus. It was surreal, the situation, the fact that she was sitting there close enough to touch him, and not a single person there to tell her not to.

No, there was just the flash of warning in his eyes that told her they were about to clash. She'd walked away from him and never given him a chance to pick apart her reasons. It had been a cold thing to do to a man like him, but something that was absolutely necessary for her to shield him from her sire. The problem was, Vitus wouldn't agree with her, and she was facing a man determined to hear her out.

And explaining was the last thing she could do.

The hot water stung, but Damascus stayed under the shower. Washing was a necessity, but she finally came out when she admitted that what she wanted to clean off herself wasn't stuck to her skin. It was clinging to her soul like an oil spill. The ooze was just as toxic too, trapping any little bit of hope and rolling it under the spill until it suffocated.

"Better?"

Of course Vitus was waiting for her. Damascus double-checked the towel she had wrapped around her body, earning a narrowing of his eyes. The scent of food distracted her from the retort she wanted to make. Her belly rumbled and her mouth actually started watering. She stared at the food, unable to look anywhere else. It actually felt like her stomach was so empty, the insides of it were stuck together.

"Eat." Vitus pulled a chair out from a small desk that was in the room. "Then we'll talk."

She'd already landed in the chair and had a spoonful of shepherd's pie shoved into her mouth when he dropped his little bomb. The mashed potatoes were steaming hot, burning her tongue and the roof of her mouth, but she was too hungry to pay any attention to caution and swallowed it, feeling it burn all the way to her stomach.

"I really appreciate—"

He held up his hand and pointed at the food. She darn near clicked her heels together in response. She drew in a deep breath and lifted another spoonful of steaming meat and vegetables up before she made the mistake of engaging with him with low blood sugar.

He'd be hard enough to deal with when her blood sugar wasn't bottomed out. She polished off the pie and ended up blushing as she realized she'd eaten it like a starving dog. The thought stung because she knew what it was like to be treated like an animal by men who so easily demoted her to less-than-human status. The need to escape was becoming more like a panicked cry, echoing around inside her head until all she could do was scream it out loud.

Colonel Magnus.

That single idea was solid enough for her to get a grip and steady herself.

"How do you know they were planning to kill us?" Vitus asked, clearly done with being a gentleman.

She looked up, locking gazes with him. Vitus was reading her expression, expertly gauging her mood by the way her emotions were showing on her face. She stiffened and then chided herself for letting him see her need to keep things from him.

"They told me." She stood up and crossed to a bed in the room. There was some clothing on it. "Do you mind?"

He lifted one eyebrow.

"Don't be presumptuous," she informed him.

"Right," he answered smoothly. "We're not in a relationship. You made that point pretty solid when you turned down my proposal."

Damascus had gathered up the clothing, but Vitus moved between her and the bathroom, the look on his face making it clear he wasn't going to let her escape. Food was a necessity, modesty wasn't.

"So why"—he took a step closer—"why did you put yourself at risk to cross town and warn me?"

His gaze was trying to slice into her. Damascus rolled her lower lip in, biting it as she contemplated her response, because it needed to be good. His gaze homed in on the tattletale motion.

"You rescued me," she said a little too fast. "I'm really not a cold-hearted bitch, but Jeb is. He saw your brother and me in a picture and it set him off. When I realized Saxon was tailing me, I had to make sure you both knew you were waving the flag in front of the bull."

Vitus didn't reply right away, which sent a ripple of sensation down her spine. He was weighing her words against her body language. The man seemed to know her better than she knew herself, which only turned that ripple into a prickle of heat that settled in her belly, her memory offering up a crystal clear recollection of just how well he knew her flesh.

She liked the fact that he knew her body language so well while she loathed it, her own personal heaven and hell in one man.

"So, that's all that really matters," she finished up.

He made a soft sound. "Not even close, Princess."

She'd made the mistake of looking away when she spoke. An attempt at hiding her true feelings didn't fool him for a second. He'd closed the distance between them while she was battling with her emotions and cupped her chin.

The connection was explosive. She jumped, feeling like he'd touched her with a live wire.

His eyes widened as she reached up to push her hair

out of her face. "Sorry." She tried to flash him a smile, but it wouldn't stick. Her lips were trembling. "Guess . . . guess I'm a little jumpy."

He nodded, falling back a pace and folding his arms over his chest. Just that little bit of space made her realize how much she didn't want to talk. No, she wanted to fling herself into his embrace and take solace in his arms.

She gasped and recoiled, realizing that she was thinking of using him.

"Damascus—"

"Stay there." She held up a single finger like it was going to do any good against him. Actually, it was her only recourse, asking him to do what she wanted.

Begging, you mean . . .

Right, dead on actually, but she didn't have enough mental strength to debate with herself. She was crumbling, feeling her sense of will falling away bit by bit while she tried to grasp at her composure. And all that happened was that it was sliding through her fingers like fine, dry sand.

She should call it the Vitus effect. Damn her hormones.

"Come here," he grunted, moving toward her, reading what was happing right off her face.

As usual.

"No, that's not a good idea." She ran into the dresser. "Using you isn't right."

"Use me?" He lifted an eyebrow.

"Yes," she snapped, her temper giving her enough strength to face off with him. "That's what you charged me with last time. How did you put it? A 'last screw'?"

He stiffened. "I shouldn't have said that."

"No, you shouldn't have," she agreed. "I haven't—" She snapped her mouth shut and groaned with frustration. She felt like she was being twisted like a wet swim towel, tighter and tighter as the water was wrung out of her.

He snorted, and a moment later she was wrapped in his embrace. He turned her so that she was facing out and his chin was resting on her head.

"Neither have I." He muttered above her head in a tone she wasn't used to hearing from him. There was a touch of uncertainty in it, something she didn't associate with him. It was hard to do so even now, with it still ringing in her ears because he was just so solid against her.

"You haven't . . . what?" Her brain was trying to shut down, making a clarification necessary.

"I haven't been with anyone else either."

It was a confession, one he wasn't very happy to be making. She let out a harsh breath and tried to squirm away from him. He snorted in her hair and let her go.

"You and I have a real problem," he said as she moved across the room, the way to the bathroom clear now.

But she stopped because she realized the last thing she wanted was to lock herself inside anywhere. In fact, she looked around, finding a window that was covered in a curtain but the glow of sunlight was still visible.

"I really want to go outside." The need took over completely. She dropped the towel and reached for the clothing without a care for the fact that Vitus got a good look at her bare body.

"Wait."

She looked up as he went past her on his way into the bathroom. She tugged a pair of underwear and a sports bra on before he returned.

He let out a grunt. "You need some disinfectant on those scratches."

"I can do it."

He held the bottle out of her reach, but she tried for it

anyway, ending up against him as he kept the disinfectant out of range.

"Is it really that hard to accept help from me, Damascus?"

His tone had deepened, touching off a ripple of sensation that made her want to hum. His touch did that to her, set her body in motion like what a musician did to the strings of a guitar. Without him, she was silent. In his hands, she was a melody.

"You've already helped me," she defended herself as she pulled back. It was hard, because it felt like she was ripping away from him. And all she craved was to touch him.

"So you want to repay me?" He sat the bottle aside and came after her. "Is that it?" He cupped her hip, somehow finding a spot that wasn't scratched.

"Why shouldn't I?" she asked as she tried to focus her thoughts on what she wanted to say in the argument she needed to formulate instead of on the way his hand felt against her skin. The sheer jolt of excitement went through her pelvis as he gripped her hip. It was bluntly sexual and thrilled her to the core.

"Because you gave me back my ring."

She heard it now, the sting of anger in his voice. She lifted her chin and locked gazes with him, feeling the connection all the way down to her toes.

"I don't want to talk about that. It was a long time ago."

There was nothing between them now. Her defenses were a pile of rubble at his feet, all of her intentions mere wisps of ideas long since turned to vapor in the face of his determination. He wanted to argue with her, she saw the distrust in his eyes along with something she hadn't expected—she clearly witnessed his pain.

She pulled away, wrenching her body from the

comfort of his touch because the memory was too painful, like a brand that burned into her tender skin. Humiliation sank its claws into her, just like it did every time she remembered those first few hours back in her father's care.

"Of course you don't," he muttered, clearly disgusted by her.

Well, that's what you want, right?

Or at least, it was what she had to make sure of if she was going to keep him alive. Vitus couldn't harbor anything except repulsion for her.

She nodded and pulled herself together. "You need to stop being so mad at me and listen. Focus on the situation details."

He crossed his arms over his chest again. "Fine. I'm listening."

"My sire . . . Jeb . . . he wants you and Saxon dead."

"No kidding," he mocked as he reached for the disinfectant, unscrewing the bottle and turning it over with a cotton ball over the open neck. "Princess, we know that."

He reached out and dabbed some of the lotion onto one of the gouges on her arm. It stung, making her pull her breath in as he made his way around her body. She pressed her feet against the floor, ordering herself to stand still and not be a wimp at this late stage of the game.

"How do you know?"

She'd waited until he was twisting the cap back onto the bottle before asking the question. He looked at her for a long moment.

"How long has Tyler Martin been heading up your father's security?"

It was a test. His face had tightened as he waited to see how she'd answer him. Damascus didn't look away. "A few months, but I used to see him, Tyler, from time to time."

"Tyler Martin was my brother's team leader until he tried to set Saxon and me up in a sting mission. Two men lost their lives in it, and Tyler had us all down for flags."

Her eyes went wide, horror nearly gagging her. Damascus shook her head, the need to protect him filling her to bursting.

"See? You have to listen to me," she insisted. "Jeb is insane, so you have to get away from me or my sire is going to think he has to remove you."

She was babbling, caught up in the need to warn him. To give him the information he needed to stay alive. Losing him she could live with, just so long as he was still alive.

He was so alive right then, so full of vigor and strength. She was reaching for him, seeking out just one last connection before he took her advice.

Just one last taste.

Vitus didn't deny her. He folded her into his embrace, giving her exactly what she knew only he could, a hard, solid shield against everything else in the world. He claimed her lips with a kiss that drove rational though into outer space while it filled her with the sweetest sensation that raced across her skin, raising goose bumps all the way down to her toes.

Right and wrong took on whole new meanings. He felt right. She kissed him back, and that felt incredibly perfect, so she rose onto her toes so that she could kiss him harder.

"That's it Princess," he growled against her lips. "That's what you really want."

"It is," she confirmed. "You are."

And there was no thinking about it. She'd dissolved into a pile of impulses, ones she was eager to act upon. It seemed like she had been longing for him, aching for him, for an eternity. She pulled at his clothing, fighting with the buttons on his dress shirt until one of them popped and sailed across the room to hit the floor. The little sound put a smile on her lips, fueled by satisfaction.

"Works for me." Vitus pulled away from her and ripped his shirt open. Several more buttons went zipping across the room.

Damascus could not have cared less. What mattered was the sight of his bare torso. Their stolen night had been cast in shadow. Today, the light illuminated every sculpted ridge. She drank in the sight of him, feeling like it was water for the dried out parts of her soul. She reached for him but he caught the edge of her sports bra and pulled it up and over her head before she laid her hands on him.

She sucked in her breath, her nipples contracting as she felt an aggressive edge in the air between them. When she raised her attention to his face, she felt her breath lodge in her throat. His expression was pure intent, solid determination, and it sent a curl of anticipation through her core.

"Strip."

His tone was tight, just like his face. Hunger was etched into his features as his eyes glittered.

"Do it, Princess . . . for me."

There was an order in his voice and at the same time, a yearning that made her feel more attractive than she ever had. Some sort of confirmation that she was more than anyone else he had ever met. She reached down, grasping the sides of her panties and pushing them down her legs. A touch of apprehension teased her, setting off a shiver that crossed her bare body once she was standing there in nothing but her skin.

"I know I don't scare you." He was jerking open his pants, letting them puddle around his ankles before he shoved his drawers down and stepped out of it all, join-ing her in bareness as she felt her belly do a little flop.

"I should scare *you* . . ." And for a moment, she re-called everything. All of her well-thought-out reasons and the logic supporting her actions.

"Not . . . a . . . chance . . . *Princess.*"

He captured her, pulling her against his body as he claimed her lips with a searing kiss. She stretched away from him, but he followed her, overwhelming her senses and dragging her back into the spinning vortex of im-pulse and action.

She craved him and didn't check herself. She reached for him, stroking him, running her hands across his shoulders as he trailed his kisses across her jaw and down her neck. He had a hold on her nape, keeping her pris-oner to his whim, lifting her head so he could taste the sensitive skin of her throat.

She was at his mercy.

And yet, exactly where she wanted to be. She stretched back, arching and offering herself to him, shuddering as he drew his teeth gently along her collarbone. His strength was transmitting through his grip but so was his control. The combination sent her senses reeling, driv-ing up her hunger a few more notches. She was bent back like an offering to him but at the same time, she settled her hips against his, purring as she felt his cock pressing against her lower belly.

He grunted, his body shuddering as he lifted his mouth and fought for control. She watched the battle in his eyes, mesmerized by her effect on him. It wasn't about power. No, the feeling was based deep down inside her, in that place where she had always wanted to matter to someone. Matter so much, that it was more important than anything else.

Selfish? Maybe, but what stuck in her mind was that at last she didn't feel alone in how much she craved him.

In that moment, she wasn't alone.

Not so long as they needed each other.

"You rip me to shreds, Princess." He scooped her off her feet, cradling her like she weighed no more than a child as he carried her to the bed and placed her on it. "So it's only fair that I make sure I have the same effect on you."

Her eyes had been sliding shut, the desire to just sink into the vortex so strong, she had no intention of fighting it. But there was a promise lurking in his tone that gripped her, jerking her away from compliancy. He chuckled when her gaze connected with his.

And then he pushed her back, the bed rocking as she ended up across it. While she was falling back, he cupped her knees and slid his hands down the insides of her thighs. Instantly, she was gripped by a shaft of need so sharp, she gasped. Her senses spun and he had her spread wide. Her brain simply refused to process anything, because it was caught in the current. She must have made some sound, because she heard it bouncing off the ceiling as Vitus settled between her thighs, his breath teasing her open folds.

"Wait." Her tongue felt like a useless wad in her mouth, the only real sounds she wanted to make were groans.

He teased her inner thigh once more, looking up her body. "You'll like it Princess."

"But you've never done . . . that." Her clit was pulsing with a crazy rhythm, her hips twitching despite her protests. "I mean, you can't enjoy . . ."

He smoothed his hand down her thigh to the curls on top of her sex, just a small patch that she left to guard her cleft. "I like the way you smell."

"Liar," she shot back at him. She tried to twist away, her cheeks heating as he chuckled and pressed her flat to the surface of the bed with one hand in the middle of her belly.

"I like it," he bit out, his tone hard and full of his determination to do exactly what he pleased with her. His eyes flashed at her. "And you'll love it."

He didn't give her a chance to argue. She gained a glimpse of him shifting his attention to her spread body, just a moment for her to twist with modesty, one last second of straining to maintain her composure before he fashioned his lips on her cleft.

She cried out, the sound a mixture of surprise and delight. There was no possibility of containing it, her self-control was a pile of ashes, floating away on the waves of heat licking at her insides. It was all centered under his mouth. He pulled her folds away from her clit, teasing the little bundle of nerve endings with the softest touch of his tongue before he lapped her from the opening of her body to the top of her slit.

"*Shit.*"

He cracked up. "So you do cuss." For a moment, their eyes met and then he was once again set upon driving her insane.

She withered beneath him, her body drawing into a tight cord that felt like it was going to snap any second. She was suspended in the moment, held in the grip of the pleasure he was raining down on her, using his tongue to drive wave after wave of intense sensation up into her core. It was churning, swirling, centering under his tongue until she felt it cresting. The wave broke, crashing into her and tumbling her. There was nothing to do but let it wash through her and drop her into a panting heap on the bed.

When she opened her eyes, Vitus was watching her,

his expression smug and cocky. Something sparked inside her, igniting a fuse. He was going to do what she wanted now, there was no room in her mind for anything else. She was consumed by the hunger, the need to not be alone. Damascus reached for him, curling up off the bed, seeking what she craved.

Vitus didn't disappoint her. He levered himself up, giving her a glimpse of his hard form before he was flattening her and she was gripping his hips with her thighs. He thrust forward, her body opening for him so much easier this time. She arched toward him, her breath hissing between her teeth as he buried himself in her.

"I want to see you," he growled, slipping his hand into her hair and straightening her head so that their gazes locked. "I want to see you take me . . ."

"Yes . . ."

It was more than just a word; it was an idea so large, it consumed her. He was riding her as she lifted to take his length, straining to make sure he went deeper with every thrust. It wasn't soft, wasn't gentle, and that was exactly what she needed. The battle was between them and yet somehow, they were fighting it together. Panting, straining, fighting to get closer, and finally, that last moment when she felt like her heart just might burst with the effort of rising up to meet his thrusts and she felt him giving up his load. It was hot against her insides, making her gasp as her body spasmed and convulsed. Pleasure ripped through her like the crack of a whip, leaving a sting behind that pulsed with the tempo of her heart. Nothing mattered.

Not a fucking thing.

Pratt waited until night fell because that was when people came out in the Quarter.

At least his type of people.

Bourbon Street was filling up, cell phones snapping away as businessmen lucky enough to score a conference next to the French Quarter eagerly set out to enjoy their few hours of free time.

Pratt watched, looking for the right people. There were two types in the Quarter—those making legitimate business and men like him. Of course they all rubbed elbows from time to time. That was the way the Quarter had always been, only now in its modern incarnation was it considered a safe place.

That was a bit of a misconception.

Legitimate strippers were moving around, going into bars to perform, but Pratt was interested in the women moving among the shadows. Some might call them prostitutes, but he knew they had more value than sex. Anyone could take a fucking but there were some who were smart enough to listen while their clients let a little intercourse loosen more than just their pants.

A woman shifted, moving closer to him, waiting to see if he wanted anything from her. He knew her; she was exactly what he was seeking.

"A woman and three men came out of my ally last night. The girl's dress was spotted with blood, ginger curls on her head. Tell me where they went."

The woman had lit a cigarette and was drawing on it as he smoked. She didn't say anything, just gave him a flutter of her heavily made-up eyes before moving down the street in a slow, sultry motion that attracted plenty of male attention. In the warm air, she wasn't wearing more than a thin dress that barely reached her midthighs but there was a polish to her, a sharpness to her skill that set her above the term "slut." She might have been a ghost from an era gone by.

Pratt ducked into a doorway, making his way to the back of a restaurant. Steam was hanging around the ceiling like a displaced cloud, the scent of crawfish mixing with alligator. The cook looked up, his short sleeves showing off his tattooed forearms. There was only one wide-eyed person in the kitchen. A young busboy who stared at Pratt until the cook reached out and smacked him on the side of his head. The cook only gave the boy a disgruntled snort, but the sound conveyed exactly what the cook intended. The boy looked down at his bin of dirty dishes and never made eye contact with Pratt again.

That was life in the back alleyways of the Quarter. At least in the ones that Pratt controlled. The cook slid a plate across the stainless-steel service counter to him. Pratt considered it before selecting a fork from the sorting bin beneath the counter and sitting down to enjoy the offering. The kitchen kept serving food, but the banter had stopped. No one looked at him except for the waitress who brought him a drink and smiled shyly at him before turning around and returning to the customers beyond the door.

Pratt tossed a photo down. "I need to find them. They walked out last night. The information will put me in a generous mood."

The cook flipped his spatula a couple of times in the air before leaning over to look at the picture of Damascus Ryland. He grinned, showing off his capped front teeth.

"No one would forget her," he said as a way of trying to assure Pratt of success.

"Good."

Pratt melted into the alleyway behind the restaurant. The noise from Bourbon Street came filtering through the separations between buildings and over the tops of them, but he was still very much alone with the shadows. He could hear his footsteps and maybe those of a few ghosts, but he was comfortable walking with the specters. A man who lived on the edge as he did needed to be on good terms with the dead, because he was always dealing with men who might send him to walk among their number.

It was wise to ensure that he would have a warm welcome when his days among the living were finished.

It wasn't that bad.

Damascus stared at her reflection, considering the missing part of her ear. Amazing how a cut so small could hurt so badly. Okay, it had been more than a cut, but in the light of day, only an inch-long spot marked where part of her upper ear had been taken.

She suddenly felt sick. Turning around, she made it to the toilet just in time. Her body heaved, sending up the contents of her stomach. She ended up draped over the toilet, a quivering mass of sweat and fear. Telling herself to get it together wasn't working. It was as though her body knew she had the time to break down now and was taking advantage of the moment.

Just great.

Well, she didn't have the time. Not really. She hadn't made it to her safe zone. Even when she made it there, she wasn't going to be able to fall apart. She would have responsibilities and no one to fall back on.

There were times she hated her sire more than others and this was one of them. She flipped on the sink and opened a drawer. There was a selection of toiletries, all still in their packages. She selected a toothbrush and broke open the plastic.

If it wasn't for her sire, she could bloody well marry Vitus.

She shot herself a glare in the mirror as she brushed her teeth.

What are you doing?

Thinking about a future that included Vitus, even one that she was going to be denied, was a one-way trip to being miserable. She knew it from personal experience.

No crying over spilt milk.

Or at least milk that she just couldn't get her hands on.

She finished up and went into the shower. It was a small one, but private. When she emerged, she took a moment to run a pick through her hair. There was no hope of controlling her hair. Once introduced to water, it curled into tight little corkscrews. Any attempt to dry it would result in a frizz cloud, so she pinned a section of it back from her face and went to find some clothing.

It was folded and laying over the back of a chair. Her memory offered up a vivid picture of Vitus pulling the sports bra off her while she was tugging it into position. Her cheeks heated as she suffered a twinge of guilt.

Honestly, she really needed to find another way to deal with stress. She highly doubted her new colleagues in the labs would be anywhere as satisfying as Vitus when she jumped them. Of course, she was hoping her life would become very sedate once she started working under Colonel Magnus.

Yeah, well, none of that is going to help you at the moment.

Nope, but Vitus would.

She didn't care for how comforting that knowledge was. Using him wasn't right and it was only going to increase how much her sire wanted to kill him. The best way for her to express her love was to push Vitus out of her life.

The problem was, he always saw right through her.

Well, you'll just have to do better.

Dare Servant crouched down, taking in details of the murder scene.

The bodies were cold, the blood clotting, which meant the killer had left them there to be found. At least that was his guess. Outside, there were bits of conversation floating through the window as the curious were kept back from the alleyway by uniformed police officers.

"What do you think?" Kagan stood in the doorway.

Servant straightened up. "I think Pratt is sending a message to his boys about how much he doesn't like to be disappointed."

"Yeah, I'm reading that message loud and clear," Kagan agreed.

"Where's the girl?" Servant asked.

"Don't know," Kagan answered easily. "Fact is, I don't want to know."

Servant sent him a long look. "Sure about that?"

Kagan straightened up. "For the moment I am. Better to have her tucked away so I can get a good look at who pops their head up to look for her."

"They might just dig in and wait for her to make an appearance."

Kagan nodded. "I've got a few days before I have to worry about testing that theory. A lot can happen in a few days."

He made sure his hat was tugged low over his head. It would only protect him from aerial surveillance but that was a good beginning. Tyler Martin had taunted him with the facts about how hard it was to remain anonymous in the modern world. It was a solid truth that weighed on his mind as he walked down Bourbon Street. For a moment, he considered a pair of women. They were tourists, their eyes sparkling with the excitement of their adventure. Naive and yet attractive, because they had no idea there were bodies lying inside one of the buildings they were busy taking pictures of.

Life was about perception. A palace might be a prison,

high station nothing more than shackles. Damascus Ryland was a prime example. Part of him wanted to see her
free but the rest of his logical mind knew without a doubt
that she had little chance of success. Even with Colonel
Bryan Magnus and his contract.

The hard fact was, her father was about to join Carl
Davis in a run for the presidency. The Colonel might be
able to fend off her father, but Carl Davis was another
matter altogether, a bigger dog without a doubt. He'd rip
Damascus right out of Magnus's grasp. It turned his
stomach, which was slightly surprising, because he dealt
with a lot of sad facts. One congressman's daughter was
hardly the most pitiful creature he'd encountered in the
last month.

But part of him admired her. Damascus Ryland had
guts and a hell of a will. It was the stuff that motivated
him to want to see her win. There really was nothing like
betting on the underdog. Maybe it was part of his soul,
that part that had wanted to put a bullet in Tyler's skull
just because it was the decent thing to do.

Well, there was more than one kind of bullet in the
modern era. Tyler Martin had made sure Kagan understood that. In the modern era, he had friends to protect
him. Well, it was going to be Kagan's absolute joy to
introduce Tyler Martin to Kagan's friends.

Kagan pulled out his cell phone, grinning as he considered the look on Martin's face when he realized
Kagan still had a few moves.

Dunn Bateson had places to be and an appointment waiting in his outer office who had flown in from Hong
Kong.

He sent his secretary a message to have them wait.

Kagan didn't fuck around. At least, Dunn had never
known him to. He picked up the call. "This is a surprise."

"Going to be a day for those," Kagan replied. "I'm sending you a gift. Interested in seeing what you do with it."

The line went dead. Dunn watched as his desktop flickered with an incoming email. He tapped in his clearance code and watched the document open up. Damascus's picture was attached, making him raise an eyebrow. But he began to chuckle as he read the information.

Now that was an interesting gift to say the least.

"You should be nervous." Jeb Ryland spoke slowly, fixing Tyler Martin with a disapproving glare.

"I wouldn't be worth a tin Rolex to you if I rattled when the shit started hitting the fan," Tyler responded.

Jeb nodded once, but his forehead remained furrowed. "Where is my daughter?"

"I don't know."

"And you admit that?" Jeb exploded.

Tyler took a moment to glance behind him, to make sure the office door was firmly shut. There was soft buzz as Jeb pushed a button beneath the edge of his desk to lock the door. "It's a soundproof door. Now what the hell do you mean you don't know where she is?"

"Vitus and Saxon Hale are not easy to manipulate. I warned you it would be better to leave them alone. Men like them don't kill easily. Especially when they know you are coming for them."

"And I made it clear—Jeb was leaning forward, slapping his open hand onto the center of the desk—"that I want them dead and disgraced!"

"I'll be in touch when I have new information."

He wasn't the first man Tyler had worked for who was slightly off balance. At that moment, Tyler recognized the twist of Jeb Ryland's features, the unmistakable mark of insanity. It was a self-inflicted sort. Something the good congressman had done to himself by believing he was so vastly superior to the men around him. Maybe his parents might be blamed for rearing him without letting him experience the life that his voters lived. Not that any of it mattered. What Tyler had to contend with was how to get what he wanted from a madman.

Outside the congressman's home, Tyler considered his contacts and what favors he was owed. A text message came in, making him smile. It seemed luck was on his side. He moved toward his car, intent on gaining the upper hand. As for Damascus Ryland, he'd find her. A woman like her didn't know how to stay hidden. It was only a matter of time.

CHAPTER FIVE

Saxon and Vitus were in the outer room when she emerged. The scent of coffee was drifting in the air but she was more interested in the view out the windows of the kitchen.

"Wow." She moved toward the glass, marveling at the expanse of green hills and the massive flow of water going past the house about a hundred feet away. It was a dull roar, even through the walls, the water white because it was moving so fast.

"So what is the next—" Damascus clamped her mouth shut, chiding herself for forgetting how completely they'd risked their skins for her. "Thank you for . . . everything."

She made a point of not looking at Vitus when she said "everything."

"But you want to know what the plan is?" Vitus supplied her question for her. She ended up shifting her attention to him.

And felt like the breath got socked right out of her. There was something about him. Actually, it was everything about him. She was surrounded by fit men, seriously ripped men, and they all were lacking compared to Vitus. Just looking at him sent a tingle down her back. Where there hadn't been a hint of sexual hunger, now there was a teasing of need in her clit.

Just from the sight of him.

So damn frustrating, and yet undeniable.

"Um . . . yes." She realized all three men were looking at her, waiting for her to grasp her wits. "I need to get back."

"For what?" Vitus demanded.

The guy turned her on and frustrated her in equal amounts. "To complete my doctorate."

"Aren't your finals finished?" Saxon asked quietly.

Too quietly, because she knew he was baiting her, just trying to lull her into a sense of comfort so that she'd spill information.

"They are," Vitus informed his brother. There was one way the two were different—Vitus took the head-on approach to everything. Damned if that didn't make him seem even sexier.

You're a nitwit . . . some genius . . .

Yeah, well, when she was facing Vitus, she felt like nothing more than a bundle of hormone-influenced reactions. Her brain went straight to base-level activity, no higher functions making it through the flood of impulses.

"I have final labs." She pushed past her rioting emotions.

"That won't lower your GPA very much if you miss them." Vitus crossed his arms over his chest. "In case you missed it Princess, someone kidnapped you."

"Because they are looking for you." Her brain suddenly snapped back into focus. She pointed at the two brothers. "Jeb is gunning for you two. I need to get away from you both, for your own good."

Saxon's eyes narrowed, but Vitus reached up and flipped her hair away from her ear, exposing the missing section. "Seems like you're the one bleeding at this point."

"Why do you never listen to me?" It suddenly didn't matter who else was in the room. The battle was between her and Vitus and it was very, very important.

"I listen." Vitus responded in a deadly quiet tone. "To your actions. Words are cheap."

"Fine. What did me refusing to marry you say?" She was getting desperate, but she had to cover up her own weakness or watch him suffer for it.

"That you're Daddy's little girl."

She felt like she'd been sucker punched. Time froze, her temper ignited, and a moment later, the sound of her hand connecting with Vitus's jaw cracked through the room. She slapped him so hard, her shoulder felt the impact. Her palm was stinging as she wrenched open the door and walked out of the house.

She couldn't wait to get back to Colonel Magnus. She needed help protecting herself from her own stupidity when it came to who she decided to fall in love with.

"Ye're an idiot." Greer's accent intensified with he was mad. He stepped in front of Vitus, blocking the door. "I've got half a mind to add a good decking to that slap she gave ye."

"Get out of my way," Vitus growled.

"Sit yer arse down. I've got her." Greer grabbed a jacket from a coat rack and shot Saxon a hard look. "Talk some sense into your brother before I have to do it."

Greer opened the door and went after Damascus. Vitus caught a glimpse of her making her way up the lush hillside before the door slammed shut. He reached for the doorknob.

"Don't. Greer called it right. You need to deal with whatever is eating you."

Vitus froze. It wouldn't be the first time he'd told his brother to shut up, but guilt was chewing a hole in him, proving that he needed to check himself.

"Why are you always so controlled?" Vitus asked his brother. Frustration was ripping him to shreds while it took every ounce of self-control he had to stay inside. All he wanted was to go to Damascus, but he seemed to do nothing but push her away when he did. Saxon was right, he needed to get a grip.

"I'm not in love." Saxon replied. "And I'm not ever planning on tumbling into that tar pit. You're welcome to it."

"You think I planned it?" Vitus snorted at his sibling.

"Doesn't seem like it. Not with the way you're trying to shove her away," Saxon observed. "Not that you're going to have to worry about it after that little remark, even if part of me was rather relieved by getting to see how much she really doesn't like her daddy."

"So now you approve of her?"

Saxon lifted one shoulder. "Blunt responses like that can't be faked, you sideswiped her with that comment. It doesn't get much more honest than that."

What he'd done was cut her to the bone. Vitus didn't need his brother to say it. He knew it. The knowledge was nearly killing him.

Well idiot, you deserve it.

He did, but he'd never been one to sit back.

"Are you sure?" Saxon asked him as he was going out the door.

"Yeah."

"I'll be sure to tell Mom you died of your own stupidity," his brother added.

"It won't surprise her—only that it took this long."

He caught a second of his brother's amusement before

he shut the door. No, it probably wouldn't surprise his mother that he'd said something lacking all sense, but what he was focused on was the fact that there was another facet of his personality that his mother knew very well, and that was that he didn't quit.

Ever.

"Now girl, you know I can't talk about work." The security guard used a soft tone, one meant to lessen the impact of his words. His companion offered him a husky little chuckle that made his cock harden. Or it might have been because she was rubbing the organ through his pants. Honestly, he didn't give a shit. Just so long as she sucked him off. The girl knew how to give head.

"You talk about work all the time, Bradford," she purred, toying with the button of his waistband. "You know when Pratt wants something, you are going to give it to him. Everyone in the Quarter does." She opened his fly, dipping her fingertips inside to tease his organ. "We can do it the nice way . . ."

The unspoken threat hung in the air. Bradford understood her completely and for a moment, it sobered him. It wasn't like he'd planned on living a life where he had to roll over for men like Pratt. There was part of him that realized he'd lost grip of every ounce of honor he'd ever possessed. He watched the way Kitten was teasing his cock. They'd both become something they shouldn't be.

But it all came back to Pratt.

The man controlled a good part of the Quarter. Only a fool didn't give him what he wanted when he asked nicely. Kitten opened her lips and closed them around his member, sending a ripple of enjoyment down his meat to his balls.

Yeah, the nice way. Kitten was sweet, but he could bet

that when Pratt got wind of the fact that he knew something about the redhead he hadn't told, the next person Pratt sent over wouldn't be asking politely.

That was the price of staying alive.

So Bradford closed his eyes and let Kitten work him over. Taking solace in the pleasure she gave his body. As for his soul? There wasn't enough balm for that. When Kitten left him, she knew all about the three men who had taken the police helicopter from the roof with the redheaded woman in tow. He went back to work, feeling hollow, trapped by circumstance. He considered the footage from the elevator, resenting the circumstances of his life. Across from his station at the far side of the reception desk, a television was on in the bar.

"Authorities are still baffled by the disappearance of the congressman's only child, Damascus. In a press conference today, presidential hopeful Carl Davis appealed to the public for help . . ."

It seemed like a sign, some sort of ray of hope reaching out to puncture the guilt currently suffocating him. He reached for the phone and dialed. Sure he'd told Pratt. That didn't mean he couldn't do the right thing and let the girl's father know where she was.

After all, he wasn't evil to his core, just a man trying to make his way as best he could. No one could fault him for that. His eyes were fixated on the reward offer being flashed across the screen. It was the escape he needed from his life, from the facts of his reality, the opportunity to just get up and go and start a new life free of the entanglements that compromised his morality.

"Hello. Yeah, I have information on that congressmen's daughter . . . but I want the reward first."

"I'm still pissed at you."

Vitus was keeping tabs on her, had been for most of

the day. Her neck was tight from the knowledge that he was there, shadowing her with the expertise she knew he had. It was enough to make her scream by the end of the day. She turned around and marched up to him, lifting her hand when he started to speak.

"P-I-S-S-E-D!" she enunciated, ending with a single-finger salute about an inch beneath his nose.

He busted up laughing.

She snorted, at least enjoying the fact that she could indulge in unladylike conduct because there weren't any cameras trained on her.

"You have a death wish."

Vitus jerked around, all hints of amusement vanishing as he found the source of the comment. Dunn Bateson offered him a lazy grin that was majorly cocky before he finished coming over an outcropping of rocks.

Dunn winked at Damascus before he pegged Vitus with a critical look. "When a redhead tells you she's pissed with you, better give her some space."

"I don't need advice on how to deal with Damascus."

Damascus scoffed at him, earning a chuckle from Dunn.

"By all means, get yourself killed," Dunn said. "That will leave the pretty lady all to me."

Vitus grunted. "Just remember you need me dead before you'd even have a chance."

"*Please,*" Damascus groaned. "I'm about to choke on the testosterone fumes."

Dunn had come closer. He actually winked at her, giving her a clear view of his green eyes. "Admitting I make you light-headed already? Come now lass, don't make things too easy for me."

"Right," she responded. "You hate being bored."

"What do you want?" Vitus inserted himself back into the conversation.

Damascus took a couple of steps away from both men because she didn't care for how much she enjoyed hearing the note of jealousy in his tone. Seriously, she was mad, but it seemed like her pride was nonexistent when it came to him.

Great. Just great. Heart on the sleeve and pathetic. Talk about the ultimate double-whammy.

"I smuggled you away from her daddy. Doesn't that entitle me to checking up on you?" Dunn answered.

"Considering what I know about you," Vitus said, "I doubt those charges would even make it onto the sheet if you got dragged into court."

"True." Dunn shot back with an arrogant tone. "I'd really hate to bore the court."

"So . . ." Vitus had closed the distance between himself and Dunn. The two faced off, neither giving an inch.

It was disgusting how attractive she found it, at least on Vitus's part. He'd put himself between Dunn and her, once more protecting her. It felt like a sliver of broken glass went through her heart, because she knew she couldn't have him. Not forever, and that was what she really longed for.

"I'm here to plan," Dunn answered seriously. "Not that I'm shoving you off my property, but we're standing on our luck at the moment and that has a way of running thin. It's remote here, but someone is going to pick up our trail at some point. We'd be idiots to assume otherwise."

"I brought that up this morning." Damascus rejoined the conversation. "I need to get back."

Dunn turned to her slowly. He'd crossed his arms over his chest and looked just as unmovable as Vitus did. Denial was glittering in his eyes. "As I said, we need a plan."

"Right, because hers isn't the right one," Vitus added.

"Agreed." Dunn delivered his opinion in a firm tone that raised her hackles.

"It's my life," Damascus argued.

"Wrong, Princess." Vitus crossed into her path and planted himself in front of her. "We're all in this. You were the one who pointed out it's me and my brother marked for bullets."

"Exactly. The connection needs to be severed." It was going to kill her but at the same time vindicate her. It was the right thing to do.

Well, she was up to the challenge.

She had to be.

"The only way this ends is by me dealing with Jeb. I'm not letting anyone else take any more shit for me."

And that was going to be the end of it.

"I hope you have something worth my time," Carl Davis said as Tyler Martin made his way into his office.

Tyler stopped and sent him a hard look. "And I thought you recognized my potential. If you were just blowing smoke in my face, I can find another man who will value me."

Tyler made a neat turn on his heel. There was a soft, electronic sound as Carl locked the door via a button on the underside of his desk. "Sit. You wouldn't have made it past the gate if I didn't respect your ability."

Tyler dropped into a padded leather chair and tossed an eight-by-ten photo onto the desktop. Carl picked it up, studying it carefully before his lips rose into a satisfied smile. It was only a small one, because the man wasn't a fool. The photo was only part of what he wanted.

"Where is she?"

"Not precisely sure yet," Tyler answered. "I intercepted a call from the tip line. The guy wants the reward for more information, but I don't want to involve anyone else."

"So you're here to test out just how sincere I am," Carl retorted.

Tyler offered him a barely perceptible nod. Carl selected a pen from the holder on his desk and used it to write down a message. He tossed the half-used pad of sticky notes across to Tyler.

SLUSH ACCOUNT. TRANSFER THE AMOUNT AND USE IT TO BRIBE WHOEVER YOU NEED TO.

Tyler considered the note. He tucked it into his shirt pocket as he stood. "I'll be in touch."

"I'm counting on that."

There was a veiled threat in Carl's voice, one that made Tyler smirk on his way out of the office. The guy had brass balls, something Tyler sort of enjoyed about him.

"Oh, by the way." Tyler turned back toward Carl. He tossed another photo on the desk. "You got a little sloppy. I cleaned up your mess, but you really might consider keeping me a little closer in your personal loop in the future."

Carl picked up the newest photo, his fingers crumbling it when he realized it was of him and his current lover.

"Explain how you cleaned it up."

Tyler opened the front of his suit and pulled a cell phone out of the inner breast pocket. "Got the cell phone the witness used to take the photos. Little journalism student with big dreams of working for CNN or some shit like that. You won't hear of him again."

"You're sure?" Carl's complexion was darker, his forehead dotted with perspiration.

"Alkaline hydrolysis. Ever heard of it?"

Carl relaxed. "Liquefaction of the body. Leaving no DNA."

Tyler pointed at him. "Going to have the ashes put into one of those tree planters." He made a gesture in the air. "That way the kid can live his dream of making the world a better place."

Carl's expression was unreadable. Tyler waited, his hand played. The ball was in Carl's court now.

Carl finally nodded. "As I thought, you'll make an excellent addition to the team. I like a man who makes sure there are no loose ends. Sees things I don't have time to."

Tyler moved back across the office, until he was in front of the desk. "I suggest you dial me in from now on. We don't want any gaps from here on out. The voters really don't need to know everything about you, but the only way that will happen is if I do. That way, I can run interference."

Carl didn't care for being told what to do. Tyler watched him battle a decision. He finally scribbled another set of numbers on the back of the photo and offered it to Tyler.

"Nice to have you on board." Carl exclaimed in a polished, public voice. Tyler touched two fingers to his temple in a half salute before he turned around and heard the outer door unlock.

It was nice. Tyler enjoyed the feeling as he left Carl Davis's house. He drove upstate, taking back roads and doubling back a few times before switching out cars with a few he had stashed. Finally satisfied that he was off-grid, he pulled into a run-down section of town, driving a beat-up sedan from the eighties. He pulled into the back of a weathered-looking brick building, considering the area before he got out of the car with a hat pulled low over his forehead. He slipped inside the narrow doorway, the air inside stale from the room being sealed.

But once inside, it was a different world. The windows were sets, like a movie production lot. On the inside, each window had a full casing that prevented anyone from seeing inside. Tyler tossed his jacket onto a chair and yanked his tie off. He cracked his neck before dropping into a desk chair and firing up the laptop sitting there.

The computer booted up. He used the cell phone from the dead journalist to connect it to the internet and logged into an off-shore account he kept as an insurance policy. There weren't many places to fall off the face of the planet anymore but if he ever had to, he was going to have the money to keep himself buried. He plugged in one of the account numbers and smiled at the amount of money in the account. A few moments later, there was a chirp as the money finished transferring. He logged out and logged into a second account to transfer the money Davis had given him for bribe.

Before he finished, his personal phone buzzed. He picked it up and viewed the incoming information. Fuzzy pictures from an airport appeared, but even the poor resolution couldn't mask the brilliant color of Damascus's hair.

"Got you."

Or at least he was closer to getting her.

And that was all that really mattered.

He really didn't give a shit about Damascus Ryland. If anything, he felt a little sorry for her. She had a good heart, but that was only dragging her down. If she'd been smarter, she'd have played the game, made sure she carved out a comfortable place for herself before she got boxed in. But in a way, that resolve to be a decent human being was the only reason she was valuable to Carl Davis. He needed a showpiece, someone people could cheer for or at the least not dig up any dirt on. It would certainly make Tyler's job easier, knowing he wouldn't have to run around cleaning up after her.

Which was why he was going to find her. Well, one of the reasons anyway. She was also his payment and, as fortune had it, she was going to be far more valuable than he'd first suspected.

Because now, Carl Davis wanted her. That was one

payment Tyler intended to take. It would secure his future.

"I really do appreciate what you have all done for me, but I can't stand by and allow you to put yourselves at risk," Damascus stated once they were back in the house. Really, it was sort of a grand cottage, with stone walls, rounded stones that had lush greenery climbing up. Under different circumstances, she would have been charmed down to her toes, but seeing the serious expressions of the men with her, there was no way to ignore the very pressing facts about her circumstances.

"What are you going to do when you get back?" It was Saxon who took the professional route, asking his question in a tone devoid of emotion.

"I will deal with Jeb." It wasn't really a lie. Of course she knew Vitus would call her on holding back information, but she couldn't afford the luxury of shielding his emotions. This was about keeping him and his brother alive.

"How?" It was Dunn who asked the pointed question.

"I will make it clear that I know what he's been up to and I will disclose it to the media."

Her response was met with three blank looks. She bristled under the hard judgment because that was exactly what it was. She could feel herself being measured and found lacking.

"Excuse me." Her temper was rising. "But I know him. Jeb will do anything to avoid a scandal. That's what this all boils down to. I told him I was going to marry you and he didn't see it as a fine enough match—"

"You what?" Vitus demanded.

Damascus shut her mouth, realizing too late that she'd spilled the beans. Vitus hooked her arm and turned her around.

"Excuse us," he muttered as he swept her through the doorway and into the bedroom.

"I didn't see that coming," Saxon muttered.

"Bull," Greer argued. "Those two hopped each other the second they were in range. Only an idiot would miss how stuck on him she is."

"And her daddy disapproves," Dunn muttered. He was thinking, rolling facts through his brain as he considered what he'd observed. "Only, she doesn't call him her father."

Saxon had been twirling a pen between his fingers. It froze as he shared a look with Dunn. "No, she doesn't." He shook his head. "Okay, she got me. I believed her this morning when she laid down that line about not wanting to marry my brother."

"You heard what you wanted to hear," Greer said, acknowledging the pitfall they all knew better than to stumble into. Damascus had managed to dupe them all. "She's protecting him."

"She's playing a game she isn't equipped to compete in," Dunn said in a hard tone.

"What makes you say that?" Saxon asked.

Dunn shifted his attention to Saxon, taking a moment to decide how much he was planning to say. "Her daddy's name is all over the press, linked with Carl Davis. I seem to recall seeing a picture of you, with her, outside of a private club where she was having a dinner date with Davis. One she looked like she wanted out of."

"She did," Saxon confirmed.

Dunn tilted his head to the side. "I seriously doubt Jeb Ryland values his daughter's happiness above his own political agenda. Carl Davis wants the carefully groomed reputation her father has made certain she has. The only blip on the radar is your brother. It's also her only soft spot. Her daddy wants him dead, so she falls into line and is traumatized enough to never step out of order again."

"I'd have to agree," Saxon answered, beginning to turn the pen once more as he thought things through.

"Only she isn't scaring too easily." Greer supplied the conclusion.

"And she decided to shield Vitus, until I showed back up on her daddy's radar," Saxon finished.

There was a thud as something hit the closed bedroom door. All three men looked at it for a moment, turning away when another thud came through the solid wood.

Dunn slowly smiled. A moment later, the pen Saxon had been holding hit him in the side of the head. He jumped, whirling on Saxon only to meet a solid, unrepentant stare.

"Can't fault me for admiring the lady's sass," Dunn said.

"She's my brother's girl, so yes, I can," Saxon responded.

Dunn offered him a grin that flashed his teeth at him before he pulled his cell phone out of his pocket.

"Get out."

Damascus turned on him, but Vitus only closed the door.

"We're going to talk," he informed her with every bit of confidence she expected from him.

She bent down and picked up a boot that was sitting on a shoe rack and heaved it at him. His eyes widened and he twisted out of the way so that the boot hit the door. The smack was somewhat satisfying, so she grabbed the second one.

"Out." She held her ammunition up, the threat clear.

"Which is it?" Vitus crossed his arms over his chest and stood his ground. "Did you refuse to marry me or tell your father you were going to?"

"It's none of your business." She launched the boot at his head. He avoided it again, frustrating her completely.

"If you had only listened to me," she hissed at him, "when I came to see you that night, we wouldn't be here."

"Oh, I heard you." His tone had dropped, setting off a ripple that went straight down her spine, leaving a trail of tingles along the way. It was the voice he used when he was touching her. She recognized it on some deep level, in that same place where thoughts stopped and reactions took over.

He stepped closer, the very way his body moved hypnotizing her.

"Every move you make gains my attention, Princess."

He was her lover in that moment. She felt her insides melting, heating for him. Facts were little insignificant things, scattered at her feet. But she pulled back, grasping at the straws of her resolve.

"He will kill you," she whispered. "Jeb is obsessed with making a run for the White House. Nothing matters to him unless it supports that goal." She spread her hands out. "I'm poison."

"You're stuck," he corrected her, "in a trap that no one should have to deal with. Your father is a massive prick."

She smiled, taking solace in a moment of commiseration. "Bad guys win, Vitus. A lot."

His lips rose into a knowing twist. "No kidding."

He reached out, gently brushing her hair back from her ear. The cut had been throbbing on and off throughout the day, but now she shied away because it seemed like a sign of her inability to deal with what life was throwing at her.

"Don't."

The single word was uttered in a low tone but it held the snap of a whip, just another part of Vitus's mesmerizing persona. He could captivate her with a rough whisper, never needing to raise his voice to get his point across. No, he did that with sheer force of will.

He was touching her again, his fingertips gliding along her jaw line, just barely making contact, yet rocking her down to her core. That's what he did to her, melted away everything and left her exposed.

"Don't shoulder the blame, Princess." He drew his fingers back along her jaw line, sending a ripple of sensation down her body. "He isn't worthy of that."

"I'm not." She knew what she meant to say, but her body was far more interested in just feeling, responding to his touch. She was arching, turning toward him as he swept her hair away from her ear again and leaned down to look at the injury.

"This," he rasped next to her ear, "is a mark of valor." He tucked her hair back, standing just an inch from her. "Proof that you didn't roll over for your daddy's plan for you, that you dug deep and found the strength to fight back."

She shivered. Her eyes flooded with tears as she absorbed the compliment in his tone. He threaded his fingers through her hair, cradling her head and bringing her face to meet his. Their gazes locked and for a moment— she wasn't alone.

That knowledge was both balm and salt in her wounds. She longed to have someone to lean on and at the same time, she yearned to be worthy of him too, which meant shielding him just as surely as he would do for her.

He was moving toward her, the fingers on her nape easing her just a little closer so that he might seal her lips beneath his.

"No." She managed a last protest, the sound of her

voice cracking broke some of the hold her rioting emotions had over her. He might have pressed the issue, taken her mouth and sealed her resistance beneath his lips. The fact that he didn't stiffened her resolve.

"I can't just take refuge in your embrace." She wanted to, ached to. It was a craving, a hunger tearing her insides to shreds as she forced herself to place her hands on his chest and push him back.

"Yes you can." He didn't release her. She felt the resistance in his body, heard the denial in his tone.

"No, I have to be better than that." She increased the amount of pressure she was putting on him. "I can't be your Princess. Always in need of saving. I have to be more. You of all people should understand that kind of need. I have to be able to face myself and know I'm not like Jeb."

He made a soft sound under his breath, his frustration clear. She was free a moment later, feeling like her knees were going to buckle without his body there to support her.

"I hear you." It sounded like those three words had been some of the hardest he'd ever pushed past his lips. Part of her enjoyed that, because he wanted to do nothing more than what she did, which was to strip down and indulge their whims.

But that would leave a sour taste in her mouth. He knew it too, saw it in his eyes as he crossed his arms over his chest and contemplated her.

"Good." The only problem is, it didn't feel right. No, when she'd been a hairbreadth from his lips, she'd felt right. Now, she had all the correct motivation and it didn't satisfy her, not completely.

Vitus shook his head, stepping toward her. She felt his approach like an encroachment, as if he was about to breach her defenses. Excitement twisted through her but there was a twinge of bitterness too. She knew she was going to give in.

"Not even close, Princess."

She bumped into the bed and sat down on it hard, the mattress swaying like some sort of preamble to her defeat. He kept coming forward until he had his hands pressed on either side of her shoulders and she was flat on her back. For a moment she stared into his eyes, those Caribbean Sea eyes, and believed that everything she longed for was close at hand. His scent filled her senses, her skin awakening with a thousand little receptors that were picking up his body heat.

It would be so simple to fold, to just give over to him.

"'Good' would be stripping you down," he said softly. "Rubbing you, the way you like to be petted, listening for the little sounds you make when I stroke you just the right way." His eyes narrowed as he straightened up. She was trembling, nothing but a mass of quivering muscles on the surface of the bed.

"You'd relax, let everything go," he continued.

She nodded, pushing herself up.

"I like to take you to that place, Princess. . . . I'm the only man who can."

"You're not a man who accepts being used," she countered. "You deserve better."

For a moment, something flashed in his eyes that she hadn't seen before. She realized she was getting a glimpse at his deepest feelings, but it was masked again before she really had time to absorb it. Vitus was taking a step back, withdrawing from her. She felt it keenly, like he was being ripped off her skin.

"I understand the need to stand on your own two feet and to know I respect your ability to do it." His tone had tightened. Vitus gave her a single nod as he took another step away, his fingers gripping the sleeves of his shirt.

"But I don't think there is anything good about it," he growled. "I want to get inside you, drive everything out of your mind except the feel of me. That would be my definition of 'perfect.' Except that I heard you loud and clear. And you're right. I actually want more than you using me as a bandage."

He got it. For one moment she was satisfied, but it shattered like a bubble of hot glass when he turned and left. The door closed, the sound vibrating through her bones, shaking her to her foundation.

Well, that was where she was, wasn't it? At the bottom, ready to climb to the top of the hill and see what was on the other side? It was a grand idea, one that would certainly fill her with hope and anticipation.

At least it would just as soon as she finished reeling from the separation.

He needed to think.

One simple idea had never been so difficult for him to wrap his mind around. Vitus was in the kitchen before he realized he was just in motion, because if he stopped, he was pretty sure he was going to toss aside what he knew was right in favor of doing what he craved.

He wanted her.

The need was pulsing through him, moving deeper than anything else and more overpowering as well. It was more than sexual hunger. He knew that bite. This was a more complex yearning, something rooted in more than just his cock. Sure, he was rock hard and needed release, but he hadn't been blowing smoke about wanting to stroke her.

So he poured a cup of coffee and sipped it as he leaned against the countertop. His lips stung, proving that his skin was still ultrasensitive. Vitus took another long drink.

"Sure you need the joe to stay awake?" Saxon asked from the doorway.

"I don't."

Saxon weighted his tone before moving into the kitchen. "It makes sense now. If she told her father she was going to marry you, it all falls into place."

Vitus nodded, his mind wrapped around a far different problem. Damascus had always been his target, the woman he'd been sent to save. Did she love him or her idea of him? And was that a fair question to ask of himself as well?

Where the hell did it leave them both? Wanting each other, sure, that was a given considering they couldn't keep their hands off each other. So was that all? Was there anywhere to go? His head was pounding with the need to know. Honestly, he was fucking desperate to discover the answers.

And he was equally aware that it scared the hell out of him, because he was pretty sure that when he got the answers to those questions, the information was going to separate him from Damascus forever.

Because she was right about one thing. The bad guys won. A lot.

"Rise and shine."

Damascus blinked and raised her head off the pillow. Vitus was standing there, looking too awake for her groggy senses. She glanced at the window and found it just brightening with dawn.

"Roll out of that rack. It's training time," he informed her.

That gained her attention, sharpening her senses. "What kind of training?"

"Hand-to-hand defense." He offered her a smirk. "So

you can depend on yourself. I think that's what you were saying you wanted, self-reliance."

"Sort of."

He offered her a half grin. "You don't want to be my princess?"

She nodded, sitting up and sweeping her hair back from her face. She was a disheveled mess but his features softened for just a moment as he considered her. Damned if it didn't make her feel beautiful. He watched her face, witnessing the knowledge work its way through her brain before he nodded.

"Ten minutes. Be ready to sweat."

It was a challenge, one that gave her the hope she'd been desperate to grasp the night before. She tossed the bedding aside and hurried toward the bathroom. She hadn't met this side of Vitus, but there was one thing she was sure of, she wanted to get to know him.

Sure about that? I thought you were leaving him.

It was a chilling thought, but one the bright light of day helped her fend off. There was also something to be said for living in the moment.

So that's exactly what she was going to do. At least until reality knocked down her house of cards.

Pratt considered the fuzzy pictures from security cameras at the airport. Relief was a welcome feeling but at the same time, he didn't stop to enjoy it overly long. He was on to thinking of ways to use the information in his hands.

"Thinking of double-crossing me?"

Pratt stiffened but held himself still, keeping his back to the Raven. There was a click as the door to the street closed.

"You'd have shot me a long time ago if that was the sort of game I played," Pratt replied. "I'm seeing what there is here, what might be useful."

"And what have you found?"

Pratt felt his heart accelerate. Now that he'd tracked the girl, he was a loose end, one of the only ones who knew truly where Damascus Ryland was.

"Bateson, he's got his fingers in a lot of business."

"He does."

Pratt considered the tablet and the personal aircraft on the screen. "I think he has the girl. A man such as him understands the value of her." Pratt tapped the screen, looking as more video was streamed. "He could have had her flown anywhere on the globe from that airfield. Three planes went out within an hour of her landing. That is by design."

"The man wouldn't be who he was without running his life in a very controlled manner."

Pratt nodded. "He's part of the World Health Association, the research division." Pratt swept his fingertip across the screen of his tablet to change what he was looking at. "That girl, she's loaded in the brainpan. A man such as him doesn't waste his time. Even when it's a sweet little girl who's been kidnapped. It was in his interest to help her."

"Very good," the Raven cooed. "I want you to go and get her. Finish your assignment. Bateson is no fool, but alone you might be able to slip under his security net."

Pratt didn't bother to answer; there really was no need. He didn't have a choice. No one failed the Raven.

"You're getting better."

Damascus resisted the urge to grunt at Saxon. He was sitting in the kitchen watching her with a tight set to his lips. But the glitter in his eyes betrayed how much he was enjoying her training sessions with Vitus.

Her elbows were bruised, her body ached, and she was probably dragging a trail of dirt and leaves with her into the cottage, but none of that seemed to matter. Nope, every pain only added to the satisfaction glowing inside her. She trudged through to the bedroom she'd been using and on to the shower.

Hot water was a necessity. One she was pretty sure she was going to perish without. She tugged her clothing off and stood under the showerhead as she let the heat ease her muscles.

But she felt time ticking away now. Another day gone, and she realized they were all on borrowed luck. She indulged in a last moment of relaxation before turning off the water and leaving the shower.

Time to face facts.

"I need to return to Washington." Damascus decided on a direct approach. Saxon, Greer, and Vitus were all clustered around a table when she emerged from the bedroom.

"At the moment, we've been told to dig in with you," Vitus replied with an unwavering look toward her. "That's what we're doing."

"I have to return," she insisted.

She had their attention now. All three of them shifted, abandoning what was on the table in favor of trying to strip her defenses down and discover what she was thinking.

"Why?" Vitus put the question straight to her.

"My mother."

Her answer wasn't what any of them expected. "I realize you didn't see that answer coming, but Jeb really is a monster. He threatened to put my mother in a private clinic if I didn't marry Carl Davis."

"You agreed to the engagement?" Vitus demanded.

"Of course not."

"He's a hell of a catch in most people's opinion," Saxon added.

"Not in mine," Damascus argued. "You saw my face when I came out of that restaurant. Did I look like I considered myself a lucky duck?"

Saxon offered her a dry chuckle. "Your face matched your hair."

"Besides, Carl is . . ." She bit back the word "gay."

"Is . . . what?" Vitus was watching her, picking up every little emotion crossing her face.

"Is just making plans with my father . . . to bring in more votes. I don't want that life," she explained. "Not that either of them is all that much interested in what I think. That's why I need to return. Jeb won't give up and at the moment, he has my mother to strike at me through. So I have to go back."

There. It was a neat, logical, truthful explanation, even if she'd held back a few bits of personal information. She stared straight back at Vitus as she felt him and his comrades assessing. They knew what they were doing too. She'd stood in front of a pack of Press and felt more confident.

"Your mother is a very respected lady," Saxon said. "Even your father will have a hard time harming her."

"What part of private clinic didn't you hear?" Damascus pressed the issue. "Jeb will do anything, to anyone, if it gets him closer to his goal. You both know he doesn't play by the rules. I can't in good conscious hide out while my mother is wearing a target because Jeb thinks it will get me into line."

"Going back will accomplish what he wants, getting you back under his thumb," Vitus said softly.

"Obviously I will have to face him and deal with this."

Vitus was shaking his head. "As you've pointed out,

Princess, your daddy doesn't play by the rules. He could just as easily have *you* admitted for treatment."

It was a solid truth, one that chilled her blood but at the same time motivated her.

"Don't tell me to sit here, putting all of you at risk," she said. "I'd far rather face Jeb and have it out once and for all. For Christ's sake, they cut off part of my ear. I've got a few things to say to him, and I don't feel like hiding. I would think that all of you could understand my thinking."

Vitus's eyes glowed with something that looked a lot like approval. It sent a spike of accomplishment through her that warmed her to the core. It was more than a compliment, because Vitus wasn't a man to give anything his positive opinion unless it was earned.

She wasn't his little Princess.

"We are assigned to you, Ms. Ryland. Let us do our job." Saxon offered a polished brush-off. She recognized the look on his face; it was the tight expression of a man who would put duty above her personal desires.

She wanted to argue but realized they were experts when it came to getting someone to spill information. Her commitment to Colonel Magnus was burning a hole in her brain.

"Classified" meant not telling anyone. Hell, Vitus was an ex-SEAL. He lived by the code of classified mission, she couldn't be less devoted.

Maybe it was better to withdrawn and wait a little. There was one thing she knew from her childhood, and that was that the Secret Service would do what they deemed necessary. Even if Saxon and Vitus were a special unit, she didn't have a prayer of shoving them off something they considered a duty.

So she'd have to hope they'd receive new orders soon or she was going to have to get creative. Her neck was tense by the time she made it back into the bedroom, because Vitus wasn't the type of man to take her going around him very well.

You know you have to leave him, maybe it would be better if he was pissed at you . . .

That thought just dug into her deeper. She knew the sting of betrayal, had felt its sting too deeply to ever want to inflict that pain on anyone else, much less the man she loved.

But she couldn't tell him where she was going. It was a choice she'd made for all of the best reasons, and she had always known that it wouldn't come without a high cost.

That cost was going to be Vitus. It always had been, which just made it so much harder to crawl into bed alone. She felt the minutes ticking by, like she was squandering her opportunity to touch him for the sake of her pride.

Well, there was one thing that was for sure. She would be getting her way when it came to protecting Vitus.

"She's not telling us something."

It was Greer who voiced the obvious. Saxon and Vitus were both brooding as they heard the bedroom door shut.

"The question is what?" Saxon added.

"Nope," Vitus argued. "What we should be asking is what is drawing her back home. It isn't a deep love for Daddy."

"Could be the mother, as she claims."

There was something else. Vitus considered the closed door of the bedroom, distracted from his purpose yet again.

He ended up smiling, enjoying the way Damascus upset his thinking.

"Can we see what Kagan makes of the mother?" Greer asked.

"Not from here," Saxon replied. "We touch base with our section leader, and someone is going to run right to Carl Davis with that Intel. It's a sure bet that if he's involved, someone is watching Kagan."

"Carl Davis puts a different spin on things," Vitus agreed. "Kagan needs to know about that complication. His back is wide open and he won't be able to keep us off-grid for long."

There were two nods in response.

"We might have to do it Dunn's way," Greer suggested softly.

Vitus wanted to argue but bit back his rejection. He managed to swallow it knowing that Carl Davis wanting to marry Damascus changed the playing field dramatically. A man in Carl's position had contacts, the types that couldn't be identified easily, which meant Damascus didn't have a chance in hell. The only thing he really could do about it was enjoy the hours they had left together. The problem was, that sounded like a really good idea.

One he didn't have a scrap of self-discipline against.

"Kagan. Meeting you is a true pleasure." Carl Davis offered his hand along with his greeting.

Kagan took it, shaking it as men shifted around them. Carl was offering him an easy-going grin that Kagan didn't believe for a second. It was practiced to the point of being flawless, like a ballet dancer. So smooth and delicate you might be duped into forgetting just how much strength the dancer had to possess in order to perform.

"I've heard some amazing things about you," Carl continued as they finished their handshake.

"Thank you." Kagan played his part. The briefing room was starting to fill up. He knew most of the men. What bothered him were the faces he didn't recognize.

"It's a real comfort to me to know you're on this team." Carl settled down into a plush leather office chair. "Damascus is very important to me."

There was a shift among the men in the room, a soft ripple of acknowledgment. In its way, it was like fear, because only a fool would miss the fact that Carl Davis had just made sure every man there knew he expected results.

"My team is doing their best to locate her." Kagan offered as he sat down and the session was called to order. Someone shifted in the corner. It wasn't unusual, but Kagan turned and caught Tyler Martin slipping into the room.

For a moment, Kagan lost control.

Oh, it was a small lapse, but one that hadn't happened in years. It was almost reassuring in its own way, some proof, small as it was, that he wasn't immune to decency.

"Decency" and "Tyler Martin" didn't exactly belong in the same sentence. Martin stared back at Kagan, shooting him a satisfied little smirk before he directed his attention to the briefing.

Won't help you any . . .

That was a very satisfying thought. Kagan let it linger in his mind because he didn't really need to listen to the briefing. There wasn't any new Intel on the table. But knowing Tyler was there was balm for the raw wound Tyler had inflicted on him earlier in the year. Tyler was a sellout and not above killing to get what he wanted from life.

Kagan considered the way Tyler was behind Congressman Jeb Ryland.

Oh yeah, he knew who had pulled the strings to get

Tyler released now. But that information was as sharp as it was satisfying. Tyler Martin had boasted about the world being a place where the only way to survive was to serve men with power.

Well, I hope you enjoy licking their boots . . .

Because Kagan was still gunning for Tyler and he was going to get him. For the moment, that meant keeping Damascus Ryland out of Tyler's hands.

It was going to be Kagan's pleasure.

It was dark.

Damascus felt it as much as she sensed it.

She hated the dark . . .

It was worse now, a hundred times more intense than it had been before. She twisted away from it, trying to break free, but it pushed down on her.

"Damascus."

She jerked, opening her eyes as Vitus's voice tore through the layers of her nightmare. His tone was as strong as the grip he had on her wrists, and she realized he was holding them because she'd tried to hit him.

"Oh . . . sorry," she muttered, horrified by how tight a grip the nightmare had held her in. It seemed she'd been tossing and turning just a minute ago.

"Easy, Princess." He smoothed her hair back, setting off a little ripple of enjoyment. It spread over the surface of her skin, feeling insanely good for so simple a touch.

God, he really was her undoing, completely and totally.

"I'm fine."

He grunted, the sound making it clear he didn't believe her. Of course he didn't, he was reading her body language. She was bathed in sweat, her heart racing, her chest heaving, but she still felt like she was suffocating. The room was black, making her feel like a thick blanket was wrapped around her, smothering her like the walls of a concrete cell.

"I'll get the curtains."

He was suddenly gone, moving across the room to the window. A moment later, there was the soft sound of fabric slipping along the curtain rod, and then the moonlight was spilling in. She let out a little sound of relief and then slapped her hand over her lips when she realized how pathetic she was.

Get grounded.

She'd taken the psychology classes. All she had to do was implement the instructions.

Find five things you can see.

Four things you can touch.

Three things you can hear.

Two things you can smell.

Vitus.

All of them ended up being Vitus, her senses fixated on him. She saw him, traced the lines of his shoulders and the way the moonlight illuminated the muscle of his forearms. Her hearing picked up the slight sound of his jeans rubbing together when he moved and the tiny sound of his shoes connecting with the floor. And then, she could smell him. God, could she. It was intoxicating, the way his skin teased her with its scent, drawing her toward him.

Which left her with touch.

She could reach out and lay her hands on him. He was so close, and she wanted the oblivion contact with him would produce. He was closing the distance between them, with every inch he crossed, offering her what she needed to survive. The bed rocked slightly as he sat down on the edge, there, within reach, so very tempting. His presence was mesmerizing, pulling her closer as she let the nightmare go in favor of what was right beneath her fingertips.

She jerked back at the last minute, realizing what she was doing.

Vitus snorted at her.

"What?" She resorted to temper because at least it helped her keep the nightmare at arm's length. "Does it thrill you to have me throwing myself at you?"

"Yes."

His tone made her tremble. She clasped her arms around herself because she didn't dare trust the need she felt. She was just projecting onto him or something. Maybe when she wasn't so close to him, she'd be able to think of the right term. At that moment, all she could manage was to bite her lower lip and grip the sleeves of her T-shirt so that she kept her hands off him.

"I've spent the last three years telling myself that you didn't give a shit about me, walked away while I lost my badge, and all I ended up doing was dreaming about you, about getting another moment with you. Like this one." He closed his eyes for a moment, shaking his head as he battled some inner demon. "I'm a bastard for it. You've been through hell and all I can think about is how much it works in my favor because it's driving us back together."

It was an admission. One she never thought she'd get from him, but secretly dreamed of it.

"Touch me." His voice was raspy. "Reach for me, Princess, before I lose my mind."

He didn't have to ask twice. She couldn't have stopped herself if there had been a hundred members of the press there. He was a need, rooted so deeply inside her. There was nothing but the desire to connect with him. He was the water she needed to survive. He drew in a deep breath, his chest filling beneath her fingertips, sending a jolt of awareness through her. She felt the connection on a cellular level.

Like becoming whole again.

"I need you." But even as she said it, she knew that she was going to fail. The reason was simple—definitions of right and wrong changed when she was touching him. What she'd decided was logical, suddenly blew away like dried up leaves that were sucked from the ground as her passion turned everything into a whirlwind.

"Yeah baby, I know the feeling," He leaned over and claimed her mouth, closing his lips over hers as she curled her hands into his shirt to bind him to her. She was pulling him closer, kissing him back as she crawled right into his lap.

Yeah, now she was grounded.

He was rock solid, more perfect than any relaxation technique. He was the pulsing rhythm of life and she craved him, needed the connection with life that only he seemed to be able to complete. He caught her by her hips, easing her around him until her knees parted on either side of him. She slipped onto his lap so that his erection was nestled against the notch of her sex.

She purred, arching back as his fingers tightened on her hips, sending a jolt of awareness through her. It was like an electric current shooting through her pelvis. She'd never realized how sensitive her hips were.

Only in his grasp.

She'd arched back, pressing her sex against the bulge of his erection. He sucked in his breath, the sound delighting her.

"You're going to drive me insane, Princess."

"Good." She brought her head back down so that she was looking at him. His features were tight, hunger making him grit his teeth. She rocked her hips toward his, enjoying the way her clit rubbed against him. "I'm pretty sure it's your turn to squirm."

She caught the hem of her T-shirt and pulled it up over her head. The night air felt perfect against her breasts, like she'd been smothered in the fabric. She wanted to be bare, free of everything. All she really needed was him. She pushed back as his attention slipped to her nude breasts, escaping his hold while he was distracted. She enjoyed the little rush of accomplishment that went through her as she stood in front of him and pushed her yoga pants down.

"I'm squirming now," he confirmed in a harsh whisper.

"Not nearly enough for my taste." He'd started to stand, but she poked him in the center of his chest, sending him back onto his butt with a little hiss. She leaned down until her face was an inch from his. "Not . . . even . . . close . . . but I have an idea."

His eyes narrowed as she slid to her knees and opened his fly. She caught a glimpse of his hands curling into the soft sides of the mattress before she settled her attention on his cock. Honestly, she hadn't really looked at it all that much. It was a full moon, the light coming through the window giving her a good view of his length. It was large. He was circumcised, the head crowned with a thick ridge that sent her clit pulsing, because she really wanted to have it deep inside her.

First things first.

She was going to cause the squirming for a change. His cock was hot and covered in smooth skin. She stroked it, drawing her fingers along its length as she heard his breathing increase. The sound was a pure shot of confidence, filling her with boldness. She leaned down, wrapping her hand around his girth as she opened her mouth and teased the slit on the top of his cock with her tongue.

"Oh shit," he grunted, pulling the sheet free. She liked knowing he was sitting there, letting her take control.

She opened her mouth wider and took another lap across his cock, this time trailing her tongue along the edge of the crown. She heard him gasping, felt his body drawing tighter, but he maintained his grip on the mattress, submitting to her.

Or at least the closest thing that a man like him could manage.

She took advantage of it, stroking his member and sucking the head deep inside her mouth. He jerked, his hips thrusting up toward her. She let his cock thrust deeper inside her mouth before he relaxed back onto the bed and her lips slid up to the crown again. He was panting and it encouraged her in a way she'd never imagined. She was sucking his cock back into her mouth, lowering her head as she cupped his balls, using her tongue on the underside of the head and reveling in every harsh, male sound coming from him.

He was hers and she was going to make him into the same ball of putty he reduced her to. Determination was racing through her veins, intoxicating her, driving her motions.

"*Princess . . .*"

She'd never heard him so strained, so completely on edge. He caught her nape, curling his hands into her hair as he lifted her head away from his cock.

"You're going to make me lose it," he growled.

"Good." She tried to reclaim his cock, but he grunted in denial and held her away from it.

"No baby. . . . I'm not going to leave you hungry."

There was a hard promise in his voice, one that tripled the pulse in her clit. She suddenly felt so empty, like she was going to convulse if she didn't crawl up and sink down onto his cock. "Well, you're not putting me on my back either. Not tonight."

She climbed back into his lap, settling over his cock and sinking down onto it. His grasp tightened on her nape, his lips curling back from his teeth as she sheathed him and groaned with the feeling of him stretching her.

Now she was grounded.

Now she was complete.

Her eyes had slipped closed, everything centering on the way she felt with him inside her. She was rocking, riding him with short, hard motions, seeking out fulfillment with instinct guiding the way.

"Easy Princess . . . don't rush." He stroked her, from her nape to the center of her back, sending a ripple of enjoyment down her spine.

"Open your eyes, Damascus." There was a firm order in his tone as he captured her hips, taking control of their pace. He eased it, refined it, insisting with a grasp that controlled her without making her submit. Only match him. She opened her eyes, locking gazes with him.

"That's it . . . no rush. . . . enjoy the ride."

They might have been anywhere in time. It was just the two of them, locked together, seeking completion.

She believed in that truth, like nothing else she ever had. It was more than an idea, it was the center of her whole existence at that moment, and the moment was an eternity that they were encased in.

Her nipples were brushing his chest, drawing into hard points as his chest hair teased them. She was lifting and sinking as he moved toward her, pulling her into alignment with a steady grip. Her heart was beating hard but in strong, hard motions that felt like it was slamming into her breast bone. It increased in strength as he moved in closer and pressed a kiss against her mouth.

How long were they locked together? She couldn't

have told anyone. Reality was a million miles away. She felt herself tensing, the building pressure promising a climax that she resisted because she wanted to remain right there, in that moment.

Her body wouldn't let her. Every motion was moving her closer to release. Vitus pulled back, watching her as she lost the battle and arched back with the explosion. She was twisting, writhing in the grip of it as she felt him jerk and begin to flood her. The hot shot of fluid sent her into another wave of intense pleasure that would have seen her falling onto the floor if he hadn't held her in place. She was being wrung, the pleasure contorting her flesh as it ripped into the deepest parts of her body. She was gasping, certain her heart was going to burst.

She was on a high she'd never thought her body could produce without some chemical enhancement.

It seemed all she needed was Vitus.

Her personal addiction.

And he'd be her ruin too, but like any junkie she was going willingly to her demise, caring only about the high she'd gain while knowing she was heading face-first into a crash and burn.

But it didn't seem too high a cost to pay for a moment of being able to clasp his hand, entwine her fingers with his, and experience the sense of completeness that she'd been seeking her entire life without realizing she was starving for it. He folded her against him, settling her head on his shoulder as the sound of his heart filled her head.

It was worth it.

She'd live on the memory.

Or at least, survive. It would be worth it because she'd have the knowledge that he was alive too.

And that would be worth everything.

* * *

She'd destroyed him.

Vitus had enough strength to pull them both onto the bed before he lost his grip on consciousness. They were both heaving, panting on top of the covers as the moment ebbed. He fought to stay awake. He didn't want to give up his moments with her, didn't want to squander the seconds when she had her defenses down. He opened his eyes and looked at her, marveling at the way the moonlight bathed her, so comfortable next to him. He reached up, smoothing her hair away from her face. She made a soft sound as she turned toward him, inhaling the scent of his fingers before she nuzzled against his palm.

Something shot through him. An emotion he hadn't realized was missing in his life.

Well, that's because you've been too busy being an ass . . .

He'd forgotten about how she made him feel, in the dark hours of the night, when the only thing that would comfort her was his presence. No witnesses, no one to impress with her conquest of him. Just the pure reaction between them, the reality of how much peace she found in his embrace.

She'd never admitted it.

And that had cut him deep.

He realized it now, was staring at the truth of what had fueled his anger. He wanted her to need him more than anything else. He wanted her to admit it and be unable to walk away from him just as sure as she would be incapable of cutting off her own hand.

Love? It was complete dependency.

Certainly more than a four-letter word or a polite term. Somehow, from the moment he'd pulled her out of that concrete hole and seen the determination in her eyes to live, he'd been connected to her completely. Even his own stubborn pride couldn't snap the link joining them.

So how in the hell was he going to get the rest of the world to leave them the fuck alone? He'd like to say he'd just tell them all to screw off, but he was smarter than that. Life wasn't fair. That was the fear he'd seen in her eyes when she'd come to his house to warn him, the sick realization that the deck was stacked against them. She hated it just as much as he did, but she hadn't been able to find a way around it.

Except to come to him.

He stroked her hair again, soaking up the details, which confirmed she was lying in his embrace. She was there and he wasn't going to let the odds shake him up.

"Quit" wasn't something he did.

Ever.

CHAPTER SIX

"You're holding something back."

Damascus had been hoping to avoid the conversation.

Yeah, like that was really going to happen.

Vitus was watching her, his gaze just as keen as always while she ate breakfast. She felt the tension building in her neck as she neared the end of the meal, her hand starting to tremble just a little as she scooped up the last of her scrambled eggs.

"What is it?" he asked the moment the fork disappeared inside her mouth.

Damascus wiped her lips and swallowed. "Good morning."

He wasn't impressed with her attempt to change the topic. He was leaning back in a chair across the small breakfast table from her, looking perfectly at ease, unless she studied his eyes. The truth was there in their blue depths. He was intent on getting information out of her.

"Talk, Damascus." He straightened and laid his hands on the table. "You want in on the planning? Fine. Disclose what you know."

"I have." It wasn't precisely a lie.

He shook his head.

"That's it," she insisted. "Just because you don't like the fact that I want to deal with Jeb face to face doesn't mean I'm holding out on you."

"No, it doesn't," he agreed.

"Oh, so what you're really saying is you don't trust me." He frowned, but she didn't give him time to dissect her comment. "Not that it matters. We can't just spend the rest of our lives hiding out and looking over our shoulders. The only logical action is to return."

She pushed her chair back and left the kitchen. Saxon was sitting in the other room listening to every word, so there was no point in arguing further. She wasn't going anywhere until Vitus and his team made the call on it.

Or was she?

Damascus considered the area around the cottage. It was majestic with greenery and snowcapped peaks in the distance. There was also a road, but there wasn't a car in sight. There wasn't another building for that matter, but Dunn had come from somewhere.

"Twenty-six miles."

She jumped and turned to discover Greer behind her. He pointed at the road. "Twenty-six miles before you come to the first town."

"That means there's a car around here." She said.

"And there are some rather nasty people waiting for you back where you come from."

"Oh please." She decided to go on the offensive. "As if you'd ever duck into a hole and hide. So why are you sitting silent while Vitus and Saxon expect me to do so?"

"Keeping my mouth shut has its uses," Greer offered. "I learn a lot that way."

She considered his answer for a moment because it sounded like there was a wealth of meaning in it. His expression suddenly changed, his attention moving from her face to the air.

"Oh. . . . *shit*," he grunted.

Damascus turned around, but the road was still bare and the water was still rushing past.

"Come on." Greer reached out and grabbed her bicep, pulling her back with an urgency she was still trying to find a cause for.

"What?"

"Drone." He pointed at a small flying craft and tugged her toward the cottage. "Walk naturally."

He draped his arm across her shoulders. "We'll hope it's a local with a splash of nerd curiosity."

She felt how tense he was but he kept their pace slow as he guided her back to the cottage. The buzz of the aircraft was intensified by the tight set of Greer's body. Making every step seem longer, the distance between the cottage and them seem greater.

"Drone flyover," he announced as he pushed her through the door of the cabin then closed it.

"Damn it," Vitus snarled. He grabbed a pair of binoculars hanging off a peg near the door and went to the window. Everyone waited while he searched the area.

"We have to assume it was looking for her." Vitus didn't like what he was saying, but he replaced the binoculars and shot a look toward his brother. "Our cover's blown."

"We can't chance it in any case. Let's clear out," Saxon agreed.

She'd expected to feel more of a sense of victory, or at least of relief, but all she really noticed was how tight her chest was.

And how truly scared she was. Her plan included her safety, and that was the only promise Colonel Magnus had given her.

Well, you hadn't expected Vitus to show back up.

True, but details didn't really matter. Life wasn't fair

and she knew better than to expect it to be kind. She'd lived all her years as a commodity, with the rare exceptions of when she was with Vitus. Colonel Magnus might be offering her a haven but only because she was something he needed.

There had been moments of wonderful sweetness, delivered up so unexpectedly by her circumstances. Last night was one.

It looked like she was going to have to live on those crumbs, because her stolen moments with Vitus were about to end.

"Shit . . . you were right dude." A happy chortle came out of the teen's mouth as he peered at the couple on the screen, his fingers on the joystick of his prized drone. "Right on. That means I get paid double, right?"

Pratt nodded. "I need a copy of that footage first."

"Sure thing. Let me set Nessie down first." He was intent on the screen for a moment, controlling the drone. There was a buzz as it came back into view, then the kid brought it in for a landing. He set it down on the road and ran over to pick it up. Pratt didn't see the need for speed since they hadn't seen a single car in the hour they'd been there.

But it worked in his favor to be on his way as soon as possible. The kid came back carrying his drone and placed it carefully in the bed of the pickup pulled alongside the road at the edge of the property line between public land and Dunn Bateson's land.

"All right then." The kid was rubbing his palms together, excitement brightening his face. He poked at the keyboard of a laptop as he transferred the flight data to a USB drive. He jabbed at the keyboard, nodding as the data transfer completed. There was a chirp from the laptop when it finished. He pulled the little drive free.

"Pleasure doing business—"

The kids face froze as he looked down at his chest. Pratt put a second bullet into him as blood soaked the shirt the kid was wearing. He made a few wheezing sounds before his knees began to give way. Pratt reached down and hooked him by one thigh, lifting the kid up and into the back of the pickup truck next to the drone.

"Nothing personal," Pratt told him as the kid's eyes started to fix and life left him. "Just business."

Pratt fished the key out of the kid's pocket before tossing a tarp over the body, making sure it was completely covered. He slipped behind the wheel and closed the door. Rain was starting to fall. He tried to establish a hotspot but the remote location defeated him. Pratt settled for turning the engine over and pulling away from the side of the road. At least there was a use for the location; it would make it easy to hide a body.

If his luck held, he'd be able to add three more to the pile within a few hours.

"I'm staying here."

Saxon turned to consider Greer.

"If they know she was here, I want some evidence." He'd changed into camouflage clothing complete with rain gear. "I'm going to stake the place out."

"Alone?" Saxon inquired.

"That's too risky," Vitus added.

"Didn't say I'd be on my own." Greer selected a high-powered rifle that was sitting in a gun rack mounted by the front door. "I'm not stupid."

He offered Damascus a wink before he slipped out the door and into the afternoon rain.

"Are you really going to let him go?" she asked.

Vitus's expression was grim, but he reached out and

hooked her upper arm. "Resources are thin, Princess. I have to move you."

There was a dedication in his tone that cut her deep.

"I'm sorry." It was the only thing she could think to say as Vitus took a look around before escorting her to a waiting car. Saxon had slipped behind the wheel and had the engine running.

"Greer may surprise you," Vitus said. He held the door open for her, and she slid in as rain splattered her in the face.

"Oh, I don't think he isn't capable. Far from it."

"Smart girl," Vitus said before he closed the door.

Saxon was watching Greer as he climbed further up onto a ridge that overlooked the cottage and disappeared into the grass. Vitus settled into the front seat next to his brother.

"Get comfortable Ms. Ryland," Saxon informed her. "We're taking the scenic route, just in case we have a tail."

Pratt decided that he hated northern California. It was too damn empty. He knew how to hide among people who were so smashed together, they ignored one another. Every time he pulled up to a town, the locals took notice of him, leaning to peer out of a window or lifting their glasses up to him in a toast. As if he wanted anything to do with any of them. Why weren't they staring at their cell phones like the rest of the modern world?

Fuck it. The only thought that kept his temper from exploding was the knowledge that he was driving around with one of their own in the bed of his truck. Bet that would raise a few eyebrows.

Darkness helped, allowing him to park behind a local tavern and hack into their internet. He pushed the information through to the Raven and Tyler Martin but made sure he put a copy in a safe place just in case he needed it. A dog started howling, loping across the parking lot to sniff at the bed of the truck. Pratt cussed, pulling away from the only promise of hot food for miles around. He consoled himself with the knowledge that nothing he might have found inside the local greasy spoon would have even come close to the food found in the French Quarter.

His belly rumbled but he headed down the road, telling himself to get on with business so that he could go back home.

"I'll get someone on locating who had the drone," Dunn Bateson said. "Around here, there can't be too many of them."

"It might have been brought in," Vitus said.

Dunn nodded. "It's a place to start while we wait to see if Greer has any luck. I sent a few boys up to help him."

Damascus felt her blood chill. "I need to return to Washington." All the men turned to consider her. "I can't sit here while you continue to risk yourselves for me."

"I told you before, Damascus, that's a bad idea." Vitus rejected her request.

"And I told you, I'm not going to sit here. It's not logical." She aimed her attention at Dunn. "Surly you can understand my argument? This won't be over until I face Jeb, so I should just get on with it. We are just treating symptoms—I need to get to the root cause of the infection. That's Jeb."

Dunn was leaning against a granite kitchen counter. On the outside, the building in San Francisco looked about a century old, but inside it was sleek and modern with everything she would have expected to find in a New York high-rise.

"I admire your spirit," Dunn replied. "But not your thought process."

"Oh really?" Damascus asked. "Where did I get off track?"

"Carl Davis," Dunn fired back. "He's involved, and he's a much bigger dog to go up against. That man is poised for a successful run to the White House because he's carefully cultivated enough support to ensure he makes it. He's decided you're part of that image. That won't be an easy thing to avoid."

"So what?" Damascus cut back. "I know where his soft spot is."

"And what might that be?" Vitus asked softly.

Damascus knew the tone. It made her bite her lip as she contemplated the man shooting holes in her reasoning. There was a knowing glint in his eyes and she realized she only had the strength to keep one secret from him.

"He's gay."

There was a snort or two and a soft word of profanity.

"According to the news, he thinks you're his fiancée," Saxon said.

Damascus held her hand up and wiggled her fingers to make sure they all saw how bare her ring finger was. "I told him no. Not that he listened to me. Of course not. He and Jeb made some pact and I'm sure Jeb told him what an obedient little wife I'd be. But he's gay. He told me so, even gave his blessing to you and me continuing to be lovers as some sort of bargaining perk."

Heat teased her cheeks at saying it out loud. Sure, she knew everyone was fully aware of the fact that Vitus had spent the night in her bed, but it still felt so personal. Not that she'd ever really had any true privacy. Vitus was the one true intimacy in her life. She didn't want to share it.

"Explain what you mean by 'continuing to be lovers.' "

Vitus's expression had gone hard. She felt the muscles running down her neck tightening.

"Um . . . he knew I went to see you." It was like a balloon popping in her face. Horror gagged her as she realized she'd led her sire's goons straight to Vitus and given Jeb more fuel for his hatred.

She'd failed.

That bit of knowledge felt like a boulder sitting between her shoulder blades. She'd meant to warn him, and all she'd accomplished was stirring up what she had invested so much effort in trying to mask. All of the meekness and shows of obedience. It had all been part of a plan to throw Jeb off the scent of what she truly thought.

She let out a sigh. "It's just another reason why I have to go back. I have to face him, deal with him directly. At least if I go back, you two can disappear."

Vitus scoffed. "You know it's not that simple, Princess. Your daddy has us marked for headstones. He'll always be worried that you'll change your mind."

"You'd have a chance," she said. "Which is more than you are going to have if we stay here. Obviously they know whose plane we left in or that drone wouldn't have found us." She shot a hard look at Dunn. "You're getting dragged into this now too."

He curled his lips back and sent her a grin that told her he'd welcome the attempt.

"That bravado won't help you."

"And you think your bravado will do the trick?" Vitus asked. "Your father just paid someone to kidnap you and cut a part of you off. What makes you think he doesn't have a good plan for forcing you to slip Carl's ring on? I'm not letting you walk back into that and I'm sure as hell not going to see you trade your compliance for my safety."

She was right back to guarding her ace in the hole. Unable to show it because of the promise she'd made to Colonel Magnus.

"What I think is that I don't like you three putting yourselves between me and Jeb. It isn't right."

"You've got one thing down." Saxon spoke up. "It isn't right, but for more reasons than what your father is doing to you. I'm in this for more than you. Tyler Martin killed two of my men when he came after me earlier this year. Your father is protecting him."

"So, you're using me?" she asked. "Nice try but I don't believe that."

Saxon shrugged. "I don't have a lot of options, and your father isn't the only one who knows how to hold a grudge."

"You're all sidestepping the fact that they know we're with Dunn. How long do you think it is going to be before they figure out we're here?"

"Longer than you think," Dunn informed her. "I don't own this place."

"Jeb's people will have a list of every friend you have."

"Which is why we're in a place that belongs to a man I hate. Officially and very well documented."

Damascus stared at him, shocked into silence. Dunn seemed to enjoy the moment. He tilted his head to the side and offered her a wink. "Shamus Campbell and I decided years ago that we'd be a lot more use to each other if the rest of the world thought we hated each other's guts. We throw a few punches at each other from time to time to keep the fire going." His eyes were glittering by the time he finished filling her in. "No one will ever think I'm here, in his place, or that he is letting me use it."

It was suddenly really clear where the guy got his arrogance from. He earned it.

"Again, how long are we going to hide?" She felt like she was trying to shoot holes in their reasoning with a straw and a spitball. "How long before your section leader has to give you up? He will, you know. He'll fold at some point because the price will just become too great. Jeb excels at that sort of thing."

She turned and left, making her way down a hallway to a bedroom. Vitus wouldn't listen to her and she just couldn't bear to watch him toss away the only chance he had to make a getaway.

"Surprised to see me?"

Kagan didn't flinch, but it was a near thing. He blew across the surface of his coffee, taking a long time to take that first sip while Tyler Martin sat next to him on the park bench. Women with baby strollers went by as old men clustered around the picnic tables across the way playing chess. Above them all, the dome of the White House was in sight.

"Nope," Kagan answered at last. "Not surprised. You're smart, even if your loyalty seems to go to the highest bidder."

"Every man has his price," Tyler replied. "You just take your worth in what you think is respect. I gave up on that pipe dream years ago."

"So it seems." Kagan turned to look at Tyler. "What do you want?"

"A trade."

"And you think I'll toss in with you, when I know you'll turn over the second it benefits you?" Kagan chuckled, but the sound wasn't pleasant, not by a long shot. Tyler didn't miss it. He considered his ex–section leader for a good long time, weighing his expression.

"I need the girl."

"Seems you need a few more of my men in the ground too," Kagan cut back. "I'm no sellout. You know that."

"It's in your best interest to bring them back now, before you get ordered to by the powers that be. Do it my way, and you'll have time to pull your men out of the line of fire."

Kagan grunted. "Now why would you offer me such a nice, pretty little peace offering? You were trying to wax them a few months ago. Think I've forgotten that?"

"If I have the girl, I can work a new deal, one that won't include cutting through the Hale brothers. I never had anything against them personally."

"Ah." Kagan returned to sipping his coffee and looking across the park. "Carl has realized your services are for sale."

"You may not like it, but as I explained to you before, this is the way the world is now. Men like us can no longer feel secure in our service. The powerful have gotten too big. We either give them what they want or get flattened when we end up in their path." Tyler ended on a heavy note. "You know it's true, otherwise you would have put a bullet in my skull while you had me chained to that interrogation table."

Kagan lost interest in his coffee, his temper straining against the hold he had on it. Tyler was so close, so damn close and he wanted to choke the life out of him with his bare hands, so that he could feel the bastard struggle for his last breaths.

"Get me the girl. I'll get Ryland off the Hale brothers."

Kagan grunted. "I'm almost tempted to say yes, just to see how you manage to pull that one off. Ryland's a crazy son of a bitch. So fucking punch-drunk, he can't see how close he is to cutting off his own nose just to get his vengeance."

"He is," Tyler agreed. "But there is a bigger dog in the fight now, one that can pull on Ryland's chain. Think about it. We've worked well together for years, no reason to burn that bridge. He'll get her anyway. We might as well profit from it."

Tyler Martin stood and started off down the path that wound its way through the park. Kagan didn't need to see the car that pulled up to the curb to pick him up. He knew it would be there; just as he expected his cell phone to buzz a few moments later. He looked at the text from Colonel Magnus and took a few large swallows of his coffee before tossing it into a trash can on his way back to his own people.

"You're not asleep."

Damascus rolled over and looked at Vitus. God, she loved the way he stood. There was something so powerful, so solid about his stance. She could have sworn she could feel his strength radiating through the space between them. The semidarkness of the room just added to his persona.

"No. How could I sleep when I know you're wasting your chance to escape?"

He moved closer, coming to sit on the side of the bed. She should have felt exposed, wearing only a nightshirt and a pair of underwear but with Vitus she only seemed to notice just how comfortable she was.

"I can't abandon you, Princess."

She heard the promise in his voice, and it made her shiver. The ripple of sensation traveled down her spine until it hit her toes and left them curled.

"You can't be responsible for me." She sat all the way up and he reached for her, stroking her cheeks with a touch that set off a pulsing need deep inside her.

"I can," he confirmed in a deep tone, one that she was tempted to take solace in.

"I'm poison."

He'd made it across her cheek to where her hair was a

bushy cloud. "You're a toxin, I won't argue the point." He was threading his fingers through her hair, sending little waves of delight across her scalp. "Thing is, I'm addicted to you."

He leaned in, holding her head so that he could press his mouth down on top of her lips, claiming them in a kiss that stole her breath. It was scalding hot and so sweet, she moaned softly as she felt her will disintegrating.

He was there and too close to deny her craving for him. She reached for him, grasping his shoulders as she kissed him back, seeking the taste of him, needing to brand it into her memory. Desperation fueled her and he answered with a vigor that left her breathless. He tore the sleep shirt up and over her head, grunting with victory as she landed back on her haunches in nothing but her underwear. He was looking at her, raking her from head to toe and then back to her bare breasts.

"I love your tits." He leaned over and licked one nipple. It puckered in response as she gasped and gripped his head, holding it to her while she arched back to offer herself to him.

He made good use of her submission, sucking the little nub into his mouth and sending a bolt of need straight down to her clit. He was drawing on the sensitive point, pulling, nursing at it like a starving man, and it released the same hunger in her.

She needed to touch his skin. "Strip."

It was an order, one that she issued in a husky tone she hadn't realized she possessed. He chuckled, releasing her breast as she caught a flash of his teeth because he was smiling so wildly.

"Yes ma'am." The bed moved as he stood, but he stopped with his hands on the hem of his shirt. "Stay."

She made a low sound that earned her a chuckle from him as he pulled his shirt up his body, reveling the cut abdomen and defined pectoral muscles of his chest. When the shirt was gone and he was looking at her again, she caught the determination in his expression.

"I said stay. As in, don't move, Princess."

Vitus reached for the waistband of his pants. He popped open the button and moved to the next one on his fly. "You're going to do what I say for a change."

"Like hell I am," she argued before she rolled back and pulled her underwear off. There was a grunt from Vitus, but she kept rolling and ended up standing on the other side of the bed. She was closer to the windows in the room, the ones that were open to let in the night air and moonlight. It cast her in a white glow, one that she knew his night vision was perfectly capable of seeing.

"You will not tell me to sit still, Vitus."

He took a moment to undo his boots before he shucked his jeans and came around the bed in nothing but skin. She bit her lower lip because she wanted to purr with satisfaction, but it seemed too dramatic, even if true.

"I'm really sick of everyone telling me what to do." Her voice had lowered because he was coming closer, closing in on her, making her belly flip as her clit pulsed and every inch of her skin felt like it was a hundred times more sensitive. Thank God she'd stripped, because she couldn't have tolerated anything against her body, except him.

"I know the feeling, " he said softly. "I'm getting real tired of you pushing me away."

He reached out, touching her belly, just above her navel. She jerked, drawing in a stiff breath as it felt like she was branded by that contact. It was all she could do to keep her eyes open because her brain was shutting down, leaving her only responses.

He drew his hand up, stroking her body between her breasts and further up to the delicate skin of her throat.

"I want to hear you tell me you want to marry me."

His voice was a husky whisper, like it came out of his soul. It was an echo of her own.

"I love you." She stepped toward him, feeling his hand slip around her neck to clasp it, capturing her even as she moved into his space. It was a vow she made with more than her words. She was committing to him with her actions, giving every inch of herself, without a backward glance.

He took her mouth, claiming it with a kiss that stole her breath. It was hard, just like him, the restraint he'd been using falling aside as their skin met. She opened her mouth for the thrust of his tongue, feeling his cock jerk against her belly as she pressed up against him completely. Somehow, she'd forgotten how small she was compared to him, having to rise up onto her toes to kiss him back. The difference in their strength should have intimidated her. Instead, she seemed to absorb it, adopting a boldness to match his.

Vitus scooped her up, cradling her as though she weighed nothing, and took her toward the bed. He rolled them across the cool sheets until he was on his back and lifted her up to sit on top of him.

"As you like it, Princess. You do the telling tonight."

He stroked her sides, cupping her breasts for a moment before he lifted her up as she reached down to place his cock at the entrance of her body. He eased her down, making sure she was ready to take him. She didn't care for him holding her back, urgency pounding through her. She gripped him with her thighs and rose up as he grunted.

"Good," she said as she seated herself completely on him. "I want to hear you, want to know you can't control yourself either."

He snorted at her and fingered her nipples, rolling them while sending her up and back down with a ragged breath.

"As if you had any doubt, Princess."

She did though. His face was drawn tight and she stared at it as she rode him, absorbed by the tension, by the need on display. It mirrored her own, somehow lending validation to all the swirling emotions he unleashed inside her. Did it make sense? No, but somehow at last she didn't feel alone. He was her companion, her soul mate, her partner in the current of pulsing need that was jerking them both toward the point where they would be tossed over a cliff and free fall into a churning pool of physical satisfaction, leaving them floating in each other's embrace.

"Tyler Martin came to you?" Saxon failed to keep his emotions masked. His tone was thick with rage.

"Shocked me too," Kagan responded.

"I'd like to shock him too."

There was a dry chuckle on the other end of the line. "Interesting thing is, he might just be making that easy for us."

Saxon had abandoned his chair in favor of pacing. He didn't need to ask what Kagan meant. All he had to do was keep his mouth shut and wait to see if his section leader was going to share his thought process. With Kagan that was never a sure thing—but it was a wise one because men who knew too much didn't live long.

"Tyler wants the girl. My guess is, he's going to jump ship on Ryland and give her to Davis as his payment into service."

"That sounds like something Martin would do," Saxon agreed. "And Carl Davis has made it clear he considers her his. However, Damascus Ryland divulged an interesting bit of information about the good presidential hopeful."

"And what might that be?" Kagan's tone was sharp and serious.

"According to Damascus, he's gay."

There was a long moment of silence. "I was about to tell you to come in, but I just changed my mind."

"Are you really considering dealing with Martin?" The question was rather insubordinate, but Saxon didn't give a rat's ass.

"You bet I am, but not quite the way he thinks." Kagan began to explain. "Situations like this, kidnappings, they don't have a good record of ending cleanly. No matter how airtight we try to make the exchange process, people still get shot."

"Yeah, I've been through a few."

"Tyler Martin is head of Jeb Ryland's security," Kagan continued. "He's in a really bad position from the way I see it."

"Just a slipup by a triggerman would mean he dies while trying to perform his duty."

"Stay put for another twenty-four hours. I want to check out that bit of information from Ms. Ryland. Because something like that could be very useful in making sure Carl Davis doesn't make a fuss over losing his new guard dog."

Kagan ended the call, leaving Saxon with mixed feelings. On one hand, Saxon wanted Tyler's blood. It was justice for the men he'd killed as well as a nice, secure feeling against a future where Tyler would be free to kill again when it served his purpose. On the other hand, that wasn't the way Saxon played. He didn't want to lower himself to Tyler's level.

Unfortunately, sometimes in order to catch a rat, you had to crawl through the gutter to get at him.

* * *

"Got you." Pratt enjoyed a surge of success. It was long overdue in his opinion. He watched Damascus Ryland through a window and took aim at the man sitting near her.

The window shattered as the bullet went through. He stayed still only a moment, to make sure he'd hit his target. He really didn't need to see the impact. Damascus whirled around and started screaming.

Pratt eased around the corner and into the building. Damascus was leaning over the downed security man, shaking him.

"Don't fucking move."

She gasped and stiffened.

"Let me see your hands."

She pushed back onto her haunches, and a moment later something slammed into the side of his head. Pratt watched the world tilt as unconsciousness claimed him.

Vitus opened his eyes. It took only a split moment for him to realize the door was open and light was shining in from the hallway. Saxon waited for him to identify him before he closed the door. Vitus eased out of bed, tucking the comforter around Damascus before he dressed and slipped into the hallway.

"Greer has someone," Saxon said. "We need to get up there."

Vitus frowned. "Why not bring him in?"

"Dunn wants to keep it out on his property." Saxon answered. "Get dressed, we're flying out. I want to see who Greer bagged."

Vitus didn't need any further encouragement. When it came to priorities, discovering the means to free Damascus from her father's control was in the number-one slot.

"Damascus?"

"I have a couple of men here to sit on her." Dunn pulled a cell phone out of his jacket and pressed his thumb against it. A moment later he tapped something into the screen and put it away. There was a soft click of the door opening at the end of the hallway. Four men came down using quiet steps. Vitus considered them before he nodded. He didn't like it but finding the link to Ryland was worth dealing with his own discontent.

Dunn's pilot set down behind the cabin. It was somewhere close to midnight. Vitus felt a chill touch his nape because there was something about the moonlit mountains that just struck him as more haunted than any place he'd ever been. A wind was whipping up, the scent of water in the air as clouds began to cluster in the sky. They made their way down the grassy embankment to the cabin.

Greer was propped in the corner, his line of sight on the door as they came in. Sitting at the kitchen table was a man with a hell of a bruise on the side of his head. It didn't seem to faze him much though. He was glaring at them as they came through the door, his eyes clear and focused. His hands were shackled in two pairs of handcuffs that were linked through a chain looped through a huge concrete block sitting on the floor at the guy's feet.

There was a motion behind Greer's captive. Vitus peered into the dark kitchen. A woman was there, sipping at a whisky glass. A red wig sat on the table as Thais Sinclair offered him a smirk.

"Agent Thais Sinclair," Greer supplied for Dunn. "Fellow team member."

Thais took a last sip of her whiskey before she moved out of the kitchen and into the living room. She passed a dummy lying on the floor with a bullet in its chest. Next to that was a large, wicked-looking cricket bat. Vitus made the connection between the bat and the damage to their captive's head.

"You put her in here as bait?" Vitus asked Greer.

"Can't expect to catch much with an empty hook." It was Thais who answered, her voice soft and sultry. "It was fun."

"It was a damn stupid risk to take," Dunn growled as he caught her by the arm. She fluttered her eyelashes at him before she dropped her arm on the other side of his and broke his grip. Dunn grunted.

"I know what I'm doing, Mr. Bateson."

Dunn didn't care for what she said, but she turned and continued toward the door.

The moment she reached the door and pulled it open, there was a round of gunfire. Vitus hit the deck as Thais fell across the floor, Greer already returning fire as they all pulled their guns. It stopped as quickly as it started, an eerie tension filling the cottage. Someone had killed the lights, leaving them waiting for their night vision to kick in. Vitus was in motion, knowing full well that whoever was trying to kill them wouldn't let them gain that sort of advantage.

Dunn had caught Thais, pulling her away from the door. She surprised him by pulling a gun out of a thigh holster that had been concealed beneath her skirt. Outside, there was a pop, followed by two more. Vitus ducked around the corner to peer out the side door. The pilot had left the helicopter and was using it for cover as he aimed down toward the back of the cottage. There was a flash as he discharged his gun. They were pinned down inside the structure, but they also had what their attackers wanted.

"Get those cuffs off him," Vitus ordered.

"Right," Saxon said. "We get to the bird, fly out of here."

There was the sound of turning metal and then Greer was shoving their captive toward the wall. "Your buddies are going to get you when they take a shot at me."

"We can't all hide behind him," Dunn said, stating the obvious.

"So set the place on fire," Thais offered. "You're running off a propane tank. Blow it. We can make the run while the night is being lit up."

"This was my grandmother's cabin," Dunn grumbled.

"If you don't, you just might get to meet her tonight," Thais advised him. "Unless you'd like to call in the emergency services to save our tails."

There was a short word of Gaelic before Dunn moved toward the kitchen. "Meet you on the high ground. You've got sixty seconds to clear out."

"You're going to move when I say to." Greer had their captive, who was resisting going through the front door. "Want to stay here and fry?"

That got him moving. They were poised in the doorway, mentally counting down.

"Go," Saxon said.

They headed into the night where it was far too silent. They made it twenty feet before gunfire started up again, the guy's comrades clearly considering it better to hit their own man than to risk losing Saxon. The pilot realized what was up and was back inside the helicopter as they slammed into it and pulled the doors open. When you were in a firefight, every second felt like an hour. Vitus recognized the feeling. It prolonged the struggle, allowing him to notice how he fought for every breath and sat poised on the edge of knowing that his next heartbeat might just be his last. He pushed his body to the limit, straining to get their captive into the bird.

The night suddenly lit up as the cabin exploded. A huge orange ball of fire rolled up from where the kitchen had been. The wall of heat hit them, singeing the skin on the back of their necks. The gunfire stopped and they succeeded in getting into the helicopter. Dunn was making his run, coming up the embankment as the pilot lifted the bird off the ground. Vitus hung out of the door, his arm extended as Saxon anchored him. Dunn leapt for his arm as a flash of gunfire showed them where one of the gunmen was. Greer came up over Vitus, returning fire as Dunn latched onto Vitus's arm.

A bullet parted his hair as he hauled Dunn aboard, and the pilot swung the aircraft into the sky. They were rolled in a mass of human bodies, the scent of sweat thick inside the helicopter. Someone shoved the door closed as the pilot leveled out, and all everyone could do was pant. The rush of adrenaline ended, dropping them all back into reality and letting them feel the pain. Vitus reached up and felt the pulsing grow in his skin. His fingers came away wet but he was content with the knowledge that it was only a flesh wound.

"Fuck."

Saxon muttered the word. Vitus turned around, looking straight into the open eyes of their captive. His pupils were fixed and dilated.

"That is going to bring some unwanted attention down on us," Dunn added.

"No kidding," Saxon agreed.

"Better call in, " Dunn continued. "There is no way I can cover a dead man."

"Or two," Thais added. She had her jacket off and was using it to press down on Greer's shoulder. His shirt was splattered with fresh blood and his lips had turned white, but he offered them a cocky grin before he looked back at Thais.

"Always knew I'd get you to take your top off at some

point. . . ." His words started to slur, his eyes slipping closed.

"What do you think of this bra Greer? Are you a lace man?"

His eyes widened, his attention fixing on the generous amount of cleavage her undergarment displayed.

Vitus decided that Thais was all right in his book. She knew how to keep her cool and be a team member when it counted.

And at the moment, every move they made was going to be measured in blood.

CHAPTER SEVEN

"You let her help." Damascus was nearly nose to nose with Saxon.

"Thais Sinclair is an agent," Saxon replied, unimpressed with the way Damascus was trying to intimidate him.

"I am not helpless," Damascus informed him.

There was a knock on the doorframe. A doctor stood there, still wearing his surgical cap. "McRae family?"

They all turned to face him. For a moment, he looked like he wasn't sure about who exactly was related to his patient, but Dunn appeared in the opposite doorway and that seemed to decide the matter.

"He's out of surgery. It looks like we got to him in time but he's looking at a couple of months of downtime."

The doctor was tired. He rubbed his eyes before he turned and left. The hospital was quiet, the early morning hours somehow managing to impact the fully lit hallways.

Relief rippled through the room, but it was a short-lived emotional state for everyone. Tension returned with a bite that was razor sharp. Damascus was certain she felt it deeper and sharper than anyone, because the hard fact was that it was all happening because of her.

"This is why I have to go back," she said.

"It's why you can't," Vitus argued with a nod from his brother.

Damascus looked toward Dunn. He was contemplating her from behind an unreadable expression. But he hadn't said no, which gave her hope, or at least an avenue of opportunity. One she was going to have to explore.

"We've got to talk to Kagan." Saxon waited to see what his brother would make of that.

Vitus nodded. "But not here. That would be a sure tip-off if anyone is watching him."

It was Saxon's turn to nod. "Which means we need to leave Damascus with Dunn."

Vitus shot him a look. "You were working up to that gem."

"I was," Saxon said. "And I'm standing across the room to keep out of your striking range while you filter the information through your brain and come to the only logical conclusion, which is to agree. We should go at first light."

Vitus ground his teeth together, but his brother was right. He didn't like it—it felt like a noose was tightening around his neck as time ran short. Resources were running thin, and their cover was now blown sky high. One dead Russian from the French Quarter and Greer in the hospital along with a murdered kid in the back of a pickup.

"I'll go talk to her. You deal with Dunn." Vitus turned and headed down the hallway of Dunn's city residence. He knocked on a bedroom door before pushing it open.

"Finally decided to fill me in?"

Damascus was pacing. There was a flash in her eyes that warned him she was in the mood for a fight. Not that he could really blame her. He'd take a straight-out confrontation any day as opposed to hiding out.

"You have to admit, Princess, making decisions without a clear head isn't a good idea."

She settled her attention on him, squaring her shoulders. "And you have to agree that you'd need to be dead in order to sit around, in another room, while your life was being decided."

"True, but that doesn't mean I don't see the wisdom—" He was cut off as he ducked out of the way of a book hurled at his head.

"Christ woman, you've got an arm on you!"

The book collided with the door behind him, the sound echoing through the room. Damascus looked a little shocked at the volume of the noise, her forehead furrowed as she frowned and her cheeks darkened with shame. "You bring out the worst in me."

Damascus was utterly charming in that moment. She was his match because every damn time he was close to her, his self-discipline went flying into a billion bits.

"Not a chance, Princess."

She stiffened, pulling in a harsh breath as he made his way closer. It was a magnetic attraction, too strong to resist. He slid his hand into her hair, feeling the connection bone deep, soul deep. All that he knew was that the feeling of her hair between his fingers was like a mind-blowing high.

"I bring out your passion. Don't you ever call that bad." He was bent over her, enjoying the feel of her nape in his grip, the pure sensation of knowing she was his. "It's more honest than anything in your life. I give you that."

Her eyes widened as she pressed her lips together like she was thinking about how much she wanted him to kiss her.

"You do that, all right." Her voice was husky, sending blood rushing to his cock. It hardened behind his fly, giving an edge to his mood.

"I'm not sure it's a good thing," she finished in a whisper, like the words had somehow slipped out of her soul.

"It's the only damn thing I'm sure of at the moment." He leaned down closer, catching the scent of her skin. His cock started to throb, the need to get inside her pressing against his brain.

Which was just the way it always was when he had Damascus in his arms. He pressed his mouth against hers, feeling her shiver as she adjusted to his hold. He kissed her, holding her steady as she flattened her hands on his chest and then slid them up so that she could grasp his shoulders. He felt every fingertip as she curled her fingers into talons and locked him in place against her.

His damn cock was granite now, his balls tightening as the need to feel her body clasping his length became urgent.

"I really did come down here to talk," he offered as he managed to break away from her mouth.

"This is how we communicate best." She rose up onto her toes to get back in contact with him, pressing hot little kisses against his neck.

Vitus groaned, lifting his chin, exposing his throat. There was no one else on the planet who could have put him in so helpless a position, but Damascus could do whatever she pleased with him, so long as she kept doing it.

He took advantage of the moment, reaching down and finding the bottom of her top. He pulled it up, earning a hiss from her as she was interrupted, and yanked it over her head. The little scrap of a bra she had on didn't last long beneath his determined fingers. It was fluttering toward the floor a moment after her top, leaving the mounds of her breasts free.

"God I love your tits." He bound her against him with an arm around her waist as he leaned over and licked one rose-crowned tip. She shuddered and he chuckled, pretty sure he'd never enjoyed anything more.

Except being inside her.

His cock reminded him of that fact, but he shoved it aside, unwilling to be rushed toward the conclusion. That was when reality would emerge again with all its specters and harsh edges.

It could wait.

Because he was in the mood to steal a moment of bliss.

He picked her up and turned around to put her on the bed. She looked up at him.

"I can walk, Vitus."

He was pulling her shoes off, making quick work of the laces as he focused on having her body bare, completely free for him to enjoy. To water the parched parts of his soul. It was more than a desire to get next to her. It was a need that was wringing every last shred of personality out of him, leaving just a bundle of hunger, and she was the only one who would satisfy him.

She snorted at his lack of response but gasped when he came toward her, pushing her back and pulling on her fly. A moment later he had her jeans hanging from one hand.

"Damned if you don't look proud of yourself," she muttered, her voice edged with uncertainty. Her teeth were set against her lower lip as she worried it.

"Don't be self-conscious."

She was, and it tore something inside him, reducing him to uncertainty, a place only she took him. She had crossed her ankles, closing her thighs as she tried to decide if she was going to lean back on her elbows or sit all the way up.

"I tore your clothes off you because I love the sight of you, Princess." It felt like an awkward wording of his e free. At his core, he was a pulsing bundle of need, craving and appetite for her.

Vitus caught her wrists and pinned them to the surface of the bed. She opened her eyes for a moment. He thrust into her, controlling the motion so that it was strong and hard. Her nostrils flared, betraying her pleasure.

"That's the way you like me, isn't it, Princess?" He pulled free and thrust back into her. "Hard and demanding. Admit it."

She snorted at him, twisting her hands as he set about fucking her with a tempo he knew she couldn't resist. But she bared her teeth at him.

"Don't be such a caveman."

He grunted and thrust against her hard, leaning down so that his breath was teasing her ear. "I'm civilized enough to hold back my pleasure until you scream, Princess." He rose up again, riding her, gritting his teeth against the feeling of her pussy gripping his cock. "I'm going to make you scream."

It was a vow, one linked to the cravings he had to empty himself deep inside her. They were like two parts of the same seed. He was breathing hard, the muscles in his ass burning as he held her in place. Listening to the sounds she made, watching the way her nipples puckered tighter and tighter, told him she was nearing the edge.

She was trying to hold onto his hands when she peaked, her body arching, straining toward his as she clamped his hips between her thighs. He felt her pussy milking him, pulling on his cock trying to claim his seed. Vitus didn't last a moment longer. He hammered into her and ground himself deep as his balls burned while sending up his load. It was harsh, slamming into his brain as he held Damascus to the surface of the bed and groaned through his pleasure. It was spine tingling and left him gasping for breath in a pile of quivering limbs. Somehow

feelings, but she offered him a shy smile and 1
onto her elbows.

"So, it seems like you know how I feel." She
her lower lip again, but this time with antici
watched her warming to the moment, relaxin
his gaze. It was more potent than white ligh
more humbling than anything he'd ever experie

"Go on, don't stop now," she encouraged.
doing a splendid job of stripping."

He chuckled and pulled his shirt off. Her a
went to his chest, enjoyment flashing through he
When he opened his belt and fly, her expression tig
as his cock sprang through the opening. It was a
fine sight, the look of hunger on her face said. Lus
there, but there was something far more attractive—r
It was a deep core sort of craving, the same one claw
at him.

"Come here, Vitus." She crooked her finger at him
he finished undressing. "Come do what your face is tel
ing me you want to do."

He was pretty sure nothing could have stopped him.
The bed rocked as he moved over her, covering her
smaller frame and lowering himself onto her. She welcomed him, opening her arms and legs and wrapping
him into her embrace. It was primitive, basic, and soul-
shattering. More honest than anything on the planet. He
groaned as she clamped him between her thighs, the
folds of her slit wet and slippery. She arched back, pushing her hips up to take his length.

"I meant . . . to go slower . . ."

"Don't," she muttered as her eyes slipped closed.
felt his cock penetrating deeper.

It was too much temptation, that slick hot fee
her body encompassing the head of his cock. E
fell aside, like a shell cracking to allow what

he landed next to her, easing onto his back as he pulled her against his side.

That was the second-most important thing he needed. This moment, when passion no long reigned supreme and he still needed her, was the most. He wanted to feel her heart beating against his side, feel the soft impact of her breath against the hair on his chest. Smell her. God, he needed to have the scent of her skin, of her sweat mixing with his filling his senses. All the little things that confirmed she was there, really there and not just a memory from a time when fate had somehow allowed him to touch a Goddess before she had to return to the realms of her kin.

Just a little while longer—hell that was a fucking lie, he wanted forever. Needed it more than anything else in the world.

He brushed her hair back from her face and watched the way her eyelids fluttered as she slept.

"I'll find a way, Princess."

Or die trying.

And it would be worth it because he couldn't face going back to living without her. He refused to. All or nothing.

Damascus stretched and felt her back pop. It wasn't sharp, just a release of sorts. She drew in a deep breath and let it out, feeling more rested than she had in, well, in forever. Something was filling her head and she realized it was the sound of Vitus's heartbeat. She opened her eyes and couldn't resist pushing her fingers through the crisp hair on his chest. He had her cuddled up against his side, the edge of the comforter pulled over her. He was toying with one of her curls, the bay area weather making her hair a mass of corkscrews. The windows were a hazy gray, announcing the arrival of dawn.

"I've got to go soon, Princess."

There was reluctance in his tone but a lazy smile on his lips. She indulged in a moment of savoring the feeling of him against her before she pushed herself up. "We got distracted."

"I like the way you capture my attention."

She offered him a roll of her eyes as she turned around and slid her legs over the edge of the bed. The floor was littered with their clothing. She went searching for hers, all the while conscious of him watching her.

"So, what's happening?"

Vitus grunted, his expression tightening. He rolled up to a sitting position and off the bed. "Saxon and I need to go touch base with our section leader, the one who sent us off-grid. We're not doing it from here in case he's been marked."

"Jeb would've had a list drawn up of who might be in contact with you."

"Tyler Martin knows. He used to work for Kagan too."

She finished dressing and started to try and get her hair under control. Vitus pulled his pants on and reached for his shirt. It felt like they were being ripped apart, the layers of clothing like blunt facts of reality all coming between them.

"You really need to just take me back."

Vitus's sent her a stone-hard look of refusal. "Let's get one thing straight Damascus. I will not ever willingly leave you to that bastard who fathered you."

She'd known he'd say that. Still, it felt like a concrete block landing in the center of her chest. The weight was crushing the breath out of her because she knew what her sire would do. He'd use that determination against Vitus. In fact, Jeb was counting on that spirit, that core of integrity to help him carry out his insane idea of justice.

That was why she had to intercede, to protect Vitus.

It simply wasn't in his nature to walk away, even knowing the risks. Actually that knowledge was only spurring him onward, fueling his determination to shelter her.

Well the truth was, a worthy princess was someone who did what was best for those who held her in such a high position.

He was finished dressing. The last thing he did was pull a gun from where he'd hidden it between the mattress and headboard. She'd never woken up when he'd stashed it, so content in his embrace.

Well, she had to shake it off now and get done what had to be done.

"Dunn's people will look after you while we're gone." He didn't like saying it. "I will be back soon, Princess."

"Got it." She moved toward him, reaching up to lay her hands on his shoulders. She rose onto her toes, stretching to kiss him. Vitus watched her for a moment before he leaned down to kiss her back, his mouth moving over hers in a slow, determined motion that made her heart race.

But he set her back, breaking off the kiss as his expression tightened and she witnessed the flare of determination in his eyes. She turned away before he saw the same thing in her, before she was given away by the fact that he could read her just as easily as she could him.

"Think I'll take a shower."

It was a shame to throw him off the scent. She would have sworn she felt him watching her, weighing her compliance against the arguments she'd made. There was a knock on the door.

"Time to roll, Vitus." Saxon's voice came through the panel.

Vitus let out a grunt before he turned and walked toward the door. "Stay inside, Princess. Don't take any chances."

"That's my warning for you too, even if I know you won't heed it."

He flashed her a devil-may-care grin that she knew well and damned if it didn't make her belly flutter. He winked at her as he pulled open the door and slipped through it.

She loved him.

It was more than an idea, more than words, more than a feeling. It was something that actually defined her, so completely merged with the fabric of her being. She would never be complete without him, but she would rather live alone, knowing he was safe, than have him risk his life for her.

She knew what she had to do, and it seemed that fate had finally decided to deliver a moment when she could put her plan into action.

Damascus indulged herself in one final moment before she went into the bathroom and washed the scent of him off her skin. She dressed with function in mind before turning her back on the bedroom and her stolen moments with Vitus.

It was time to take charge of the situation.

Time to face her sire.

In shadow games, camouflage was key. That meant Vitus didn't go blindly into whatever situation he'd been instructed to. He crouched down, considering the dock. It was stacked high with steel shipping containers. The type that could be loaded straight onto a rail car or a Big Rig truck. They were muted shades of brown, rust, blue, and black, most of them dented and scraped.

He and Saxon listened for a moment, making sure they were alone before they moved toward one of the containers. There was a chirp as Vitus pressed his hand against an identification pad and his prints were scanned.

Amid the rusty and dented containers, the high-tech equipment was misplaced, until a section of the container opened and they both slipped inside. It was like moving through a portal into another universe. The interior of the container was a communications center, equipped with the latest in computers and satellite links. Inside, an agent was watching them as they entered, his gun drawn.

"Identify yourselves please."

There was a second set of hand scanners inside the container. Saxon flattened his hand on one while Vitus used the other. The agent waited for the chirp from both units before replacing his gun in his shoulder harness. The communications bunker was top secret. The agent wouldn't have hesitated to shoot them. There were deep cover teams that relied on the container when they needed to come in.

"Your section leader is online," the agent said before he slipped on a pair of noise-cancelling earphones. He looked at the screen in front of him, completely ignoring what was happening behind him. It was a hell of a post to end up on but a vital one nonetheless. Vitus looked down to see Kagan on a screen.

"Your dead man is a guy who went by the name of Pratt," Kagan supplied. "A Russian who had a reputation in the French Quarter."

"He was a long way from home," Vitus said.

"So are you," Kagan answered. "And it's time to come in."

Vitus frowned. Kagan didn't miss it. "As much as I'd like to think no one is going to leak this conversation, I know that's hoping for a lot. There are too many connected players on the board at the moment. Better to bring you in while I still have some sort of control."

"That's a stretch." Saxon added his opinion. "I don't think any of us has control at this point."

Kagan nodded. "Maybe you're right, but I have an opportunity. One I plan to make use of."

It was a risk. Vitus felt the sting of that knowledge and bit back the denial he wanted to voice. It was an emotional response, and he couldn't afford such a lapse. Not with Damascus on the line. He needed to be clearheaded.

"What is the plan?" Vitus asked.

Kagan shook his head. "Not on this line. Bring the girl in. Instructions will be waiting for you when you land."

Kagan cut the line. Vitus wanted to smash his hand through the screen in some vain attempt to grab hold of something, anything. The entire operation was like oil floating on the surface of water. All you could manage to do was get your hand covered in it.

But that was a real problem, because that meant he and Saxon could be incriminated just as easily as they might be judged heroes. Saxon was watching him, his eyes full of indecision.

Vitus grunted and straightened up. "We don't have any other options."

He had to force the words out, and his brother didn't like hearing them any more than he enjoyed saying them.

"I'm really going to enjoy shooting Tyler Martin," Saxon said as they left the bunker.

Vitus was used to his brother sticking to the line, the one they'd both lifted their right hands and sworn to uphold when they had accepted their badges. But he knew another side of Saxon too, the part that took a whole lot of shoving to push over the line.

They were both at that point. The problem was, Vitus had no idea if fate was planning on being on their side. The harsh facts were that the deck was stacked against them.

He slowly grinned as they made their way through the

dark docks. It was also a fact that he liked kicking "challenged" in the nuts.

And that was exactly what he was planning on doing.

The opportunity to talk to Dunn should have pleased her. Instead Damascus felt a wave of reluctance that swept her in the opposite direction.

Well, that would be the coward's way out, and one that was likely to land Vitus and Saxon in early graves.

Her blood chilled with the harsh edge of reality that thought unleashed in her. She wasn't being overly dramatic, wasn't playing some sort of game. No, unlike so many of the girls she'd grown up around, she knew the difference between a real problem and a first-world inconvenience.

Jeb wanted blood.

Well, she was going to make sure Jeb was disappointed this time.

Damascus squared her shoulders and moved down the hallway to the office. Dunn's complex had an interesting silence to it, like it was soundproofed. Mostly likely it was, but she admitted to not caring for the feeling it gave her, like she was trapped or imprisoned. She was lifting her hand to knock on the door when it slid open.

"Come in Ms. Ryland." Dunn called from inside an impressive office. "I've been expecting you."

She frowned as she forced herself to cross the threshold then heard the door slip shut behind her. There was a husky chuckle from Dunn. He was sitting behind a massive desk that captured her interest because it looked like it was several centuries old. She couldn't help it, the thing was carved with an elaborate hunting scene complete with three-dimensional horses, hounds, men, even hawks.

"It's Victorian," Dunn supplied. "A family heirloom."

"And you use it?"

He pushed his chair back and stood. Unlike the desk, the chair was modern. with wheels on the feet so that it slid out of his way with a whisper. "I believe in luck, Ms. Ryland. I worked my first business deal on this desk, in the attic where it was collecting dust because my step-mother didn't think my ideas held any merit and she thought the desk was better suited to a museum. She just hadn't found one willing to pay what she knew it was worth." He tapped the top of it with a fingertip. "I went up to the attic, to hide from her judgment. I think you understand what I mean when it comes to overly critical and controlling kin."

Oh boy did she . . .

There was a flicker of satisfaction in Dunn's eyes that she understood. In fact, at that moment she felt it warming her blood, chasing away the hesitation that had been slowing her down.

She locked gazes with him. "Guess I'd use the desk too under those circumstances."

He came around and perched himself on the corner of it. The pose seemed too relaxed for his persona and she contemplated him suspiciously. His lips twitched, finally curving into a smug grin. "Not fooling you, am I?"

She shook her head. "You're trying to put me at ease." It set off a warning bell inside her brain.

"Some people would call that polite," he offered, sounding less than sincere.

Damascus sighed, recalling her purpose. "Most people wouldn't be in this situation."

He offered her a shrug. "How we respond to the challenges life flings at us defines our character."

She laughed. Just a single bark of amusement, but it

gained a smile from him. "I can see how that would be the way you would look at this situation."

Dunn was enjoying the moment hugely, his lips parted in a wide smile.

But she was off-topic again. "I need to discuss business with you."

His demeanor changed instantly, just as Damascus had intended. He stiffened, and eyed her sternly. It was exactly the mood she needed him in.

"I need to leave before anyone else gets caught in the line of fire. You can help me make sure no one else ends up hurt." There, she'd said it. Vitus would be furious, but she had to keep her focus on what he needed as opposed to what he wanted.

Neither of them was going to get what they wished for.

"Except you."

She stiffened her spine. "I am more resourceful than you give me credit for."

His lips curved again, only this time, it was more of a male-appreciation sort of grin. The sight sent a little ripple down her back because she got the impression that he had anticipated her.

Proving her correct, Dunn reached for something on the desktop.

"What is that?" Damascus didn't care for the confidence on Dunn's face. It wasn't a gleeful sort, more of a dead-serious kind and it chilled her blood. He pressed his thumb against the screen, and it flickered to life.

"Whatever you think of me Ms. Ryland, know this. I tell people what they need to know even when I know they aren't going to like it."

The tablet displayed a newscast.

"Earlier today, wife of vice-presidential hopeful Jeb Ryland was taken to Mercy General. The only official report is that Ms. Ryland is suffering from extreme anxiety stemming from the kidnapping and disappearance of her only daughter, Damascus Ryland, who has been missing since last Saturday. Sources inside the hospital claim the congressman's wife's condition is critical and life threatening. The congressman was joined by Carl Davis, both men clearly overcome by concern. Carl Davis's appearance fueled the growing speculation of a joint run for the White House between the two and the possibility of them being united by a soon-to-be-announced engagement. When questioned, Carl Davis had this to say: 'Now is not the time for announcements, unless it's the news we all long for—news of Damascus's whereabouts.'"

Damascus felt her heart stop. She must have held her breath, because one moment she was fixated on the tablet and the fuzzy footage of her mother on a gurney and the next Dunn had her by her upper arms, his grip biting into her because her knees had started to sag. He was muttering as he lifted her up and deposited her into a chair.

Damascus did a little cussing of her own. The profanity earned her a scoff from Dunn, who turned to consider her. He grunted and settled himself against the edge of his desk.

"You love your mother. That much isn't fake about you."

"And you doubted that?" she demanded.

Dunn merely shrugged. "It was a reasonable question to ask. You could be enough like your father to play the innocent."

She bit back the response she wanted to make because she needed to focus and not get her panties in a twist over what was in fact a logical argument.

"You wanted to shock me," she concluded.

He tilted his head to one side and eyed her. "Are you accusing me of being blunt? I'd take that as a compliment."

"Of course you would." The guy had charm oozing out of him. She wasn't blind to it, just wasn't as into it as she was Vitus's head-on approach.

He laughed at her and offered her another shrug as he contemplated her from his perch on the edge of his desk.

"Fine. To the point suits me. I need help getting back to Washington," Damascus stated clearly. "Running isn't my style. Neither is hiding out while other people get shot because they are protecting me."

He enjoyed her answer. She watched his features reflect that before they hardened, hiding his thoughts from her.

"With Carl Davis pairing up with your father, you don't have much of a choice. Unless you've decided to fall into line with their plans and go pick out your wedding dress."

She didn't care for how much truth was in his statement. He knew it too—she saw it flickering in his eyes.

"Well, I am not going to be reduced to hiding in a hole and keeping Vitus and Saxon there with me," Damascus insisted. "I want to go back there and get my mother out of that hospital."

"Something tells me you're asking me for help because you know the Hale brothers are going to have a problem with that little plan." Dunn was up, walking toward the wide expanse of windows that made up the far wall of his office. It gave her a prime view of his back. Honestly, the man was worthy of more than a second glance. Except her fickle emotions just kept comparing him to Vitus and finding him lacking.

"My plan helps them too," she countered. "I need your help because they won't let me cover their tails, but it's the only logical solution."

She heard Dunn chuckle before he turned to look at her. "I believe you're right on that account. I might even consider tossing in with your little idea, just to enjoy seeing them out-maneuvered."

"So what's stopping you?" She was out of the chair and moving toward him. "You've lost an amazing cabin, had to deal with a dead body, and Greer is in the hospital. Come on Dunn, let me define my character. Fate decided that my sire is a scumbag."

"You've sure enough been flung into a mess." His tone had deepened.

Damascus nodded, once. "It's time for me to take action."

"Interesting choice of words," he said as he took a step toward her. "Carl Davis can't marry you if you've already got a husband, and one that he can't make disappear. Marry Greer McRae. He's a Scottish national."

"Oh for Christ's sake. What is it with men and the idea that I need to be married?"

Dunn didn't take offense. He watched her, his eyes starting to sparkle with amusement.

"You know what? Forget I asked you for help," she informed him.

Dunn shook his head. "I never forget, and it's a good solution. You want out of your father's world. Marrying Greer would get you there."

"And my mother will be stuck."

"I can take care of her too," he continued. "Greer is family. I take care of my family."

"So what's in it for you?" The question was out of her mouth before she really thought about it. But she didn't regret giving into impulse. She got the impression she'd get a lot further with Dunn by taking the direct approach.

His expression became unreadable, but another chill touched her. A man like him didn't know how to do anything except play for keeps. He had something up his sleeve all right.

"Let's deal with the immediate issues first," he said.

Damascus recoiled. "I will not marry Greer."

"That's fucking right," Vitus said from the doorway.

Dunn growled, but Vitus only flashed him a look that made it clear he'd enjoy Dunn starting a fight because it would give him an excuse to finish it.

"It's a good solution," Dunn said as Saxon and Vitus came into the office. "Admit it."

Vitus lifted his hand and flipped Dunn the bird before he moved closer to Damascus, planting himself in front of her like a shield. What pissed her off was just how much she enjoyed knowing he wanted to mark his territory. Why in the hell did he always reduce her to such primitive emotions? She had a PhD for Christ's sake. She had a cultivated and educated mind. But with him, she was nothing but a bundle of receptors, and all of them were hardwired to her sex drive.

"No," Damascus interjected. "Admit that I need to go back and face Jeb. That's what I came in here to discuss."

"I hate that idea too." Vitus sent her a look that made it clear he was furious. Damascus sent it right back, but her damn nipples started puckering, undermining her resolve completely.

"My mother is in a hospital. I won't ignore that."

Vitus surprised her by nodding. "We don't expect you to, Princess."

For a moment, she felt a sickening twist in her belly. She could take a lot of things from life, but having Vitus turn into her jailer was one thing she was pretty sure she couldn't deal with. He was the man she fell apart in front of, the only soul on the face of the planet who had seen her stripped down to the core.

"Don't tell me you're going to make me stay here." Her

voice was a mere whisper because she knew she'd lose it if she spoke any louder.

"I want to," he confirmed in a solid, firm tone.

"But we have orders," Saxon interrupted. "So, none of us are getting what we want today."

Vitus's expression cracked, giving Damascus a glimpse at the raw pain he was feeling. Her knees nearly buckled, because she'd never seen him afraid, never even suspected he felt such an emotion. But there it was in his eyes.

No matter what happened, she was going to carry that look with her because it told her what she meant to him, confirming that she was as destructive to his world as he was to hers. What did that mean? She wasn't sure she could put it into words, only feel the burn of it as it traveled through her, leaving behind a brand that she knew she would cherish for the rest of her days.

The fact was, she was going to have to live with it because fate wasn't going to be kind enough to let them have a happily ever after.

No, she couldn't ask for that much. Reality was too sharp for anything so wonderful, but maybe, just maybe, she might be able to trap her sire into hanging himself. One thing was for sure—she was going to make sure he had enough rope for the job.

Tyler Martin looked at his phone as it buzzed. The line was restricted, giving him hope that something was about to break. He needed it, more than he cared to admit. Carl Davis was getting impatient, which meant his confidence was falling.

That was something Tyler couldn't afford, not when he was so close to getting everything he wanted. He wouldn't allow it.

"Meet me," his ex-boss stated clearly. The line went

dead a second later so that Tyler wouldn't have time to trace it.

Tyler slipped the phone back into his suit jacket pocket and started toward the door. Jeb Ryland's office door opened.

"Where are you going?" Tension was showing on the congressman's face. There were deep circles beneath his eyes and a pinched look to his features.

"Running down a possible lead."

Tyler was gone before Jeb had a chance to question him further. Tyler was getting close to being out of patience with the man, something else he admitted he really couldn't allow himself the luxury of. He'd burned a lot of bridges to get into a good position with Jeb Ryland. Bridges that people like Kagan wouldn't forget Tyler had torched.

But Kagan had called him. Sure, it might be a setup but Tyler kept his mind focused on the facts that were stacked against Kagan. His ex-boss might be devoted to justice, but not completely. If Kagan had been unshakable, Tyler would be dead. It was a hard, cold fact, one that sent a little shiver down his spine while he was driving. He'd been helpless, completely in Kagan's power after he'd failed to take out Vitus and Saxon Hale the last time. It would have been simple for Kagan to shoot him and make apologies after the fact. Tyler had to admit that it was very possible Ryland would have let the matter go. After all, dead was dead and there wasn't anything much to be done about it once the trigger had been pulled.

But Kagan hadn't done it and that revealed something about him that Tyler intended to use. Kagan wasn't the all-American Boy Scout he put on he was. No. There was part of him that was just as realistic as Tyler was. A core that Kagan had kept to himself.

Well, today was the day to exploit that part of Kagan.

Who knew? It might just be the beginning of a very
lucrative partnership.

The plane they boarded had a bedroom in the back. Damascus eagerly went into it, ripping the wig off that Vitus had insisted she wear. Red hair was such a pain in
the ass at times. She sat down on the bed, realizing she
was avoiding Vitus. More to the point, she was putting
off the argument she knew he was spoiling to have
with her.

She sighed, feeling drained—and the hard part was
yet to come.

Okay, maybe that wasn't quite so. Dealing with Jeb
wasn't going to be taxing on her emotions, but Vitus? She
was pretty sure she would carry those scars with her for
the rest of her life.

That made her sigh again. She didn't want to fight with
him, didn't want to squander their last few hours on bick-
ering. So she sat on the bed as the plane taxied and the
jets revved up for takeoff. It made the moment more real,
her mouth going dry as she watched the clouds come into
view through a small oval window next to the bed. Time
felt like it was slipping through her grasp, which only
made her more desperate to grip it.

When the door opened and Vitus joined her, one look
at his expression was enough to nudge her closer to the
edge of depression.

"You're mad at me," she said without hesitation.

Vitus hadn't knocked. He had come in and closed the
door behind him, standing for a long moment just considering her with his blue eyes.

"That's right, I am. 'Furious' is actually a more ac-
curate word," he confirmed. "And hiding back here isn't
going to keep me from following you so that we can discuss it."

She was sitting on the bed, still looking out one of the windows. For a moment she contemplated whether or not to talk to him.

Vitus folded his arms over his chest. "What? The silent treatment now, Princess? Telling me what you think suddenly scares you?"

"I don't want to fight." She suddenly smiled and shrugged when his eyes narrowed. "That's one reason, but every time we start to have a conversation in a bedroom, we get . . . distracted." She blushed.

Understanding dawned on him instantly, his expression tightening in a purely sexual way. She recognized it, in more ways than just with her vision. It was like some unspoken communication between them, some critical need that overrode everything else when the opportunity was at hand.

Yeah, like going into heat.

"You shouldn't have gone to Dunn." He was fighting to keep his focus.

She heard the wounded pride in his tone and recognized her mistake. Only it wasn't really an error, not when she recalled just how much her sire wanted Vitus dead. Both of them were going to have to learn to live with reality.

"I love you, Vitus."

He pressed his lips into a hard line, his eyes narrowing.

"So don't fault me for having the same need to protect you. Jeb will kill you, and I can't let that happen. I'll use any means of stopping it, even if it you hate me for it."

He wanted to argue with her. She watched the desire glitter in his eyes.

"You'd do the same," she continued.

"That doesn't mean I like it," he grunted.

"I didn't think you would, but I'm not going to sit by helpless. You'd get mighty bored by that sort of woman."

Direct hit. She watched her words impact, saw the moment when his pride reared its head, before he ended up shaking his head while embracing the fact that she'd called it right.

Damascus smiled. She really shouldn't have, but it was a compliment, and one so completely suited to Vitus. It warmed her from the inside out, cracking the ice that had been freezing over her heart at the prospect of returning home.

"You don't have to leave me."

He was reading her face again but there seemed little point in trying to hide anything. Very soon, she'd have all the time in the world to sit in silence.

"Believe me, Princess." He was darn near shouting at her, but he was also holding her hands. Vitus Hale, who drove her insane with lust and pushed buttons she hadn't known she had, was gently cradling her fingers like a devoted suitor.

It sent tears into her eyes. He made another sound in the back of his throat and leaned forward to kiss her. It was a soft, lingering kiss he pressed against her lips as he rubbed her fingers.

"I love you, Princess." He sat back and dug something out of his pocket. The light coming through the window glittered off a diamond. "Wear it, say you'll marry me."

"I remember this—" her voice caught as tears stung her eyes and her fingers trembled as she reached for it.

"That's not an answer," he said softly, hiding his emotions in a gruff whisper.

Damascus locked gazes with him as she pushed the ring down her finger with a firm motion. She watched his lips lift into a very satisfied grin.

"How's that?" she asked.

Vitus lifted Damascus's hand, looking at the ring on it for a long moment. Victory glittered in his eyes, killing whatever she had been thinking of saying. All she wanted to do was soak up the look of happiness on his face, let it seep deep into her core, where she'd be able to remember it.

Damascus leaned forward and pressed a kiss against his neck, the scent of his skin filling her senses, intoxicating her. She went into it willingly, eagerly reaching for him, finding the buttons on his dress shirt and working them loose.

"You're redirecting, Princess. . . ."

"So tell me to stop." She'd opened four buttons and undid his tie, giving her a magnificent view of his chest. She stroked him, smiling as he sucked in his breath.

"It would be a bald-faced lie," he confessed as he stood up and opened the cuffs of his shirt before shrugging out of it.

She kicked her shoes off before standing. She'd started to grab the sides of the dress when he shook his head and clicked his tongue at her.

"Easy now, Princess." He cupped the sides of her face, holding her still as he locked gazes with her. "This time is going to be slow and steady."

She trembled from excitement and anticipation. The firm connection of their lips curled her toes. The sensation shot down her spine, through her core and along her legs as he worked his mouth against hers, coaxing her to open and let him tease her tongue with his own. The moment became an eternity that she was a willing captive inside of. There was no desire to leave, because she was inside a bubble of pure bliss. She was twisting, writhing with all the points of stimulation and in no hurry to rush to the conclusion.

"That's it." He was trailing kisses along her cheek and then onto her jaw line. "I want to taste you."

And she wanted to touch him. Damascus threaded her fingers through the hair on his chest, enjoying the crispness of it, the sheer maleness. His skin was satin but covered muscles that were rock hard. She purred softly, feeling herself melting. The heat was rising from inside her, making her dress the most uncomfortable thing she'd ever worn.

He sensed it, moving his hands down her body to grasp the fabric and pull it up. She let out a little sigh of satisfaction when it was gone and tossed aside.

"You're so perfect, Princess." He reached out and cupped her breasts, brushing his thumbs over her nipples as they drew into tight points. "I saw these in my dreams for three fucking years. Every damn time I closed my eyes, you were there." She heard the frustration in his voice, or maybe she felt her own. Once again they were counterparts, two sides of the same coin. He leaned over, opening his mouth and sealing his lips around one of her nipples. She gasped, enjoyment racing along her nerve endings. He'd slipped one arm around her back, supporting her as she arched and offered her breast.

"Yeah, three damn years." He scooped her up, cradling her for a moment before laying her on the bed. In the back of her mind, she heard the steady drone of the engines and felt the vibration of flight, but she was much more interested in the way Vitus was opening his pants and shucking them off.

His cock sprang into sight, hard and thick, exactly what she craved. The bed rocked as she flipped over, getting her knees under her before wrapping her fingers around his length.

"Christ," he growled as she stroked, closing her fingers around him and pushing her hand down to the base of his cock as she leaned over and licked one side of his ball sack.

It was bluntly sexual, which she craved from him as much as the tenderness of that first kiss. Now, she wanted to make him squirm, wanted to feel his cock jerk in her grasp and taste his cum because he couldn't hold back.

"Damascus."

His teeth were grinding as she licked around the ridge of flesh that crowned his cock, his body drawn tight as she stroked him and licked the slit on the head. She heard him cuss when she closed her lips around the head and listened as he groaned when she started to suck.

His hand was in her hair, holding her in place even as he made a halfhearted attempt to get her to stop.

"Princess . . . ease up . . ."

She had no intention of doing so. She hollowed her cheeks, sucking harder on him as she used her tongue on the underside of the head, rubbing against that little cluster of nerve endings as she used her hands to stroke the portion of his length she just couldn't get into her mouth.

His grip tightened as he lost control, his cock giving up the load from his balls. She sucked him through it, reveling in the sounds coming from him. Deep male ones that set off a wave of satisfaction inside her.

He pulled her head back, forcing her to release his cock. She looked up his body, enjoying the glitter in his eyes.

"Proud of yourself, aren't you?"

She nodded, forcing him to release her hair or pull it. He let go, but a moment later he was pushing her back onto the bed, parting her thighs and spreading her folds wide. It was a swift reversal of power, an instant transition that left her gasping as she felt vulnerable beneath him.

"I think you should share that sense of victory, Princess." He was watching her, looking up her prone body with a smug curve on his lips. "Since you've made sure I can focus now, I don't plan on wasting the opportunity to induct you into the mile-high club."

He was teasing the curls on the top of her sex as he spoke, sending little ripples of excitement through her clit and across her belly. There was a flash of victory in his eyes before he shifted his attention to her spread body.

"Copper curls," he cooed as he teased them again. "Guys talk about these, know that?" He looked back up her body, flashing his teeth at her.

"No, I wouldn't know that." She choked on her amusement.

"They do, like it's a myth."

Vitus chuckled and pressed her flat on her back with one large hand in the center of her belly. An insane little twist of anticipation went through her as he watched her.

"Can't let my opportunity get away," he muttered before leaning forward.

She felt his breath against her wet folds, a prelude to the first touch of his lips, which sent a shaft of pleasure through her core. She twisted again, unable to remain still. It was simply impossible. Her body was a mass of receptors, all firing off in rapid succession. Vitus gripped her hips, pulling her to him, his shoulders making it impossible for her to snap her thighs shut. She gripped him as he plied his tongue across her clit and closed his lips around the little bundle of nerve endings, sucking until she was crying out with rapture. It was sharp and hard, shaking her to her bones and leaving her a panting mess in the middle of the bed.

Vitus was chuckling with victory. He pushed back onto his haunches, taking a good long look at the state he'd reduced her to. "Now *that* is a very good look on you, Princess."

She snorted at him, trying to compose herself, but his cock caught her attention and her body clenched as she realized she wasn't really satisfied. She wanted him inside her, deep, so that he pushed every bit of reality aside. He knew it, craved it as well. The desire was glittering in his eyes as he cocked a finger at her.

"Come here baby . . ."

It was all the encouragement she needed. Damascus sat up, reaching for his shoulders as he guided her onto his length with a firm grasp on either side of her hips. She was slick and ready, mounting him with ease.

"God," he groaned as she sheathed him. Vitus moved his hands around so that he was cupping both sides of her bottom, lifting her up and letting gravity take her back down. "Goddamn that's good."

It was. Although "good" just wasn't the right word. "Intense" came to mind, right before she lost all grasp on thinking. They were back in that moment, that little wonder-filled bubble where all that mattered was the way they made each other feel. The sheer heights the connection between their bodies produced took command and she was a willing servant, striving toward him as he worked beneath her, driving them toward a final eruption that blew both of them into tiny shards.

Somehow, she ended up on the bed, Vitus curled around her back, his arms locking her in place. She fought off sleep, needing to soak it up, but there wasn't any room in her for fear—even though she knew they were flying toward a date with reality, she just couldn't rise above the security of his embrace. So she didn't, and lay in his arms as sleep claimed her.

So perfect.

It was too bad they were going to have to come back down to earth.

* * *

"Don't look too pleased with yourself."

Tyler didn't bother to change his expression. At least, not at first. Then a hard look from Kagan wiped it clean.

"I'll expect something for that girl." Kagan got down to business. "I'm not stupid enough to not be able to figure out that you're getting a good amount for her."

"So don't cheap you out?" Tyler asked.

Kagan nodded a single time, his attention on the people moving through the park. He liked the view, enjoyed knowing there were still inhabitants of the city who had no idea what other reasons the park was used for. They were content to walk their dogs, push their kids, and take selfies without ever questioning what other people were doing there.

Yeah, that was why he did what he did. For the people who didn't even know he was alive. He wanted to keep it that way, ensure they never had a reason to step outside their own personal snow globes.

"Look at it this way." Tyler Martin laid out his reasoning. "You can't do shit about the way Ryland wants this to end for your men. I know someone who can influence him, maybe go so far as to jerk his chain."

"Carl Davis, no doubt."

Tyler stiffened, giving Kagan a moment of pure enjoyment. "You know I'm not stupid, Tyler. Don't get cocky at this stage of the game. Besides, I'd like to get a bite of that girl myself. She's a ten all the way. Davis has good taste."

Tyler relaxed and even offered him a nod. Kagan hid his revulsion behind a smirk that Tyler mistook for male enjoyment.

"She's got a great package," Tyler said. "But she's out of our league. You're smart enough to know to keep your hands off."

Kagan nodded and kept his lips sealed as he waited for Tyler to spill some information.

Tyler hesitated, clearly rolling the facts through his head before opening his mouth. Kagan didn't say a word, just let the pressure build as time grew longer.

"Fine. Get me the girl, I'll get Ryland off the Hale brothers."

"I'll need some assurance of that," Kagan said, pressing the issue.

Tyler didn't care for it. His lips turned white because of how hard he was pressing them together.

"What? Did you think I would just do it on your word?" Kagan demanded softly. "You waxed two of my men. They were just kids."

"Only because I was ordered to get at the Hale brothers. And if you want to work with me, better get used to handing out a little meat from time to time. At least when we're on top, it won't be *our* blood on the pavement." Tyler was cracking, talking too fast as he jumped to defend himself.

"And you're still under those orders." Kagan tightened the noose. "Maybe I'll just let Dunn Bateson keep her. That man made a very persuasive argument and he'd make a good friend. It's not like it will be very hard for me to convince her it's in her best interest to stay off American soil. Besides, Dunn could just keep her, all I have to do it put it to him the right way. Convince him that she'll come around given enough time with him. Not that I doubt that, she's smart enough. She'll toss in with Dunn when she realizes he can keep her in the style she likes."

"I'll get you what you want," Tyler snapped.

He was off the bench a second later, cutting around people who were moving too slow to suit him.

"That was brilliant." Thais Sinclair spoke into the

microphone taped to the face of a doll she was cradling like an infant against her breast. Kagan didn't look over his shoulder at her, maintaining his position in case Tyler had someone watching him.

Now all they had to do was wait and hope that Tyler went to Davis to expose their link. Without hard evidence, it was nothing but hearsay, and Tyler was right about one thing: the powerful didn't answer to the same set of rules that he did. Carl Davis would walk away without so much as a scratch, even if both Hale brothers were lying in a pool of blood in his entryway.

Not that Kagan expected any evidence to go very far. It was a hard fact that Davis would continue to enjoy his life no matter how much dirt he got caught with on his hands. But maybe, if they got enough luck tossed their way, Saxon and Vitus wouldn't have to die. That wouldn't come for free though.

But both men were worth sticking his neck out for.

"I trust you're here to tell me about a happy event soon to take place in my life."

Carl Davis didn't mince words. He squared off with Tyler, showing off some of his character. Tyler had to admire the man's brass. It told him a lot about just why he was in line for the White House. He was the sort who got things done, no matter the means necessary. The man didn't mind getting his hands dirty. Tyler was getting sick of working for turds like Ryland who ordered shit but wouldn't lower themselves to doing the actual job. It just seemed to him that if Ryland was so hell-bent on seeing Vitus Hale capped, he should be man enough to pull the trigger.

"She's on her way back." Tyler tossed out a sample of what he could do. Davis cracked a smile that he controlled quickly because he wasn't stupid enough to think it was going to be so simple.

"And you need what from me?" Davis inquired smoothly, as easily as he might have ordered a whiskey on the rocks.

"I need Ryland handled," Tyler said. "He has this notion of seeing the Hale brothers dead. I never had anything against them. I set the girl up as bait to satisfy him. Seems it should be *your* call now, since she's going to be your wife and he's lined up as your running mate."

"He's a loose cannon all right," Carl Davis said as he was thinking. "I like the way you think." He'd stepped away from his desk and was pacing. "I like it a lot. Once Damascus is back, I'm going to need you to make sure she keeps that spotless reputation intact."

Carl had stopped pacing and locked gazes with him. Tyler nodded firmly. "Her daddy's obsession is counterproductive to that. Jeb goes off the deep end, and it will splatter onto her."

"Agreed." Carl rocked back on his heels and drew in a stiff breath. "Thank you for bringing it to my attention. I'll deal with it directly."

Carl started reaching for the button that would unlock the office door.

"Just one more thing," Tyler said. "I'm going to need a little time with her, to ensure she returns to you under the conditions you laid out. So the exchange is going to be private."

Understanding crossed Carl's face. For a moment, Tyler Martin witnessed a flare of disagreement, but Carl masked it quickly.

"So long as she's happy to be home and wearing my ring." Carl Davis made his demands clear.

"I will make sure of it."

Carl offered him his hand. Tyler shook it, enjoying the moment a great deal because it was a sure bet that Ryland would never shake his hand. No, he was an underling to Ryland.

"And just as soon as Damascus is attached to me, I'll need you to come on board full time," Carl finished up. "I can't trust my bride to just anyone."

"It will be my pleasure," Tyler answered.

Carl pressed the security button and the outer door popped open. "I look forward to the conclusion of our business, Mr. Martin."

Tyler did too. Of course, there was no way to go but forward. Not that he regretted anything. Damascus Ryland might have a few scrapes and a little less of an ear, but she'd hardly known a harsh life. Born into the elite, she'd been raised with better-grade toilet paper in her bathroom than men like him. It was the new world, the reality he'd warned Kagan to embrace or run the risk of having it flatten him when he refused to clear the path. No one was going to stop the men of the ruling class from doing exactly what they pleased. The best that men like him might hope for was to secure a position in their employ.

Tyler refused to feel guilty about what price he was going to pay for that position. Damascus would settle in. Sure, at the moment, she wanted her lover. Tyler chuckled, not begrudging her that desire. They all got the itch for someone, and she was used to getting what she wanted out of life more so than most people.

Tyler consoled himself with the fact that her fascination with Vitus Hale wouldn't last. A woman like her didn't play by the same rules as the rest of the world. Monogamy was nothing more than a necessary sham, used to make people beneath her think she was a good person. In reality, she didn't even have the same definitions of the word "good."

At least Kagan had come around. That was a relief. It also opened up a whole lot of doors that would led to opportunities once Damascus was back in her world. Then Tyler could get on with carving out his niche with the help of Kagan's contacts, which were numerous and varied.

He grinned as he pulled away from Carl Davis's house, looking forward to a bright future. It was a double shot of good luck to realize that he wasn't going to have to silence Kagan. Hell, the man really was connected better than anyone Tyler knew. Leaving him alive while Kagan counted him among his enemies wasn't the wisest idea.

But as someone he could do business with? Well now, that was definitely something Tyler enjoyed the idea of.

CHAPTER EIGHT

"We're doing what?" Vitus was using his quiet voice. Damascus felt a tingle go down her spine because she knew he was enraged.

So did everyone else in the room. It was a nondescript room, nothing but a desk and a few chairs, but what was laid out on the desk drew her attention. Vitus's section leader had brought along a selection of tiny cameras, and she didn't need anyone to explain their purpose. No, she'd been reared with one simple ideology: Never, ever, let anyone get evidence on you. Her father's office was soundproofed and had a door that locked like a safe just to make sure what went down inside its walls stayed secret.

"Tyler Martin came to me and wanted to work a deal." Kagan said. "It's the break we've been looking for."

"Actually." Saxon was deep in thought. Vitus turned on him, but he shot his brother a hard look. "Think it through. We've got nothing but his word."

"Which won't stand up against her father threatening her mother," Kagan added. "Now that Pratt is dead, there is no one to tie the kidnapping to Tyler Martin."

"We know he was behind it," Vitus said.

"We suspect, " Kagan corrected. "Which isn't worth a wooden nickel. It's only a matter of time before my hand is forced and she's returned to her father. He'll make her roll over once that happens."

Dunn offered a solid nod in agreement.

Damascus bit her lip. Her pride wanted to rear its head, but she decided that listening was more important than telling them that she'd rather die than toss in with her sire. But Kagan didn't miss it. His attention shifted to her for a moment as he noticed her teeth worrying her lower lip. When Vitus looked her way she lost her grip on her self-discipline.

"I'm in," she said firmly, reaching for one of the cameras. "Where does this go?"

Vitus lifted it out of her hands. "It's not that simple."

She faced off with him. "I didn't think it would be, but I came back here to face Jeb and that is exactly what I plan on doing."

There was a crusty chuckle from Kagan. "I like her."

Vitus looked back toward his section leader. "Tyler Martin arranged that kidnapping." Vitus returned his attention to her. "He has no conscience. If you're somehow in the dark about that, just reach up and feel your ear."

"What I am, is ready to deal with this."

There was a flicker of approval in his eyes. She saw it and offered him a smug smile in response. Vitus cussed softly under his breath. "I hate the idea of it, Princess. Your father is no novice and neither is Tyler Martin. Once he gets you back on his ground, it's going to be very hard to protect you."

"Really hard," Dunn added, looking at a three-dimensional model of her father's estate on a big screen.

"I know," she offered as she tried to ignore the shiver that went down her spine. With Vitus agreeing, reality was happy to start flooding her brain with doubt. "But it isn't your fault I was born into this family. I want out and honestly, isn't it only fair that I have to earn that? I'd be just like my sire if I thought otherwise."

"Glad to know we're a team again." Kagan took charge of the meeting. His gaze seemed to be even stronger than his massive physical person. If there was a weak spot on the man, she couldn't find it, unless she factored in his devotion to the team. A man like Tyler Martin would exploit that honorable trait and use it against him.

"Tyler Martin thinks I'm going to trade Ms. Ryland for him getting the congressman off you two," Kagan elaborated. "He's smart enough to know where to aim when it comes to me."

"Still have trouble swallowing the fact that Tyler came to you," Vitus said with a shake of his head. "Didn't see that one coming."

"To his way of thinking," Kagan explained, "he's just helping me accept the way the world works."

"I don't doubt it." Damascus put herself back into the conversation. "There are an awful lot of people in Washington who don't know how to relate to one another unless they are buying or selling."

"Your father is one of those." Kagan stated his opinion as he held her stare. It was a test, one she didn't flinch away from. She looked straight back at him before pointing at the cameras.

"Like I said, I don't expect to get out without facing him. I told your men this in Scotland. I will not hide behind them."

Vitus grunted and Saxon shifted closer, clearly unhappy with her statement.

"Not that I am not grateful."

"Shut it, Princess," Vitus interrupted her. "You don't want to hide behind me? Too bad. I am not stepping aside."

"Neither am I," Saxon added in a tone she'd rarely heard from him. Saxon was always the cool-headed brother, the man with a grip on his emotions. It was slipping now, giving her a glimpse at what he'd kept hidden. She recognized it because he had a whole lot in common with Vitus. God help anyone who got on his bad side, and Tyler Martin clearly had.

She was hoping that God would let Tyler get what was coming to him. The slimeball had ordered someone to cut her. It was going to be her pleasure to help bring him down.

"Well, you can't do this without my help," Damascus told them both. "Jeb will never spill his guts anywhere but in his office, and I am the only person here who can get inside that room."

Vitus didn't like it, but she watched him accept the logic of her words. She turned back to Kagan.

"Want to show me how these work? I earned a degree in microbiology. They didn't cover surveillance cameras."

Kagan's lips twitched, and she got the impression that was very telling. He wasn't a man who let anyone see his true feelings easily. He picked one up and began to explain it.

Damascus felt a chill go down her spine, but she decided she liked the sensation because it meant she was moving forward. It was a path that would separate her from Vitus but give her the knowledge that he was safe.

And that was worth everything, even risking her life.

He still didn't like it. Damascus felt Vitus's disapproval like there was a wire connecting them. The tiny camera was tucked into her bra with a second one attached to the dragonfly. She looked at herself in a mirror, trying to stand naturally and not give herself away. Vitus finally

sighed, even if the sound came out as more of a dissatis-
fied male grunt.

"Give us the room." There was solid authority in his
voice and the rest of the team didn't hesitate to respond
to it. Even Kagan made for the door, closing it firmly
behind him.

Damascus turned to look at Vitus and found herself
being scrutinized. He was in a pose she recognized, feet
braced shoulder-width apart with his arms crossed over
his chest. His expression was stone and gave nothing
away, but his eyes, those Caribbean blue eyes, were full
of emotion. What warmed her most was the flicker of approval. It made her confidence grow, giving her a sense
of ability to see the mission through.

"You'll do just fine, Princess."

His tone was husky and warm. She didn't hear his feet
touch the floor but he was suddenly there, in front of her,
his hands smoothing across her cheeks until they settled
into a firm grip on the side of her head. She knew he was
going to kiss her. Time slowed down, allowing her to notice every second of his approach. Sensation went tearing through her, warming her blood and leaving her skin
tingling. Only his touch did that to her, awakened her
senses like she'd been locked in a dark cell prior to the
moment when he put his hands upon her. It was the purest definition of life, the essence of it, and the substance
that restored her soul.

Vitus withdrew, but he lifted her hand and looked at
his ring winking at them both from her finger.

"Kind of wish I'd be there to see your father notice
you're wearing my ring." He lifted her hand and kissed
it gently. "I'm sure that's going to be entertaining."

She snorted at him.

There was a rap on the door before it opened. "Time
to roll," Saxon said.

He wasn't happy, but what shocked her was the look of confidence in his eyes. It was the last bit of encouragement she needed to walk through the door. The future was gray but she moved into it without hesitation.

The reason was simple: she had to. There was no room in her mind for anything that didn't include freeing Vitus from the mess that meeting her had saddled him with.

Her sire better get ready. She wasn't a little girl anymore.

"Ready?" Kagan asked.

Damascus flashed him a smile that earned her a raised eyebrow. "I doubt you ask Saxon or Vitus if they're ready."

It was just her and Kagan in a nondescript, tinted-window sedan. She'd spent her life riding around in similar ones. They had bulletproof glass and enough horsepower under the hood to make quick getaways when the need arose. There were also handy pockets designed right into the doors and the center console for guns of all calibers.

The driver turned the corner, bringing a deserted section of the dock into view. There were puddles of water and bits of cardboard littering the cracked asphalt. Ahead was another tinted-window sedan. They eased up as they got closer, stopping a hundred yards from it.

"Showtime," Kagan muttered.

He pushed open his door and climbed out. The other man started walking toward him. They met between the cars, stopping to talk for a moment.

"Sorry miss, but I need to put these on you."

The driver had turned around and had a pair of handcuffs dangling from his fingers. Damascus nodded, a shudder moving through her as she stuck her hands out and felt the cold metal slipping around her wrists. She flinched when the driver snapped them closed, but succeeded in drawing in a deep breath.

"And this."

Damascus looked up to see the driver holding a small caliber handgun. He held it up, making sure she got a good look at it before he slipped it into a holster. "It straps around your thigh."

He had secured only one side of the cuffs, allowing her to slip the strap around her thigh and lower her skirt before offering her hands to him again. She was quivering, the knowledge that she just might have to shoot Jeb almost overwhelming, though not in a bad way. There was a deep solace in it, a confirmation that things would then truly be over.

Would she be damned to hell for it? Maybe, but Vitus would be free. Part of her toyed with killing Jeb just because it would be far more final than getting evidence against him.

Well, you'll be just like him if you do . . .

That thought sobered her, making her return to their plan. Vitus couldn't love a cold-blood murderess. Kagan opened the door next to her and reached in. He hauled her out like an errant child.

"To tell the truth, I'm glad to be rid of her." Kagan gave her a shove. She stumbled and ended up running into Tyler Martin.

"Yeah, I have the feeling I'm going to be real happy to turn her over to her daddy," Tyler agreed.

The disgust in his voice caught her attention. Damascus started blubbering as she reached for Tyler's shirt, clawing at him. "You have . . . have . . . to take me home! I need my dad!"

"See what I mean?" Kagan said. "Honestly, the money better be good or I'll tell you straight out, man, you picked the wrong team to work for if she's what you have to put up with. At least I can shoot people in my job."

"Tyler . . ." Damascus whined. "You have to take me home now!"

Kagan chuckled and waved Tyler off. Damascus bit her lip to keep from laughing. Tyler wheeled her around and strong-armed her into the waiting car. She dropped into the backseat and stuck her wrists out.

"Unlock me," she demanded.

"Not a chance." Tyler Martin slammed the door in her face. When he climbed in beside her, she sniffed indignantly at him.

"You have to do what I say."

Tyler aimed a cold, smug little smile at her. Her belly tightened, threatening to heave with disgust.

"You will be the one doing what your told," Tyler informed her. He was enjoying himself too. She witnessed the flare in his eyes that reminded her a whole lot of the way her sire looked when he was getting on with trying to impose his will on her.

A sick flash of personal entitlement.

"You are going to marry Carl Davis," he informed her as calmly as he might have instructed her on the proper use of a soupspoon.

She lifted her nose into the air and sniffed. "Of course I am. Do you think I'm stupid or something? He's going to be the next president."

That surprised Tyler. He recoiled just a tiny bit as the driver pulled them around the corner and into traffic.

"Please . . ." Damascus rolled her eyes. "I was only making sure I had his full attention. At least until the engagement was announced. Is that too much to ask? I know he's screwing that little press bitch and her boyfriend too. I just wanted my fair slice of his time."

He dug some keys out of his breast pocket and opened the handcuffs. "Give me one moment's grief, and I'll truss you up again."

She gave him what she hoped was a "get real" look before she yanked a tissue out of the center console and started to fix her face in a mirror. "Honestly, I look like roadkill. Better make sure no one gets a picture of me. Carl will have a fit."

"She's not bad," Kagan said.

"Got to agree," Dunn added.

Vitus didn't say anything, but it was the honest truth that he was proud of Damascus. She had Tyler fooled. The car was making steady progress toward the Ryland estate. There was a bitter taste as a memory stirred.

'The bad guys win . . . a lot.'

He knew it, had been face-to-face with that harsh edge of reality more than once. He just hoped that today wouldn't end up being another one of those cases.

"Baby!"

Damascus hadn't expected her mother to be home. It was a relief that nearly swept her off her feet. Miranda Delacroix was out the front door before Damascus got out of the car.

"Mom!"

For one, blissful moment, she was in her mother's arms.

"Now Miranda, you shouldn't be up." Jeb came through the double doors that connected to his office. "Where is that nurse I hired to look after you?"

"Oh really, Jeb." Her mother let her go and looked at her husband. "I don't need a home nurse."

"I will be the judge of that," her sire snapped, but he stepped back when her mother sent him a stern look.

"Well now," her sire backpedaled, "I'm just so worried about you."

"You're so sweet to be concerned about me," her

mother cooed but turned back to Damascus and slipped an arm around her waist. "But I have to be a mother right now. Our daughter needs me."

Her mother swept her right past Jeb and into the house. Somewhere, Tyler was whispering to her sire, but that didn't keep Damascus from seeing the way his complexion had darkened.

For sure, the second shoe was going to drop just as soon as Jeb could figure out how to get around his wife. For just a moment, a tingle of suspicion went down her back. There was something in her mother's smile that hinted at her being more aware of the undercurrents surrounding her than she'd ever let on.

You're just seeing what you want to see.

Maybe. But one thing was certain: her sire was going to take issue with her the second he could.

Well, bring it.

The congressman's security was good.

But Vitus was better.

He waited, listening to the footfalls of the guard rising up behind him like a shadow. The man never knew what hit him. Vitus locked his arm around his throat, cutting off the blood supply to his brain and holding still until he slumped into an unconscious heap.

Saxon pulled the cap off a syringe and injected the contents into the guy's arm before Vitus dragged him behind a row a perfectly clipped shrubs.

They moved closer to the house, skirting along the edge of the shadows and taking out the surveillance cameras with an infrared laser. Dunn kept pace with them expertly well. For a half second, Vitus pondered just where the man had gotten his training. No one came by knowledge like that by instinct. It was drilled into a man. Dunn knew it, had experienced it, which left Vitus curious as to the man's past and his relationship with Kagan.

Vitus returned his focus to the mission. He couldn't falter now. Before, it had only been his life on the line. Now, there was so much more.

Kagan dialed Colonel Magnus's personal cell phone. It buzzed a few time before he answered.

"Should I be surprised that you have this number?" Bryan asked.

Kagan chuckled. "Be surprised that I have a picture of you in a pirate costume holding a parrot."

There was a clipped word on the other end of the line before the Colonel chuckled. "Every man has his form of letting loose. But considering one of your teams was investigating my daughter earlier this year, I can understand why you have those pictures. The parrot's name is Harley. Why did you call?"

"I just returned Ms. Ryland to Tyler Martin, sort of thought you'd like to know your asset is back on home soil."

There was a long pause. "I'm an hour outside of Washington. Magnus out."

Kagan didn't get surprised often. He sat there, looking at the disconnected call and discovered himself blindsided. He checked his Intel again and it clearly showed Colonel Magnus in California. It was a telling bit of information, one that he enjoyed knowing. Dunn Bateson was the only link to Magnus. One Kagan needed to remember.

"I've sent your mother to bed."

The other shoe had dropped. Damascus turned to see her sire coming through the doorway of her bedroom, Tyler Martin on his heels. It wasn't the presence of the security man that chilled her blood, it was the absence of any other personnel. The house was eerily quiet, as in dead silent.

Well, it was a fitting backdrop. It also suited the feeling of the gun against her thigh. Keeping the weapon hidden had been a chore as her mother tried to help her. It had been worth it. Without a doubt, it was do or die time.

"And this time, her nurse has made sure she'll stay there," Jeb informed her with a nasty little sneer.

"You should be ashamed," Damascus admonished him. "My mother has always done exactly what you wanted."

"Yes, she has," Jeb answered with a frown. "Until today. That's one more thing you are going to answer for, Damascus. Mark my words on that."

"Actually, it's going to be your turn to answer for a few things." She stood her ground, enjoying it far more than she'd anticipated she might.

Her sire was less than impressed. He offered her a slow, amused smile as he spread his hands out. "How do you propose to do anything of the sort?" He backhanded her. The blow sent her staggering, but she recovered quickly. Martin was waiting for her, reaching out to grab a handful of hair. She cried out as he wrenched her in front of her sire.

Jeb grunted, satisfied like a glutton at a buffet table. She struck in the moment, lifting her knee and kicking her foot up into his throat. The front snap kick worked as well, granting her a shot of confidence as she mentally thanked Vitus for training her.

Jeb recoiled, sputtering as Tyler jerked her back. Pain tore through her scalp, but she ended up tumbling away and gaining her freedom. She scrambled to her feet, kicking her useless shoes off. But when she turned to face her sire, she was looking down the barrel of a gun. Tyler

Martin had it leveled at her face, just far enough away to keep her from making a try at disarming him. She needed him off balance, mad enough to spill information.

And the truth was, she was going to enjoy every second of pushing his buttons.

Jeb was wiping his lips with a handkerchief, his complexion pale. There was a tremble in his fingers as he shoved the soiled linen into his suit jacket pocket. "I had really hoped to avoid this, Damascus. Truly I did, but it seems I must take you in hand." He looked at Tyler. "I believe some privacy is in order. My office if you please."

"She was right," Saxon said. "Bastard has a sealed office."

"Will the link still work?" Vitus demanded.

Dunn looked up from the tablet he was watching Tyler Martin and Damascus on. "It should."

"That's not fucking good enough," Vitus bit out.

"I know," Dunn countered. "We'd better get in there."

Saxon was already overriding the house security system. Vitus pulled a pair of pliers out of his pants pocket and watched his brother, judging the timing before he reached into the loosened security panel and jerked a wire free. There was a soft buzz before the whole thing went dead. Dunn jammed a crowbar into the door, and wood split as it gave.

The lack of response from anyone inside the house sent a chill down his spine. It had all the makings of a perfect unsolved crime. No witnesses and he and his team had been the ones to take out the security systems. There was going to be a body on the floor, and it chilled his blood as he considered just whose it might be.

"You see Damascus, your duty to me has always been to bring attention and votes."

Jeb Ryland's words fueled Vitus's effort as he took off

into the house, scared for the first time in his life as he undertook a mission.

Fucking scared to death that he was going to fail.

One chance.

One last chance.

The feeling was strangely euphoric, an unexpected mixture of anticipation and gut-wrenching dread.

It felt like her brain was moving in slow motion. She could clearly hear each beat of her heart, could notice the way she picked up each of her feet, bent each knee, and then lowered each foot to the floor while the office door got closer and closer.

It was the point of no return, like a pit where she and her sire were going to enter to fight, and only one of them was going to be left standing when the door opened.

She felt Vitus's frustration, would have sworn there was a current connecting them as Tyler marched her through the doorway. They were sealed inside, her fate in her own hands.

Well, it was the way it needed to be. If she didn't walk out, she would die contented because she'd been worthy of the man she loved.

The house echoed with the footfalls of men running like in some sort of action movie. Outside, the rain was thrashing against the windows and hailing down on the roof. Inside, the heavy pounding of booted soles was muffled by double-cushioned carpeted hallways.

But the connection of a fist against the outer door of Jeb Ryland's sealed office ricocheted through the house. If will alone could have taken down the barrier, it would have crumbled.

"Fuck," Vitus snarled. He checked the cell phone, gaining a horrifying glimpse of what was happening on the other side of the wall. The image froze and flickered as it bounced off a satellite and back down onto his screen.

He stepped back and kicked the door. Saxon joined him, but the door held.

"It's reinforced," Dunn snapped. "Nothing short of C-4 is getting through it."

"We'd better find some and fast," Vitus snarled. "Kitchen." It was the only place in the house where there might be something they could use to make an explosive.

"Now." Jed Ryland was clearly feeling back on his turf and in control. He shrugged out of his suit jacket and tossed it toward the huge, padded chair behind his desk. He moved back toward her and sent her reeling with another hard strike across her face. Damascus made a show of stumbling and falling.

"I won't do it," she snapped at him, taking solace in the feeling of the gun against her thigh. She stayed on the floor, reaching for it.

"You will do whatever I say!" Jeb snarled.

There was a click as the door popped open. Damascus bit her lip to keep from crying out. It was too soon. Her sire hadn't said anything yet. But it was her mother who calmly walked through the door and pressed a small remote that she tucked back into her pocket as the door began to close behind her.

"Mom?"

Her mother offered her a smile but this one wasn't soft and it wasn't unknowing.

"Miranda. Really, what are you doing here?" Jeb was knocked for a loop, reeling as he brushed his hair back and blinked as though that would somehow make his wife disappear.

"I told you Jeb, I'm here to be a mother," Miranda

informed him. "You seem to not understand what being a parent means. I've been very disappointed in you for several years now, but I truly never thought you'd go so far as kidnapping."

She shook her head and removed the remote from her pocket. "Still, one must always be prepared for the bumps in the road life offers up."

Jeb gaped at his wife. "How?"

"How did I know you arranged for our daughter to be abducted?" Miranda smiled softly. "I am a Delacroix. Everyone who is anyone wants to be connected to my family. That's why you married me after all."

Jeb Ryland pressed his lips into a hard line. "Quite right. And"—her sire returned to his objective—"she is going to marry Carl Davis and I will be his running mate, putting us in line for a run in another eight years. Exactly what your family would approve of."

Her sire had raised one finger into the air, as if he was instructing pupils in a private school.

"Don't be ridiculous Jeb. Carl is gay. That sort of thing will get out," Miranda Delacroix admonished her husband. Damascus struggled to her feet, blinking in astonishment as she looked at her mother.

This certainly was a side of her Damascus had never seen.

"Miranda," her sire sighed. "Really, this simply must be done. I thought to have it over and finished while you slept. You're too soft with Damascus, always have been. I've been driven to these measures."

Her mother offered Jeb a smile that was very knowing for a change. "Ah yes, while I slept. With the help of those pills you had your man hand me. Or, dear me, I mean personal nurse? Really Jeb, you must think me an idiot." There was a fire in her mother's voice that intrigued Damascus. Her mother sent her a look that was bright with impending victory. "I drank a cup of vegetable oil before going upstairs. It's going to go right to my hips, but it coated the lining of my stomach. So, if you think you are going to get up to any shenanigans with our daughter, you are sadly mistaken."

Her sire scoffed at his wife. "Miranda, don't make this harder on yourself than necessary. You're setting a bad example for our daughter. "

"On the contrary, I seem to be the only one showing her how to behave," her mother shot back. "I've played the part you wanted, but now you've gone too far."

Jeb snorted at his spouse. "Too far? The hell I've gone too far! You always knew what I wanted. The White House. We had an agreement, one your father shook my hand over." He pointed at Miranda, his complexion going dark. "And you are going to continue to hold up your end of the deal? You will be everything I want you to be! Both of you will."

"My father would have drawn the line at having me admitted to a hospital and pumped full of drugs, and he certainly would have baulked at having his granddaughter kidnapped." Her mother was facing Jeb, steady and confident.

"She was being put in her place," her sire snapped. "That's the job of any parent. Your father was man enough to not pull his punches. I witnessed him getting his hands dirty plenty of times. Why do you think he agreed to our marriage?" Jeb snickered. "You've played the innocent well, but we both know you're not as innocent as you make out."

Her mother only raised an eyebrow. "What I have to hide is nothing anymore. It certainly isn't murder or kidnapping."

Her sire was shaking his head and offering her mother a smirk. "Exactly Miranda. You were smart enough to know that you couldn't follow your heart, are you going to stand by while our daughter does?" He cast a look at Damascus. " I expect your full support in getting her under control. By any means necessary."

Tyler Martin was there. Damascus felt his hand grip her nape, turned and found herself looking down the barrel of a gun. She steeled herself and reached for her own, forcing herself not to think about having to shoot her own blood. She'd do what had to be done to protect Vitus.

She touched the top of her pistol, pulling it free of its holster.

She wouldn't have done anything differently. She drew in a deep breath and straightened, accepting her fate while staring straight at her enemies. She tightened her grip on the gun, settling her finger over the trigger.

Her mother reached out and stroked her cheek. "My sweet baby girl."

Her mother finished stroking her cheek, all the way to her jaw line. A second later, she'd wrenched the gun from Tyler's grip, turned around, and fired at Jeb.

The discharge was deafening, echoing through the office. Her sire flopped back like a fish, floundering on the expensive carpet as blood bubbled up onto his lips. Tyler grabbed the gun and than cussed when he realized he'd put his prints on top of her mother's. He dropped it before moving toward her father's desk. There was a click as a portion of the wall opened. Tyler Martin was gone in a blink of an eye.

"Good riddance," Miranda said.

Damascus's mother was calmly shrugging out of her clothing, dropping it all into the fireplace. The flames caught the cotton garments easily, reducing them to ashes in moments. She walked to the closet, pulled out one of her husband's coats, and slipped it on, all the while ignoring the lasts struggles for life that Jeb made. Bright red blood had been pushed out and over his chin, dripping down into the perfectly pressed collar of his shirt. His body stiffened, his hands contorting into claws as he fought to hold onto life. But there was no fending off death. It stole him away with his eyes open as if he refused to surrender.

Her mother knelt down and closed them for him. Damascus stood there, the little gun in her hand, shocked to her core. There was an explosion, and the door to the office flew open. A cloud of hot air rushed at them as Damascus coughed and covered her eyes. When the dust settled, Vitus was there with a gun leveled at her mother. Saxon and Dunn were right on his heels. Miranda surprised them all by maintaining her composure. She waited until everyone had time to see her before she stood up and moved away from the body of her husband.

"Are you injured?" Vitus was in mission mode. He reached out and grasped Damascus's wrist, pulling her behind him as he scanned the rest of the office.

"No," she replied. "My mom—"

"Was a witness to it all," Miranda interrupted. "Truly terrible, but I do suggest you get after that Tyler Martin. He's escaped down the hatch under my husband's desk, but you will find his prints on the murder weapon."

"Ah . . . Mom," Damascus said softly, "I was wearing a camera."

Her mother looked at her for a long moment and then surprised her again by offering a little sound of approval. "Of course you didn't come in here unprepared. You are a Delacroix."

It was the sort of compliment she'd never expected to get from her mother.

Miranda cast a look toward the body of her husband. "Do put that gun away, Damascus. If any member of this family was going to shoot Jeb, it was going to be me." Her mother's attention was on the gun in her hand. Mother and daughter looked at each other as if for the first time.

"We couldn't get through that damn door without a bomb." Vitus sent her a glare. "You could have been killed."

"As if you have never risked your neck." Damascus replaced the gun, once again feeling like it didn't matter who was in the room, she only had eyes for Vitus.

"Not without damn good reason."

"Fighting my own battles is a very good reason. So is making sure my wacked family doesn't kill you," Damascus fired back. "I am not your princess."

"The hell you aren't."

He pulled her to him, intending to kiss her, but all Damascus ended up doing was getting crushed against his chest. Her head was filled with the sound of his heart and there was no way to miss the tremor in his arms. She sighed, the scent of his skin filling her senses, triggering all of the emotional responses that she always had for him.

Why was it impossible to have a future with him?

Because you signed a contract with Colonel Magnus . . .

She dug her fingers into his shirt, intent on holding on to him just as long as possible.

But it had to end. She heard more people arriving, their footsteps sounding like the pounding of a gavel. The sharp sound one designed to separate her from the man she loved. Tears stung her eyes and she forbid herself to let them escape.

She couldn't.

Mustn't.

Vitus had been strong for her and now she needed to repay him in kind. She drew in a last, deep breath, trying to savor the moment, before she pushed against him. He let her go, reluctantly allowing her to place distance between them. She blinked away the tears, determined to face their parting with the same courage that he would if he was doing the same for her. That idea gave her the strength to take a step away from him and look him in the eye.

For the last time.

"Welcome back Ms. Ryland."

Damascus turned to discover Colonel Magnus watching her. He seemed perfectly at ease with a body laying a few feet behind him, not even sparing it a glance. She was having a hard time grasping the situation herself. She looked at her sire, needing confirmation that he really was dead.

"Nice work, Hale."

Vitus actually clicked his heels together and snapped the colonel a salute. "Thank you sir."

The Colonel's attention moved to Dunn. "Well done, for a civilian."

Dunn cracked a grin in response and offered Magnus a double-finger obscene gesture. The colonel's eyebrow rose, but so did Dunn's lips. The colonel decided to shift his attention back to her.

"You have precisely one hour left, Ms. Ryland."

Vitus looked between them, a frown on his face that quickly turned deadly. "I don't follow."

Damascus got a glimpse of a rare sight—surprise flickering across Bryan Magnus's face—before he offered her a pleased expression. "I am pleasantly impressed; didn't think you had it in you, Ms. Ryland."

There was a note in the colonel's voice that made her want to preen, because Damascus knew without a doubt he wasn't a man to say something he didn't absolutely mean.

"Have what, in her, sir?" Vitus demanded as he moved in front of her. He wasn't happy, and Saxon moved back toward them as he heard the tone of his brother's voice.

"The resolve to keep her involvement with me from you," Colonel Magnus replied.

"You said it was classified," Damascus defended herself. "And I might add, you outlined some rather nasty reprisals I should expect if I didn't keep my mouth shut."

"All of it true," Magnus confirmed. "But I was just doing my job."

"Are you telling me."—Vitus was piecing it together quickly—"that you contracted—"

"With my team." The colonel interrupted. Dr. Ryland is going to be working in my classified germ lab," he said firmly. "And she has one hour before I have her remanded into custody for missing her report-in time."

"I was in protective custody," Damascus defended herself again. "Hiding from the bad guys, and your men didn't exactly ask me if I wanted to go."

"Yes. Considering the circumstances, we'll skip the trial this time." Colonel Magnus lifted his wrist to reveal an actual wristwatch. "Fifty-nine minutes."

Damascus drew in a deep breath and locked gazes with Vitus. "I didn't see any other way out of my father's plans for me."

"You mean any other way of protecting me," Vitus answered back.

"Yes, and I don't regret it." She began to work the engagement ring off her finger. Vitus clamped his fingers over hers.

"We have fifty-eight minutes to get married, Princess."

"Didn't you hear me?" she asked. "I have to report or be arrested. You know what a classified lab is."

"Sure do," Vitus replied with a grin on his face that confused her completely.

Dunn was choking on his amusement and Saxon was rolling his eyes, but Vitus was simply aiming that bright, happier-than-she'd-ever-seen-on-him smile at her. It made her believe anything was possible, the way his eyes sparkled, driving a bolt of hope straight into her heart. It didn't make any sense, but it was Vitus, so there wasn't really a point in trying to understand.

"So, we just get married and it's no problem?" It sounded lame because it was just too simple and she was some genius for having never asked about spouses.

Vitus nodded. "Because I also hold a classified clearance level."

"That's the way it works," the colonel confirmed.

"He can come with me?"

"Yes, I can," Vitus double assured her. "We just have to get hitched."

It was surreal moment, one in which it felt like water suddenly started flowing uphill, because what had been impossible was now somehow achievable, so amazingly within reach. Damascus realized she was trembling, petrified by the idea of making a grab for the thing she'd spent so much time trying to convince herself was impossible to have.

"Fifty-six minutes." The Colonel cleared his throat and held a folded paper out to Vitus. There was a crinkle as Vitus opened it.

"Knew you'd be on a tight time schedule," Bryan Magnus explained as they both read through the marriage license, "so I came prepared." He checked his watch again. "Fifty-four minutes remaining."

But she stopped and looked past Dunn to where her

mother was watching. There was a bright smile on her lips, only this time it seemed more sincere.

"Mom . . ."

Damascus had gone past the colonel but her mother caught her hands and clasped them. "I am so happy for you, baby. You are so clever, slipping out from beneath your father's nose."

"Really?" she asked.

"Why do you think you are an only child, Damascus?" Her mother surprised her yet again. "One year into my marriage and I knew your father was a monster. I was so happy you were a little girl, who wouldn't feel the need to be Jeb Ryland's son. I only stayed in this marriage to make sure I could be your mother. If I'd divorced him, he would have made it difficult to see you, and I needed to be under the same roof to truly know what was going on. In case I had to make sure he couldn't hurt you."

"I never suspected."

Miranda nodded, satisfaction glowing in her eyes. "Good. It was my mistake, being duped into marrying Jeb." She looked past Damascus. "I realize I have committed murder, but I wonder . . . is it possible for me to see my daughter's wedding before you have me arrested?"

The men in the room were frozen. Damascus wished she could have appreciated the moment more because it was for certain they weren't the type to get shocked often. It was Kagan who reached over and took the iPhone Saxon held. There was a crunch and a snap as he folded the thing in half. "The thing about sending away all your personal security is you never know who just might be waiting for an opportunity to get you alone."

"You'd think a congressman would know better," Colonial Magnus added.

"Well, he was knee deep in some sort of shady

business with Pratt," Dunn added. "I came all the way over here to confront him, but he was already dead. Seems Tyler Martin has a few things to answer for."

"He slipped out sure enough," Saxon said.

"Really," Miranda interrupted. "I am fully aware of my actions."

"Now Mrs. Ryland." Kagan cupped her shoulder. "Seems to me that you were given a very heavy dose of medication by a certified nurse tonight. No one will expect you to have any information to add to the investigation in the morning."

Her mother sighed. "Tyler Martin knows the truth."

"We'll make sure the Secret Service questions the nurse first," Kagan confirmed. "Which gives you time to witness a wedding before getting back to your room while that nurse is sleeping. As for Martin, I have a murder weapon with his prints on it. If he comes forward, my evidence will blow his testimony out of the water."

Miranda brightened. "Thank you, and a Delacroix never forgets a favor done for them."

Damascus was shocked all over again because her mother was someone to be reckoned with.

Colonial Magnus cleared his throat. At some point, he'd pulled a sash out and had it draped over his shoulders.

"You're a justice of the peace?" Damascus asked incredulously.

He nodded. "Back when I made captain, I wanted to be able to perform weddings. Looks like it's coming in handy tonight."

Dunn considered the private nurse. The guy was hugging a bottle of tequila as he snored. Men like him turned his stomach. Any medical professional who would dope a woman for a paycheck wasn't a real man in Dunn's book.

The nurse would wake up with a hell of a headache, but Dunn really wished he could kick his ass instead.

Beyond the doorway, Mrs. Ryland was settling back into her huge bed. He walked toward her, pressing a syringe into her arm so that her blood would show the evidence of being under the influence. He left just as silently as he'd arrived and heard her sigh behind him in the dark.

"She'll do just fine," Colonel Magnus said beside him.

"I know she will," Dunn said as he turned and left the suite. "She's earned it."

"That's something you like," Magnus said as he kept pace with him. "Careful, it's your weak spot."

"What is?" Dunn countered. "Admiring people who earn their way? I don't see that as something to worry about. Save your concern for those who try to fake me out."

The Colonel chuckled. "Oh, I've got concerns about you. Plenty of them. That's what makes you interesting."

Vitus was holding the door open for his bride. A happy smile was on her lips as she slipped inside and turned her back on her father's house. They'd left the body of the congressman lying on the floor of his office, waiting to be discovered by his people in the morning. The rain was washing away their footsteps, as if fate herself was giving a resounding approval to the night's events.

Sometimes, the good guys won.

"Not too bad for government work," Damascus considered her quarters.

"It's a far cry from your father's place," Vitus said.

She winkled her nose at him. "I signed away the better part of my life to escape that, thank you very much."

Her new husband was laying on their bed in nothing

but skin. She indulged herself in a long, slow look that gained her a husky male chuckle.

"I'm impressed," he said.

"Really?"

He nodded, considering her with a flicker of admiration in his eyes. "It took balls hooking up with Magnus. A brilliant maneuver on your part. I never considered it. You blindsided me."

She smiled, feeling the compliment warm her. Damascus took her shirt off, baring her breasts. His attention shifted to them, his features thinning with hunger. The sight sent a tingle through her. He lifted a hand and crooked his finger at her.

"Come here, Princess. Your husband wants to adore you."

She shivered with anticipation. "Say that word again."

He grinned. "Husband." He enunciated each syllable, sending a shiver down her spine to curl her toes.

"Perfect." Just perfect. In a world that was far from it, well she was happy to be surprised by fate.

Perfectly happy, that was.

CHAPTER NINE

Carl Davis valued disappointment. He let it sink deep into his soul while he absorbed the impact and let it resonate through him. Everything in life held a lesson. He was a firm believer in that truth. Learning from those cosmic instructions was how a man claimed victory. Life was a vicious sport—the greater the risk, the higher the possible gain.

Of course, there was also the increased penalty for failure.

That was all part of the sport. He was a master at playing, had always had a fascination with the real-life version of gaming. Sitting in front of a screen while he looked at a virtual world didn't interest him, but learning how to manipulate the movers and shakers of the political world, well that made his heart race.

He looked up, making eye contact with Tyler Martin. "You know something? I like a man who isn't afraid to look me in the eye when things have gone badly."

Tyler didn't relax, and that pleased Carl even more. The man was no fool and he understood the game. He knew there had to be retribution and he was there, willing to pay it.

"Pratt did a lot of things for me."

Tyler began to shift, catching the hint of an offer to square things between them. His eyes narrowed because he wasn't stupid enough to believe it was going to be a simple thing to achieve.

"Most importantly, he was my main contact between the Raven and myself."

"Right," Tyler said. "I understand the Raven is exclusive."

"He's got an image to protect," Carl supplied. "Something I understand the value of." He flattened his hands on the desktop. "I need you to assure the Raven that the loss of Pratt is something I will make amends for."

Tyler sat for a long moment. "He might just shoot me to make sure you understand how unhappy he is."

Carl sat back in his chair, the thing groaning. "It's a possibility. The Raven likes to keep his contacts guessing."

Tyler rolled it around in his head for a moment, before he stood. "I'll be in contact."

"Good," Carl said. But he didn't release the security lock on the door. Tyler turned back around.

"The Raven was bringing a lot of votes to the table. In the event that he doesn't shoot you, find out what he wants to continue that service. I'll let him know I'm sending you down."

Carl pressed the button and watched Tyler leave. It was possible it would be the last time he set eyes on the man, but personally he was hoping for a better outcome. He really needed the Raven on board with his election plan. His face tightened as he considered how many votes he was likely to lose as well as money.

Well now, Damascus would discover one thing very quickly if he lost those votes. She'd come face-to-face with the fact that her haven wasn't as safe as she believed it to be.

Reprisals had to be swift and hard, or no one respected you.

"Where are you off to?"

Vitus was leaning against the doorway, watching his brother load a duffle bag. "I thought Kagan ordered you to take some leave. Thought that was why you were crashing with us."

Saxon looked up, locking gazes with Vitus. Damascus felt the charge in the air between them, moving under her husband's arm so that she wouldn't miss whatever Saxon might say. Vitus was tense, his body ridged as he waited for his sibling to explain.

Saxon reached for something and tossed it onto the dresser by the bed. It was a photo printed from security footage. "That was taken this morning in New Orleans."

Vitus picked it up and studied it for a long moment. "Tyler Martin."

Saxon nodded and pulled open the dresser to scoop out his socks. "I replaced the guard at the Hyatt with someone who would feed me information."

"The guy who tipped off Carl as to how we left the French Quarter?" Damascus asked.

"Exactly," Saxon clarified. "With a guy who looks a whole lot like Bradford. I want to know what people tell him."

Vitus tapped the picture. "Not a bad start."

Saxon pulled the zipper closed on the bag and slung it onto his shoulder.

"You need a wingman."

Damascus bit back a denial. She knew who her husband was and couldn't very well expect him to leave his brother's back unprotected. Not when they were talking about Tyler Martin.

"He has one."

Vitus pushed her through the doorway out of instinct because whoever had spoken came up behind them.

"You remember Bram Magnus?" Saxon made the introduction.

Vitus nodded. "Aren't you set to deploy, Captain?"

"Not for a few more weeks." Bram offered Vitus his hand. Vitus shook it.

"Does the colonel know you're going with Saxon?" Damascus asked the question on everyone's mind.

Bram offered her a wink. "Just going down to New Orleans for some fun."

"Right." Saxon hooked her around the waist and gave her a quick hug on his way out the door. "You two could use a little privacy. Bram's sister is newly married. Seems us bachelor men need to clear out before our blood gets thinned by all this matrimonial bliss in the air."

"I see," Damascus said. Saxon turned and shot her a look. She lifted her hands into the air. "Fine. Got it. I know nothing about men roaming through the French Quarter looking for—"

"Women," Bram informed her as he nodded. "And booze."

Damascus rolled her eyes and tried not to shift.

Vitus reached out and caught his brother's forearm. "You'll tag me in if you need help?"

Saxon's expression went serious as he nodded. "Oh, and Greer is taking a little personal time, so don't go looking for him."

Vitus didn't like watching his brother leave. Damascus watched him fighting the urge to follow.

"I understand if you need to go," she offered, hating how she had to say the words but somewhat proud of herself for getting them out. Loving him meant accepting him for who he was, and Vitus was a warrior. He wouldn't be settling in to become her lap dog.

Vitus turned around to look at her. She caught a shimmer of regret in his eyes but it dissipated quickly, leaving behind a flicker of need that she recognized.

"No, Princess, my brother's right. We could use some privacy." He ripped his shirt off and tossed it aside. "Now, I can chase you down the hallway . . ."

"You will do no such thing," She'd stuck her finger out at him, and he bit the air between them in warning. "I mean it."

"So do I!" He opened his fly and shucked off his pants. She lost her confidence, along with her breath, as his cock came into view, shifting her entire focus back to what his touch reduced her to. He pawed at the ground, making a snorting sound and she turned to run, a squeal filling the hallway as he caught her from behind and hoisted her up over his shoulder.

"Barbarian!" she accused in a breathless tone that left no doubt in either of their minds as to just how much she was enjoying being carried away.

He tossed her down onto the bed and she turned around, coming up onto her knees as he stood over her, so very proud of himself.

"*My* barbarian," she clarified in a husky tone. "Mine."

His eyes flashed with approval. "That's right, Princess. Very, very right."

Read on for an excerpt from Dawn Ryder's
next *Unbroken Heroes* series

DEEP INTO TROUBLE

Coming March 2017 from St. Martin's Paperback

Her mind must have snapped.

There really wasn't any other explanation for the fact that Saxon was suddenly there, holding her, smoothing her against him with long strokes of his hands along her back and hips. She'd never even suspected that a man's touch could feel so amazingly good. It was bone deep and a little sound bounced off the walls of the bedroom, one that escaped from her lips a moment before Saxon kissed her.

She'd thought he'd kissed her good before but she'd been mistaken. All of the strength was there in the way he took command of her lips but there was a touch of need too, a coaxing that sent a shaft of heat straight through her. He was waiting for her to meet him, to rise up against him and join him in surrender.

Ginger had no intention of disappointing him or herself. She curled her fingers into the soft jersey of his T-shirt, pulling him toward her even though they were already pressed against each other.

It wasn't close enough, not nearly so. She realized that she hated the fabric of her shirt. Somehow, her skin had become ultra-sensitive, to the point that she felt like the

T-shirt was scratchy and needed to go immediately. She pulled it off and he cupped the sides of her face and held her still so that he could reclaim her mouth.

This time, there was no hint of coaxing. There was only determination as he opened her mouth and teased her lower lip with a swipe of his tongue before boldly thrusting it inside to tangle with her own.

She shivered, twisting in a storm of sensations that felt like they were ripping her in too many directions at once. There was white hot need clawing at her insides so intense she couldn't stay still, couldn't focus. There was only the overwhelming multitude of opportunities to touch him and be touched in return. She was frantic to not miss an inch of him. The need to be closer to him was pounding through her, making her dizzy as she rose onto her toes to kiss him back.

"What's good for the gander . . . ." He lifted his head. "Is good for the goose . . . ."

She felt the brush of cool air against her skin. Saxon didn't let her suffer it long. He was folding her back into his embrace, pressing his skin to hers and stealing her breath with the contact.

It blew everything else out of her mind, leaving her awash in sensation.

He knew his way around her clothing, unhooking her bra and easing it over her shoulders before it went sailing across the room to hit the floor in a forgotten heap.

"Christ." He'd cupped her breasts, the word coming out as he kneaded them.

The exclamation bounced around inside her head because all she could do was arch back as he leaned over and fashioned his lips around one of her nipples. She gasped, the sound echoing inside the room, certain she was going to combust.

Stripping became a priority. One she set to with zeal.

She was too damned hot to deal with clothing, both hers and his.

"Yes ma'am." He growled as he followed her lead, their clothing ending up in piles. Saxon turned away from her for a moment, setting their guns on one of the side tables. It afforded her a moment to realize she was bare. She felt exposed and inexperienced.

"Don't."

She was used to him commanding her but now his voice was a soft enticement instead of a blistering demand. He moved closer, easing back against her as he smoothed his hands along the sides of her face and found the pins she'd stuck into her hair.

His breath teased her temple as her hair became heavy and finally sagged free.

"Don't doubt yourself Gin . . . ."

He caught her hair, gripping it and sending a little tingle through her at the taste of his strength. His chest was hard and covered in hair that teased her nipples and the delicate skin of her breasts. Her clit was throbbing, her senses had seemed to turn on the moment she met him.

"So . . . kiss me . . . because I can't think when you do."

He chuckled, leaning down until his breath was teasing the wet surface of her lips. "I know the problem myself."

Ginger rose onto her toes to end the conversation. She didn't want to talk, she wanted to do. Impulses were firing off inside of her and she longed for nothing more than to give over to them. Sure, there would be a reckoning, there always was. Honestly, what she feared more was not getting the chance to experience what she could in his embrace. Now that, would be a true regret.

Saxon didn't disappoint her. He kissed her hard and completely, leaving her senseless as she twisted against him, eager to make sure she was in contact with him as much as possible. Beside, remaining still was impossible. She wanted more, needed it. The craving was a living force inside her, melting away everything she'd been taught about behavior and its rights and wrongs. At that moment, there was only him and the way he felt against her.

The way he could make her feel if they got even closer . . .

His cock was hard against her belly. She reached for it, humming softly at the sound he made in the back of his throat. Satisfaction surged through her as she stroked him from base to tip, loving the way she affected him.

"Two can play that game," he warned her before he scooped her off her feet.

For a moment he cradled her, making her feel as light as a feather before settling her on the bed. She only had a moment to feel uncertain before he was covering her and reclaiming her mouth in a kiss that shattered every little thought that had started to push through the thick cloud of sensation settled inside her skull.

"And I can't wait to toy with you . . ."

There was a thick promise in his voice. She caught a glitter in his eye.

"I'm really starting to enjoy your rules, Gin." He stroked her, moving his hand down her body, across her belly and right into the curls guarding her folds.

"Ah . . . rules?" It was a stupid question but her brain wasn't working and she didn't want it to.

He teased those curls, making her twist and writhe as she gasped, stunned by just how intense it felt.

"Good for the goose . . ." He sent one thick finger into the folds of her sex, leaning over her to keep her on her back and at his mercy. "You sound like that felt very good . . . ."

She was biting her lower lip, holding her breath as he made contact with her clit. It was mind blowing, making sweat pop out on her skin. She felt her nipples contracting as he rubbed the little bundle of nerves, drawing the fluid that was seeping from her body up and over it.

"It feels like you like it too . . ."

"Would you stop talking?" She demanded. "I thought guys hated chicks who babble."

Saxon chuckled, choking on his amusement. "Glad to know I'm not like your other dates, Gin."

There was the ring of smug satisfaction in his tone. He liked being unique to her.

"I want to make sure I blow every one of those memories out of your head . . ."